pretty ugly

Also by Kirker Butler

Blue Agave and Worm

pretty ugly

KIRKER BUTLER

Thomas Dunne Books
St. Martin's Press
New York

This is a work of fiction. All of the characters, organizations, and events portrayed in this novel are either products of the author's imagination or are used fictitiously.

THOMAS DUNNE BOOKS.
An imprint of St. Martin's Press.

Printed in the United States of America. For information, address St. Martin's Press, 175 Fifth Avenue, New York, N.Y. 10010.

www.thomasdunnebooks.com
www.stmartins.com

Designed by Omar Chapa

Library of Congress Cataloging-in-Publication Data

Butler, Kirker.
Pretty ugly : a novel / Kirker Butler.—First edition.
pages cm
ISBN 978-1-250-04972-8 (hardcover)
ISBN 978-1-4668-5068-2 (e-book)
1. Satire. 2. Domestic fiction. I. Title.
PS3602.U872P74 2015
813'.6—dc23
2014037218

St. Martin's Press books may be purchased for educational, business, or promotional use. For information on bulk purchases, please contact the Macmillan Corporate and Premium Sales Department at 1-800-221-7945, extension 5442, or write to specialmarkets@macmillan.com.

First Edition: March 2015

10 9 8 7 6 5 4 3 2 1

For my mother,
who, when I was in seventh grade, said, "Hey, you should choreograph this pageant for me."

For Indie and Cleo,
who inspire me every day with their beauty, innocence, and humor.

And always, for Karen,
who said, "Hey, you should write a book."

pretty ugly

chapter one

Miranda Ford never expected a simple trip to the drugstore to change the course of her entire life. She'd really just popped in to pick up her mother's Klonopin refill, but when she saw that stack of applications on the counter next to the fishbowl of complementary cigarette lighters, something deep inside her shifted. Urgent letters streaked across the page: "The 18th Annual Miss Daviess County Fair Pageant Is Looking for Contestants!" Until that moment, beauty pageants had seemed as foreign and exotic as Mexican food, but this felt different. At fourteen, Miranda was too much of a teenager to want to appear genuinely interested in anything, so she skimmed the application while projecting an aura of boredom and indifference, the same look she'd perfected while staring at Mike Greevy in algebra class and Kandy Cotton's boobs in gym. The headline was followed by the alluring question: "Are *you* the next Loni King?" Miranda raised an eyebrow.

Loni King, a superfriendly strawberry blonde, had been crowned Miss Daviess County Fair a few years earlier and then became a star. Soon after graduating salutatorian from Apollo High School's Class of '89, Loni left her hometown of Owensboro, Kentucky, and moved to Nashville, where she quickly landed a recording contract with Ichthus Records, an independent label specializing in praise and worship music and Bibles on tape read by celebrities. *KING,* her debut album of contemporary Christian music, sold more than two million copies and won three Dove Awards. Hoping to expand her music and message to a wider audience, she recorded a love ballad with Daryl Hall from the secular rock band Hall & Oates: a man who was not her husband. The song reached number eight on *Billboard*'s Hot 100 and completely alienated Loni's Christian fan base. In June 1991 she married a bank executive who, threatened by her celebrity, encouraged her to quit music and start a family, which she did, for six months. After the couple's "scandalous" divorce, Loni quickly released an ill-conceived comeback album of honky-tonk-flavored country songs that sold a disappointing fifteen thousand copies and further turned off her godly fans. One of Loni's cousins had recently told Miranda that the singer had rededicated her life to Jesus and was in Atlanta recording an album of traditional Christmas hymns. Maybe Miranda wasn't supposed to be the next Loni King, but she was pretty sure she was supposed to be the next something.

The application continued: "Make New Friends While Competing Against Them for Cash and Prizes!" Miranda *did* like cash and prizes. She read on: "Learn poise, confidence, and public-speaking skills you may use for the rest of your life!" Miranda's guidance counselor had told her that without good public-speaking skills one had *zero* chance of becoming successful in *any* career. Her interest fully piqued, she read the rules:

1. *Contestants must be at least 14 years old and no older than 19 years old by July 1 of this year.*
2. *Contestants must be a resident of Daviess County, Kentucky. (U.S. citizens only, please.)*
3. *Contestants must not currently be married, or have ever been married.*
4. *Contestants under the age of 16 must have written consent from parent or guardian to compete.*
5. *All races, creeds, and ethnicities are encouraged to participate. (Again, U.S. citizens only, please.)*
6. *A $25 registration fee is required of all contestants. Corporate and/or business sponsorship is accepted/encouraged.*
7. *Contestants must not currently be pregnant. (Girls with children are eligible to compete if they are single—see rule #3.)*
8. *Contestants will be judged in three categories: sportswear, prom/evening wear, and bathing suit. (Tasteful one-piece suits only! Two-piece suits will NOT be allowed! This is a family event!)*
9. *All decisions made by the judges are final and cannot be challenged in any court of law.*
10. *Failure to comply with any of these rules will result in immediate disqualification and banishment from the Daviess County Fairgrounds for 1 calendar year.*

But it was a simple line at the bottom of the page that really hooked her: "All body types welcome!" As a proud member of the Interfaith Christian Alliance—an after-school fellowship group tasked with the seemingly impossible goal of bringing together Baptists, Methodists, Pentecostals, and even Catholics—the statement appealed to Miranda's egalitarianism. Miranda had learned "egalitarianism" as a vocabulary word the previous semester, and liking both its meaning and sophisticated sound applied it to herself whenever possible.

Miranda took an application from the stack and slipped it into her backpack. Years later, while writing her memoirs, she tried to explain why she felt compelled to enter that pageant.

"Maybe it was fate. I don't know. Maybe it was a desire to try something that scared me. Maybe it was God opening the door to the next part of my life. Either way, it just felt like something I needed to do. And why not? It was right there in my hometown, and the local girls weren't *that* much prettier than me. Besides, maybe I'd been wrong about the kind of girls who did pageants. Maybe they weren't all dingbat, stuck-up phonies. Maybe they were smart, and interesting, and down-to-earth like me."

As soon as Miranda decided to enter, she began plotting how she could win. Sportswear wouldn't be a problem. She'd always been active and owned many casual shoes. For evening wear she could reborrow her cousin Denise's prom dress she had worn to the previous year's eighth-grade dance. *But the bathing suit,* Miranda thought, looking down at her figure, *the bathing suit is going to be a problem.* Flat chested and hipless, the girl's fourteen-year-old body looked more like an eleven-year-old boy's. The A-cup bra she insisted on wearing gave her more of a psychological lift than a physical one. She knew she had a cute face, and she'd even been called "attractive" by some of her dad's friends, but if she was going to compete against girls as old as eighteen, she'd need to figure out a way to augment what little she had. All body types may have been welcome, but not all body types could win.

She collected her mother's pills and crossed to a shelf stocked with vitamins and dietary supplements, scanning it for anything labeled "female" and "enhancement." The bottles promised stronger bones, shinier hair, and healthier skin, but Miranda didn't need that. She needed boobs. Pendulous, award-winning boobs. And she needed them right now.

A product called Nu Woman, a homeopathic hormone supplement for postmenopausal women, looked promising, so she dropped it in her basket and continued browsing. X-trogen promised to "promote and enhance all aspects of the female anatomy," but the woman on the package, an obviously naked Asian with the contorted face of an orgasm, totally freaked her out. She looked away, embarrassed, and that's when she saw it: a long-forgotten tube sitting alone on the bottom shelf. Peering coyly from the dusty, time-faded label, a buxom Tinker Bell–ish wood nymph waved her magic wand over the tempting words, "Her Curves All-Natural Breast Enhancement Cream." Miranda looked around, then leaned over pretending to study a bottle of children's multivitamins.

"Noticeable results in as little as 30 days! Guaranteed!"

Perfect. That gave her a month to grow them and a month to get used to them before she debuted them at the pageant.

The line at the pharmacy counter was now six deep, and Miranda felt a rush of panic. Mr. Wiggins, the pharmacist, was a family friend. He'd had coffee with her father every morning back when her father was still alive. He would know the cream wasn't for Miranda's mother, whose breasts were years past the point of concern. There was another register in the front of the store being manned by Mr. Wiggins's son, Jed, a good-looking basketball star at Miranda's school, but she'd sooner have Jed ring up a hundred boxes of ultraabsorbent maxipads than a single tube of magic breast-growing cream. But she could not leave the store without it. It had suddenly become the single most important thing in her life. Looking again at the sexy sprite's heaving bosom, Miranda felt a singular focus overtake her, and with a flush of guilty adrenaline she slipped the tube into her backpack. And to make sure she was completely covered, she took the Nu Woman pills as well.

It was her first crime, and Miranda could feel her heart pounding through her soon-to-be enormous chest. Hoping to mask her guilt, she casually meandered through the aisles, stopping to admire a new arthritis cream, a porcelain figurine of former University of Kentucky basketball coach Joe B. Hall, and a *Fangoria* magazine before making her way to the exit.

"Bye, Jed," she said a bit too loudly to the disinterested boy behind the register, and slipped out the door.

Miranda sprinted the half mile to her house, then raced to her room, tearing off her shirt and bra as she went. Standing topless in front of her full-length mirror, she studied her prepubescent form and tried to create a mental "before" picture. She then smeared a generous dollop of Her Curves All-Natural Breast Enhancement Cream all over her chest. Instantly, her skin began to tingle, and she couldn't help but smile. Buzzing with expectation, Miranda lay back on her pink canopy bed and waited for a visit from the boob fairy.

Six weeks later, a few red streaks were all that remained of the second-degree chemical burns caused by the unholy Her Curves All-Natural Breast Enhancement Cream. The tingling that had so excited Miranda quickly evolved into a searing pain that felt like a fire-breathing cat clawing its way out of her chest. She spent the rest of the afternoon under a cold shower, praying for forgiveness and an end to the torrent of angry blisters erupting on her skin. Only after covering her entire torso with plastic bags of frozen deer meat did she finally get any relief.

Miranda knew it was God's punishment for her shoplifting and vanity, but the truth was much less supernatural: Her Curves had been recalled by the FDA nine months earlier for being "deceptive and dangerous." After losing a class-action lawsuit—which revealed, among other things, that the cream had no set formula and was manufactured in an unsanitary former munitions factory in Vietnam—the now bankrupt parent company of Her Curves had been mandated by a federal judge to immediately recall all of its North American products. But Mr. Wiggins, who spent most afternoons drinking whiskey and shooting guns in the alley behind the drugstore, ignored the notice. To the product's credit, the girl's chest did noticeably swell up, if only for a few agonizing weeks.

Because Miranda had stolen the cream, she was forced to hide her shame with high-neck sweaters and scarves: a peculiar look for an oppressively humid Kentucky June, but she really had no other choice. If her parents had found out, they would have insisted on taking her to the doctor, and that nightmare was *not* going to happen. Despite being a teenager, Miranda still went to her pediatrician, a kindly old man who had also been her Sunday school teacher since second grade. Odds are he would want to know how she'd acquired the burns, and how was she supposed to explain that?

"Well, Dr. Johnson, I wanted to enter a beauty pageant,

because I think I'm so beautiful, but there's no way I could win with my tiny little mosquito bites so I shoplifted some cream from Mr. Wiggins's drugstore that was supposed to give me enormous boobs, but it was defective and burned my little-girl chest and now I have scabs on my nipples. Would you please look at them? Thanks!"

The thought of that conversation was worse than nipple scabs, so Miranda chose to suffer in silence.

With the pageant now just weeks away, Miranda found herself right back where she'd started: flat chested and desperate. Undeterred, she charged ahead with her backup plan and took two Nu Woman pills. After an abrupt and painful period that felt like a gallon of spicy salsa fell out of her, she decided just to go with what the good Lord gave her—toilet paper, to stuff her top. It wasn't very original, but she was pretty sure it also wouldn't burn the lining of her uterus, either.

Two weeks later, Miranda sat backstage at the Miss Daviess County Fair Pageant nervously curling her hair. In the off months, the unairconditioned barn wood building served as storage for the fairgrounds' numerous maintenance vehicles as well as home to an ever-growing family of rats. The sweet smell of gasoline and cut grass mixed with the oppressive humidity made the air feel thick and flammable. Even the slighest breeze would have made a world of difference, but in 1991 a local judge fell out of a nearby tree while taking pictures of the contestants changing clothes, and since then the doors were ordered to remain closed during pageants. Putting on makeup was like trying to paint a waterfall. Thankfully, the pageant itself took place outdoors with the closest audience member a good fifteen yards away.

Halfway through the pageant, Miranda was feeling like a contender. Her sportswear outfit looked great, much better than what the other girls, even the rich ones, wore, and her interview question was practically gift wrapped: "Who in your life do you look up to the most?"

Smiling confidently, she answered, "I would have to say my grandmother, because she's the one who took me to church for the first time and introduced me to Jesus Christ, my personal Lord and Savior."

The crowd ate it up like deep-fried pickles. The only acceptable role models for young girls in a Kentucky pageant were their grandmothers and Jesus, and Miranda had name-checked them both without sounding like she was pandering. The audience was on her side, and based on the judges' approving nods she'd obviously impressed them, too. But none of that mattered. The bathing suit competition was next.

At her dressing station—a three-quarter-inch slab of plywood on a couple of sawhorses—Miranda nearly shit a Chevy when she reached into her bag and found an unfamiliar bathing suit.

"Who stole my suit?" she yelled.

Most questions shouted backstage began with "Who stole my . . ." and were usually ignored save for the random "not me" barked from Nikki Rummage a bucktoothed, spaghetti-thin redhead hoping, at the very least, to come out of the experience with an attractive friend or two. When no one responded, Miranda scanned the room and mentally accused, tried, and convicted several girls she didn't like.

A note was pinned to the suit, and she quickly snatched it off. "Thought you might could use a little lift! You are a beautiful champion. Have fun and good luck. Love, Mom."

Padding had been lovingly sewn into the bust, filling it out to a generous and tasteful B-cup. Miranda swallowed the sour knot growing in her throat. *What a reasonable solution,* she thought, shoving the Her Curves incident to the back of her mind, on a very high shelf, where it would be ignored and then forgotten about forever. Slipping into the modest turquoise one-piece, she checked herself in the communal full-length mirror and was charmed by the tastefully bosomed young woman smiling back at her. As a finishing touch, Miranda rubbed two arcing streaks of dark foundation onto her chest, hoping that from a distance it would create the illusion of cleavage.

Perfect, she thought. *Now . . . let's go show 'em what you've got.*

With a chestful of confidence, Miranda strutted across the asphalt stage and relished the audience's polite applause, exuberant cheers, and wildly inappropriate catcalls. Miranda's smile, like her breasts, had never been bigger.

When the time came, all nineteen contestants lined up across the stage and waited for special guest judge Kentucky State Representative Donnie Lane Mather (D-Beaver Dam) to announce the winners.

"Look at these girls up here," Representative Mather said. "Don't they just look good enough to eat?"

Marlene Martin, the pageant host and county's best church singer, smiled through her glistening teeth. "Delicious, Donnie. Just delicious."

"And now the winners," Representative Mather continued. "Miss Congeniality *and* Fourth Runner-up goes to . . . Rose Maddox!"

The audience clapped as Rose, an inexplicably popular

gossip who'd gone to college the year before and had apparently traded her virginity for sixteen pounds of leg fat, fake-cried as the reigning queen, Kitty Price, handed Rose her trophy and fifth-place sash.

"Third Runner-up is . . . April Morgan."

An audible gasp rose from the crowd. April was a popular cheerleader who was dating the son of the pageant director, and she'd been expected to finish much higher.

"Our Second Runner-up is . . . Miranda Ford!"

When Miranda heard her name, she accepted her third-place sash from Kitty with a warm smile and sincere hug. However, she wasn't quite sure that any smile would be able to mask her disappointment. After everything she had been through, Miranda had convinced herself that not only *could* she win but that she *deserved* to win. Her disappointment, however, would not last long. The Daviess County Fair Pageant wasn't quite done with Miranda Ford.

Three months later, the winner of the pageant, Missy Hale, was forced to relinquish her crown after informing the pageant committee she had married her boyfriend, who she was "pretty sure" was the same guy who got her pregnant. Promoted to First Runner-up, Miranda was told she should be ready to take the crown in the unlikely event that the new queen, former First Runner-up Alexandra Black, was not able to fulfill her duties. And then, just as if God Himself had ordained it, six days before Christmas, Alexandra—along with her uncle, sister, mother, and mother's boyfriend—were arrested for felony production of crystal meth with intent to distribute.

Miranda's reign lasted only seven months, but it was one of the most exciting periods of her life. Her picture was in the paper almost every other week, and everywhere she went little kids asked for her autograph. At school, she immediately skipped several rungs of the social ladder and soon went from being a dedicated yet anonymous 4-H member to being recruited for Drama Club vice president. Her prefame friends accused her of becoming "two-faced" and "conceited." Miranda just shrugged it off as jealousy, but they weren't wrong. She *was* acting different, because she *was* different. Miranda was a local celebrity now—and she liked it. A lot.

"Look," she told Lori Caldwell, a close friend since kindergarten, "I have responsibilities now. People count on me. And that means I'm going to have less time for my friends. And if you can't accept that, then maybe it's not me who's being conceited. Maybe it's *you* for not understanding what *I'm* going through."

It's like she said in that interview with the school paper, "Being me can be overwhelming sometimes. I mean, I can totally relate to the pressures of someone like Princess Diana." She paused to let the scrawny sophomore reporter, who had once tried to kiss her on a church hayride, really *hear* her. "It just never ends, you know? Someone's always wanting a picture or a hug or just a kind word. But that's my job now, I guess, touching people's lives and stuff. And I'm just grateful to have it."

For seven glorious months, Miranda got to breathe the rarified air of royalty. It's like she said in her memoir: "I was famous, which meant I was special. And in a world that reveres such things, why wouldn't I want the same for my daughter?"

chapter two

"Of course your children are beautiful. But are they *sexy* enough?" Miranda Ford Miller repeated the words out loud to make sure she'd read the ad correctly. *What an appalling question,* she thought. "As if I don't already have enough to think about."

After eight and a half years and three hundred sixty-three pageants, Miranda was pretty sure she'd thought of everything, but *this* had never even occurred to her. What kind of pageant mother was she, anyway?

"Dammit," she whispered, drumming her fingers on the faded yellow Formica of her kitchen table. If she'd overlooked something as fundamental as her nine-year-old daughter's sex appeal, what else had she missed?

To be sure, Miranda had done a lot right. Her daughter, Bailey, was a legend on the Southern United States pageant circuit, having racked up one hundred twenty-eight wins and ninety-six runner-up titles in her career, placing her fifth on the all-time winners' list according to the Southern Pageant

Association's Web site. A born competitor and naturally (for the most part) beautiful, Bailey had a commanding stage presence and carried herself with the grace and elegance of a high-heeled gazelle. Her talent, a grueling tribute to Cirque du Soleil's KÀ set to Fleetwood Mac's "The Chain," was provocative and perfectly executed, and no child flirted with the judges as intuitively as Bailey Miranda Miller. She was the total package. But according to Glamour Time Photography Studio, that wasn't enough. Apparently, she also had to be sexy.

Are your children sexy enough?

The words stuck in her head like a bad song.

"I can't deal with this right now," she said, and tossed the ad aside like everything else that bothered her. Adjusting the pumpkin and turkey table runner, which was only a few months from turning a corner and being appropriately seasonal again, Miranda pretended to ignore the three days' worth of dirty dishes snaking out of the sink and across the cracked tile of the counter to focus on what was important: the weekend and the 29th Annual Little Most Beautiful Princess Pageant. Bailey would be relinquishing her crown as Junior Miss Beautiful, and not a moment too soon. What with her pushing seventy-five pounds and all.

Miranda was not proud of how she judged her daughter's appearance, but the harsh reality was that the average nine-year-old girl weighed sixty-three point eight pounds. Bailey was in the eighty-fourth percentile for weight, and *that* made her vulnerable. No doubt the other mothers had noticed Bailey's extra bulk just like Miranda noticed the numerous flaws in their girls. Melody Norton's hair extensions looked (and smelled) like the horsehair they were; Karliegh Sandefur's flipper (the dental prosthetic that filled in the gaps of her missing baby teeth) only highlighted the fact that her new adult teeth were stained and crooked; and all the makeup in the world couldn't hide the fact that JoBeth Kanton was just plain ugly. But all of that was better than fat. Fat was unforgivable. Fat was fatal.

Parents who entered their overweight children in beauty pageants were worse than parents who encouraged their handicapped children to play sports. They think they're doing the right thing, showing the kids that they're "just like everyone else," but everyone else, including the handicapped kids, knows they're not. It just slows everything down and makes people uncomfortable. "Some parents," Miranda liked to say, "shouldn't be."

Most overweight girls who participated in pageants did so because their parents thought it would be good for them, which was akin to saying, "Hey, honey, you know how everyone at school makes fun of your weight? Well, I think you'd feel much better about yourself if you put on a bathing suit and stood next to a cheerleader on a stage under a spotlight in a room full of strangers." Miranda called them charity girls. Parents of the serious competitors were usually pretty tolerant of charity girls because they never won anything except maybe Congeniality, and there wasn't a cash prize for that. And that was the problem. Pageants were expensive, and if Bailey didn't remain diligent, and count every calorie, she would balloon right out of a career.

Miranda had started to suspect Bailey was eating an extra lunch at school. At the very least she was consuming more than the four-hundred-calorie meals Miranda had paid a nutritionist to prepare and deliver every morning. And she was very close to proving it before being asked to leave the school grounds for loitering. Miranda had tried everything to help her daughter lose weight: a gym membership that came with ten private pole-dancing lessons; a consultation with an overly puritanical plastic surgeon who refused to even discuss performing liposuction on a child, even when Miranda offered to pay double; and the "health clinic" in Puerto Rico where Tina Murray had taken her seven-year-old daughter Sephora to get excess fat removed from her love handles and injected into her lips. Miranda decided to put a pin in Puerto Rico when Sephora contracted a still unidentified infection that left her seventy percent deaf in one ear and half of her bottom lip permanently blue.

She then tried a fourteen-hundred-dollar custom-made neoprene sleep suit that was promised to sweat out excess water weight. But after a series of night terrors where Bailey dreamed she'd been thrown in the trash, followed by a two A.M. trip to the emergency room for dehydration, the suit was put on eBay. Despite her best efforts, the sad fact remained that Bailey was getting fat, and Miranda would just have to add that to the growing list of disappointments in her life.

She glanced again at the Glamour Time Photography ad sitting like a cherry atop a shit sundae of past-due bills. Again, Miranda tried to ignore it and looked around her kitchen wishing it were bigger. And newer. And part of a larger house. In Thoroughbred Acres. If Bailey hadn't won that new dishwasher at the Gorgeous Belles and Beaus Pageant (Augusta, Georgia), the room would be downright shameful. Miranda briefly considered washing a few dishes, just to take her mind off her failure as a mother, but the ad wouldn't leave her alone. Needing a distraction, Miranda decided she should start packing for the weekend, but a sharp kick in her stomach nearly took her breath away. Rubbing her belly, she realized she hadn't eaten in nearly four hours.

"Brixton," she said quietly, feeling her baby move inside her, "you've got to calm down, sweetheart. Lunch isn't for another"—she looked at the clock—"half hour."

Aggressively nontraditional baby names had become a trend at pageants all across the South, each one desperately transparent in an attempt to be quirky and memorable: Maelynn, Shelsea, Brinquley, LaDoris, Braethern, Gradaphene, Hendrix, Stylus, Dorsalynn, Orabelle, Gunilla, Kindle, Haylorn, JubiLeigh, Harlee, Davidson . . . Ridiculous all, but Brixton was different. Brixton was divinely inspired on a road trip to the Prettiest Girl in the World Pageant (Valdosta, Georgia).

Trailing a battered yellow dump truck filled with charred bricks from a razed crematorium, Miranda thought, *There must be a ton of bricks in that truck.* The words "bricks" and "ton" tumbled around in her head, and when she put them together it sounded a lot like poetry. A bumper sticker on the back of the truck asked WHERE IS YOUR DESTINY? and listed the Web site for one of those Six Flags Over Jesus megachurches Miranda disliked so much. Seeing the word "destiny" as the name "Brixton" formed itself in her brain was such an obvious and powerful sign from God that even an atheist would be compelled to rethink some things. Miranda decided right then and there that if she ever had another girl, she would name her Brixton Destiny Miller.

Her husband, Ray, wasn't so sure. "Don't you think it sounds a little . . . porny?"

Miranda did not.

When Bailey won her first pageant, Baby Princess Bar-B-Q Fest (Owensboro, Kentucky), at the age of seven months, Miranda told Ray she was ready to have another girl.

"All I want to do is make princesses, Ray! I want a houseful of princesses!"

Within two months she was pregnant, but when the child was born, a healthy and happy little boy they eventually named J.J. (which didn't stand for anything), Miranda fell into a bout of postpartum depression so deep she could barely see the sun. For the first four weeks, Miranda could not bring herself to hold her baby boy for longer than a few minutes at a time. Six years later she still found it difficult to speak to him in anything longer than curt, declarative sentences. When their second son, Junior Miller, was born fourteen months later, her despair multiplied exponentially.

Spending quality time with her sons became a never-ending struggle. Little girls liked shoes, playing dress-up, having their hair and makeup done, things Miranda understood and was good at. Little boys liked frogs and dirt and farting. How could she possibly be expected to relate to that?

Every now and then, Miranda's pastor would drop by to check in on her. They'd sit on the screened-in back porch and chat. She'd offer him a piece of pie and a glass of sweet tea, and he'd attempt to explain how the mother/son relationship is one of the most sacred in all humankind, using Jesus and Mary as his primary example.

"First of all," she said, laughing good-naturedly, "I dare you to spend ten minutes with these boys and then compare them to Jesus. I'm kidding, of course. They're good boys, and their father looks out for them. Not unlike Jesus. And my mother watches them a lot, too. So they're fine. I'm not worried."

The young pastor smiled and sipped his tea, and tried to explain that Miranda was neglecting sixty-six percent of her children.

"Well, first of all, I wouldn't say I'm neglecting them," she said. "I love them. I love them more than anything. They're my children, for heaven's sake. I just don't have anything in common with them." *And besides,* she thought, *when Brixton is born, that number will drop to fifty percent, which is probably pretty close to the national average.*

When the ultrasound technician pointed out Brixton's blurry gray fetal vagina, Miranda practically leapt from the table. She rushed home, dragged Bailey's old baby pageant outfits from the attic, and meticulously laid them out on every available surface of the living room. Most of the outfits, like the furniture they lay on, were shamefully outdated and needed to be replaced, but just seeing the tiny dresses with their starched crinolines and ruffled bloomers, or the hand-stitched beadwork on the Indian headpiece and matching sequined leggings, made Miranda giddy for the first time in years.

Mistakes had been made with Bailey, obviously, but Miranda was determined not to repeat them with Brixton. And if that meant starting in utero with a strict meal schedule, then so be it.

"If Brixton learns in the womb that meals are to be eaten at specific times," she explained to Ray, "then maybe she'll be born with the nutritional discipline that Bailey obviously lacks."

Ray just nodded. He'd learned to not question Miranda's plans for the girls.

"Mom, what are you doing?"

Miranda jumped and grabbed her tummy.

"Oh, my God, Bailey!" Miranda said, catching her breath. "Don't sneak up like that, sweetheart. You're going to give Mommy a miscarriage."

The nine-year-old stood in the doorway and shrugged. "Sorry."

Her honey blond hair hung in front of her face like a veil, and she made no effort to move it. The pink Juicy sweat suit she'd won at last year's Pride of Paducah Pageant (Paducah, Kentucky) had become a bit snug, but it perfectly matched the running shoes Miranda got free with Bailey's gym membership. "I'm hungry."

Miranda took a deep breath and tried to be encouraging. "I'm sure you are, sweetie, but you're competing this weekend, and we talked about this. You're up to seventy-five pounds. Which is a lot more than those other girls."

"Yeah, but most of those girls have been bulimic since birth. They'll probably never be seventy-five pounds."

"Well, honey, not everyone can be blessed with an eating disorder," Miranda said. "Some of us have to work to stay thin."

Bailey pushed the hair from her face so her mother could see how genuinely appalled she was. "Mom, that's not funny."

"You're right. I'm sorry. I'm just a little hormonal." Miranda sighed. "Okay. Go do your workout, twenty minutes on the elliptical, and I'll steam you some carrots."

The girl stared at her mother before letting her hair fall back into her face and trudged across the kitchen to a door on the far end of the utility room.

"I love you, sweetie!" Miranda called after her. "You're a beautiful champion!"

"Yep!" Bailey called back, her fist raised in mock triumph. "I'm a winner!"

"See if you can push yourself and do twenty-*five* minutes," Miranda yelled, but her daughter slammed the door, cutting her off.

Bailey took a deep breath and locked the door behind her. Kicking off her shoes, she dug her toes deep into the thick white shag carpeting and looked out into a sea of rhinestones. Every surface was covered with trophies, sashes, plaques, and crowns. In one corner, an old toy chest was filled with smaller, lesser trophies that didn't warrant prime visibility: Best Hair (First Runner-up), Best Smile, Daviess County Second-Grade Spelling Bee Champion. Framed photographs of Bailey being crowned, holding fans of cash, and posing with "celebrity" judges (regional TV news anchors) covered the walls. The ceiling was a rainbow of contestant ribbons. It looked like the rec room of an elegant hoarder. The only nonpageant items were an old futon and a SOLE E35 elliptical trainer Miranda got from a neighbor who'd caught her husband cheating and was giving all his stuff away.

The asymmetrical room was an obvious add-on, made with cheaper materials and less skill than the rest of the house. It would have made a decent walk-in closet if it had been connected to any of the bedrooms, but instead it grew off the utility room like an architectural tumor.

Bailey set the elliptical machine for a twenty-five-minute workout and sat on the floor next to it. A large dusty trophy from the Little Miss Sass and Sand Princess Pageant (Gulf

Shores, Alabama) sat in the back of the room: an anonymous peak in a mountain range of awards. Bailey carefully twisted off the bottom, and a Snickers bar fell into her lap. The elliptical machine beeped impatiently, and Bailey started pushing the foot pedal with her hand. The distance and calorie counter slowly began to rise as Bailey tore into the candy bar, jolting her body with the satisfying rush of sugar and defiance. From under the futon, she pulled a Kindle she'd won in an online photo contest and swiped to page seventy-eight of *Looking for Alaska*. A poster-sized glamour shot—Bailey's most recent pageant photo—looked down at her from across the room, and Bailey stared back, mocking it as she finished the candy bar in an earnest attempt to destroy the girl in the photo from the inside out.

Meanwhile, Miranda took a worn overnight bag from the cabinet over the washing machine and caught a glimpse of herself in a mirror. Her highlights needed some serious attention. Her hairdresser, Garo (who also styled Channel 7's popular new weather girl, Giselle Lopez-Beard), had overdone the blond streaks in Miranda's mocha hair, making her look like a jaundiced zebra. Thank God her body still rocked. Despite having three kids, her boobs were holding up pretty well. Having one small B-cup and one full C was a constant source of embarrassment, but pregnancy rounded them both out to a satisfying and nearly symmetrical D. At seven months, Miranda had barely gained twenty pounds. Although she was dangerously close to her lifetime high of one forty-seven, she was determined not to reach it.

"Not bad," she said, rubbing her belly. She turned to the side and shot a quick, furtive look at her butt. Every pregnancy had expanded her backside a little bit. She didn't like to dwell on it, but she did want to be aware of any changes. Miranda Ford wasn't dumpy, but at five foot four, she certainly could not afford to get any wider. One more baby and she would likely have to permanently go up to a size six, and the thought of that was more depressing than having another boy.

Tossing the overnight bag (substandard swag from the even more substandard Little Miss Kentuckiana Sweetheart Pageant—Jeffersonville, Indiana) onto the kitchen table, Miranda shook her head in disgust. "Second Runner-up," she muttered, still not over it. "Never trust a judge from Indiana."

Pulling Bailey's socks and underwear from the dryer, Miranda shoved them unfolded into the bag, then stopped. Even with something important to occupy her mind, she couldn't stop thinking about that ludicrous photography ad.

"Are your children *sexy* enough?" she practically spat. "How dare they?"

Storming to the freezer, Miranda reached past the tube of frozen tapeworm eggs (a gift from a pageant mom whose own daughter had experienced an unfortunate weight gain), and pulled out a three-pound block of ice that encased the family's last usable credit card. A financial adviser had suggested she and Ray freeze their cards to help reduce impulse spending and rein in their mounting debt.

"When you want to use your card, just set the ice on the counter and let it thaw," the man advised from behind his four-thousand-dollar oak desk. "It should take about ninety minutes. If after that time you still want to make your purchase, then go ahead. If not, it probably wasn't that important."

Miranda put the chunk of ice in the microwave and set it

on High for three minutes. Brixton kicked. "Ooh, sweetie, did you think Mommy was making your lunch?" She chuckled, patted her bump, and checked the clock by the fridge. "Eighteen more minutes."

Fishing her phone from her purse, Miranda called the number at the bottom of the ad and sighed, disappointed in herself and humanity. As the phone rang, she fiddled with the magnetic poetry on her fridge, picking through limitless combinations until she'd written: *i hate stupid people*

"Glamour Time Photography Studio. How can I help you?"

"Yes, my name is Miranda Miller and I saw your ad in the pageant newsletter? I'd like to schedule a sitting for my daughter."

Bailey may have been getting fat, but there was still a chance she could be sexy.

chapter three

Ray Miller peeled off his white New Balance cross trainers and relished the cool air on his damp socks. The pedometer clipped to the waistband of his scrubs read eight point six miles. He was too tired to process that number, but he knew it was nowhere near a record. It was Ray's fifth consecutive twelve-hour shift, and he couldn't remember most of his day. But that was okay. He was just happy to have something to do.

As he added up his total mileage for the week, a familiar voice screeched from the intercom: "Nurse Miller, please report to the ER. Nurse Miller to the ER."

"Fuck." He sighed heavily and considered slipping out the back door by the used-needle incinerator where he used to smoke, back when he smoked, back when he did nice things for himself. Instead, he slid his swollen feet back into his warm, moist shoes and stood up. Resetting his pedometer, he laced his fingers behind his head and slowly twisted his back, exhaling when he felt the deeply satisfying pop of his spine.

The tiny nurses' lounge reeked of stale sterility, like it had been cleaned with sour towels and hand sanitizer. When the doctors' lounge received a multimillion-dollar remodel two years earlier, the nurses inherited a museum of outdated sofas and easy chairs. Most were threadbare and musty, but Ray slept better on them than he did his own bed.

A blister pack of sample pills left by a pharmaceutical rep sat on a stack of old magazines by the twenty-seven-inch TV that hadn't worked since the world went digital. Ray quickly popped two of the orange caplets without reading the label and swallowed them dry. New sample packets arrived daily like junk mail, and Ray tried every one he found. It had become a game he played to pass the time: take a pill, wait an hour, then try to figure out what he'd taken based on the side effects. *Everyone needs a hobby,* he told himself. After a decade as a respected medical professional, he could now identify most medications on sight, so taking something new was always exciting.

A standard tox screen would have shown his blood to be a cocktail of muscle relaxers, painkillers, amphetamines, benzodiazepines, depressants, antidepressants, antibiotics, anti-anxieties, steroids, blood clotters, blood thinners, finasteride, Valium, Zoloft, lithium, Percocet, Depakote, Soma, Adderall, Xanax, Vicodin, Focalin, Lortab, Paxil, Coumadin, Estrace, OxyContin, Effexor, Ambien, Ativan, Flexoril, tramadol, Provigil, Nuvigil, Proscar, prednisone, Klonopin, Lexapro, Lipitor, Lunesta, Valtrex, Ritalin, Dexedrine, Prozac, Wellbutrin, Tylenol with codeine, codeine without Tylenol . . . The list went on and on, and so did his boredom.

Ray had stopped keeping track of how many hours he worked. He just showed up, punched his card, and did the job: six days a week at the hospital and five nights working hospice. At thirty-four, he felt at least ten years older, and with small gangs of gray hairs starting to bully the remaining brown ones, it wouldn't be long until he looked it. Miranda said his gray hair looked "dignified," but she said it in the way one might tell a bald man that his toupee looks "natural." To be honest, Ray didn't care.

"Better to turn gray than turn loose," one of his hospice patients said right before she died.

The walking kept Ray fit, and the pills kept him balanced enough to deal with the few hours he spent at home with his family.

People often praised Ray for his hospice work, casually throwing around words like "noble" and "hero," but those people were full of shit. Nothing about Ray's life bore even a passing resemblance to nobility or heroism. He worked hospice because it paid. After nearly a decade, Miranda had spent roughly $89,687 on Bailey's pageants, winning a grand total of $49,406 in cash, prizes, and "scholarships" (a label designed to make parents believe the pageants were contributing something to their child's future besides emotional instability). Ray had done the math. If Miranda never spent another dollar on pageants, and Bailey won every competion she entered for the next twenty-six years, they would ultimately break even. Ray would be sixty years old and would have walked 109,287 miles, four and a half trips around the circumference of the Earth.

Splashing water on his face, Ray looked at himself in the

shatterproof mirror over the federally mandated handicapped sink and tried to remember the last time he shaved. Two days ago? Three? What day was it?

"Nurse Miller. Please report to the ER."

"Jesus, I'm coming," he said, and dried his face with one of the surgical masks someone had stacked in place of paper towels, which because of recent budget cuts were locked up tighter than the pharmacy. Again, the voice shrieked from the intercom, "Nurse Miller, report to the ER. STAT!"

"Fuck off, Nancy!" Ray shouted back, then clipped his pedometer to his pants and shambled out the door.

Walking quickly past the patients' rooms, Ray kept his head down. Owensboro was a relatively small town, and if he wasn't careful he might see someone he knew, and Ray didn't really like anyone he knew. Somewhere, he imagined, there were people he might enjoy spending time with, people with similar interests, but he didn't know where they lived or how to meet them. He reluctantly went online, dipping a toe into the social mares' nest that is Facebook, but after a few months, Ray's handful of Facebook friends were just the real-life friends he was hoping to replace. Ray had always held that the Internet was at best just an expensive porn delivery system and at worst the most loathsome thing ever created by mankind. So he gave up, abandoning his Facebook page like an office he never fully moved into, at a job he never really wanted.

As Ray reached the ER, he felt the unmistakable signs of an impending erection. "Shit." He sighed. The pills. *Must be a new ED medication,* he thought. *I probably shouldn't have taken two.* Everyone needs a hobby.

Working a code with a drug-induced erection was the worst, not that he hadn't done it before, but Ray had been on his feet for twelve hours. He *really* wasn't in the mood. Ducking into the men's room, he darted past a waiting room refugee vomiting blood into a urinal and locked himself in a vacant stall where he tucked his penis into the waistband of his scrubs. He tightened the drawstring to hold it firmly in place, then stepped back out into the chaos that was the ER.

Victims of a drunken boat race laid on gurneys as orderlies led equally drunken family members to the waiting area. Ray sighed without emotion and absorbed the too-familiar sights and sounds of avoidable tragedy.

Once upon a time Ray enjoyed nursing, even though everyone he met assumed he was gay, which didn't bother him nearly as much as the people who thought he became a nurse because he wasn't smart enough to be a doctor, as if all nurses were just failed med students. It was particularly bothersome because in his case it happened to be true. Ray never wanted to be a doctor, but since the Civil War every firstborn male in his family had been one.

"In fact," his father, Dr. Benjamin Miller, once told him, "Dr. Sam Mudd, the physician who set John Wilkes Booth's broken leg after he shot President Lincoln, was your great-great-great uncle." Ray wasn't sure if it was pride or shame he heard in his father's voice, but it didn't matter. "My son is not going to waste his time playing music. You're going to be a doctor."

So Ray struggled through premed at Western Kentucky University and graduated near the bottom of his class from an inexpensive, low-tier North Carolina med school. Thanks to his father, Ray landed an internship at a war-zone public hospital near downtown Detroit. Within six months, his substandard education and slow recall were at least partially responsible for the deaths of seven patients. Ray didn't sleep much after that. Overwhelmed with guilt, he'd spent his nights studying, cramming, literally forcing too much information into a too-small space.

"It was like a guy in a bad sitcom closing a door on an overfull closet," he'd explained to Miranda. "And later someone opens the door, and everything comes spilling out all over the floor. That was med school for me. Everything was in my brain, but it was just all over the place."

The resulting wave of malpractice lawsuits eventually forced the ninety-eight-year-old hospital to permanently shut its doors. Ray knew it would have been impossible to defend his intelligence, so at his medical board hearing he tried defending his dead patients instead.

"They were all very old and had been treated repeatedly by other doctors, hospitals, and clinics. One of them had been shot twice in the past three years. In my professional medical opinion, they had—at best—a combined twenty years among them. And I believe that most, if not all, of those years would not have been quality. So, if I may answer your question with one of my own: Is life itself more important than quality of life?"

The board didn't think much of Ray's professional, medical opinion, or of his "decidedly European" attitude toward patients' quality of life.

"Your primary responsibility was to save lives, and you failed that responsibility," said an elderly physician who looked like a melting wax sculpture of Ronald Reagan. "Therefore, this board believes that the most appropriate punishment is to ban you from practicing medicine in the United States."

Ray felt like he'd been granted a divorce from an arranged marriage. He'd wanted out from the beginning, but looking back, he couldn't say he hadn't learned *something*. Reluctant to squander what little knowledge he *had* retained, Ray moved back to Owensboro and enrolled in a nursing program at the community college. Having a nurse for a son would have killed Dr. Ben Miller if he hadn't dropped dead of an aneurysm at a tobacco auction two years earlier. And while Ray was a total failure as a doctor, he soon discovered that he was a very competent nurse.

"I really like it," he e-mailed an old med school buddy, "less pressure, less responsibility, I don't have to cure anyone. I just have to help. I can do that. Plus, there's a lot less stuff I have to know. It's doctor lite."

Ray moved to Owensboro when he was ten. His father had been lured to the area to head up Bluegrass Memorial Hospital's new Spinal Action Team, a title that exuded more positivity than Dr. Miller ever had about anything in his life. While very proud of being "the Barbeque Capital of the World," the people of Owensboro always worried that the rest of Kentucky thought of their beloved town as just a smaller, shittier Louisville. Both sat on the Ohio River, but Owensboro was downstream, which created the distinct feeling of being constantly pissed on by the larger city. Louisville was fast becoming a major force in the health-care industry, and Owensboro was not going to stand idly by while its smug, more successful cousin cornered the market on health care *and* tobacco. A call to action was declared by the Department of Economic Development, charging the city's four hospitals with the goal of making Owensboro synonymous with back pain. Money soon started flowing like piss down a river.

THE BACKBONE OF AMERICA bumper stickers started appearing on ambulances and Cadillacs. Hospitals raced to see which could expand faster, one even convinced the city to declare eminent domain on an adjoining neighborhood that overlapped with its planned multimillion-dollar spinal rehab facility. Lawsuits followed, but "progress" won the war, and four blocks of residents could only stand by and watch as the homes they'd lived in their entire lives were bulldozed to make room for someone else's dream. Six months into the crusade, Baptist Hospitals of Louisville bought Bluegrass Memorial and established the Bluegrass Baptist Spinal Center, "a revolutionary spinal treatment facility that will work hand in hand with our world-class spinal center in Louisville to provide quality care to patients throughout the Commonwealth of Kentucky." The battle was over. Owensboro got its spine center, and those four blocks of razed homes gave the town something else to brag about: the largest parking lot in the state.

Ray liked Owensboro well enough. It was a nice place to raise a family: safe, good schools. It had the feel of a city—there were four colleges, three Starbucks, and five McDonald's—but it was really just a town. You could be anonymous if you wanted, or you could be popular if you tried. Like everything else in life, it was kind of like high school.

The desperate moans of the boat race victims provided a haunting sound track to the brusque demands of the doctors.

"BP 80 palp! Let's get two of O neg, and move her to Trauma 3!"

In their expensive words, Ray could hear the interest accruing on their student loans, and he allowed himself a fleeting moment of gratitude for his failure in Detroit.

Commencing CPR on a thirty-year-old Asian man who probably wasn't going to make it, Ray realized he'd tied his scrubs too tight, cutting off circulation to his rapidly growing erection. He also realized that the head of his penis was visible over the top of his scrubs. Unfortunately, another nurse noticed first.

"Oh, my God, Ray! I can't believe I just saw that! Why is it purple?"

"It's fine, Christie." Ray deadpanned, embarrassed. "If I try really hard I can make it any color I want." He tucked his penis back into his pants without missing a single compression.

Christie was Ray's only real work friend, and like most of his other friends, he didn't like her very much. An insufferable do-gooder who spent every weekend volunteering at the county animal shelter, Christie was the kind of person who made you feel terrible about yourself for not doing more to help save the world but was so immensely off-putting about it that you wanted to hasten the end of the world just so she would shut up. The thought of an animal being put down for any reason was too much for Christie's fragile critter-loving heart to bear, so every weekend she would "rescue" some two-legged dog or cat with AIDS, then spend the next week trying to convince someone at the hospital to adopt it. The fresh claw marks across her face, arms, and neck made this increasingly difficult to pull off.

"I thought your shift was over."

"It was. It is," Ray answered.

"So why are you still here?" Christie asked, as if talking to a stupid person.

"I got paged."

"Ah. You working hospice tonight?"

"Soon as I'm done with him."

Ray looked down and noticed that with every compression, the erection now tenting the front of his scrubs was rubbing across his patient's unconscious face.

"Jesus," Ray screamed, and turned around.

Christie looked at the patient, mistaking Ray's shame for grief. "Is he dead?"

Ray turned back around. "Yep."

Sighing, he peeled off his latex gloves, loosened the strings on his waistband, and adjusted his throbbing penis.

Christie gave a good-natured chuckle. "The Angel of Death strikes again. How many is that now?"

Ray just shrugged. "I don't know," he said. But he knew. Since those first seven in Detroit, Ray had kept a running total of how many people he'd been physically touching when they died. This was number three hundred sixty-five. *I've killed a whole year of people,* he thought. Ray stood silently for a moment, reflecting on his newest milestone.

"He your first Asian?"

"Hm? No. I don't know. What's Filipino?"

Christie shrugged and looked at the clock on the wall. "Time of death six oh nine P.M."

"Shit," Ray said, "I gotta get to work."

"Try not to kill this one, will you?" Christie laughed.

"It's hospice," Ray said, forcing a smile. "Those ones are supposed to die." *But it's still early,* he thought. *Maybe I'll get a leap year before sundown.*

Heading toward the parking lot, Ray passed the nurses' station and spied two unattended pills in a tiny paper cup waiting to be delivered. A rack on the nearby wall was filled with informational pamphlets left by various pharma reps: "Stop Suffering from Depression," "How to Cope with Stress," "Why Be Anxious About Your Anxiety?" They looked trustworthy, like they'd been lifted from the pages of the *New England Journal of Medicine* or *The Lancet*. Informative, in that everyone who read them could easily diagnose themselves as having that particular disorder; and comforting, in that they could recommend an effective new medication that could help! None of them suggested exercise, or a change in diet, or turning off the TV. Just drugs. Ray shook his head and threw back the tiny paper cup like a shot of tequila. In an hour he would be feeling . . . something. It was something to look forward to. Just then his eyes landed on a pamphlet he'd never seen before. Three smiling, ethnically diverse women sat in a gazebo surrounded by wildflowers: "The Breast Self-Exam Guide." Ray stared at it and tried to imagine the breasts of the women in the picture. They were just models, probably never even had cancer, so thinking about their breasts didn't seem inappropriate. Ray looked at his watch: six fourteen. He was going to be late. Adjusting his still erect penis, nurse Ray Miller snatched a copy of "The Breast Self-Exam Guide" from the rack and quietly slipped out the back door by the used-needle incinerator.

chapter four

Stiff-arming the horn, Miranda slammed on the brakes of her 2002 Chrysler Town & Country and slid into her mother's driveway, an unwelcoming patch of dirt and gravel that had spent the last twenty-five years winning a war of attrition against the backyard. It was seven forty-seven, and Miranda was already behind schedule. The boys had refused to share a bath again, so they didn't get one, and the drive-thru line at McDonald's was too long so they didn't have breakfast, either.

"Why don't you enter the boys in pageants?" Ray had once suggested. "They'd probably enjoy it, and it might help you connect with them a little more."

But Miranda just sighed and shook her head. Yes, there were little boys who competed in pageants, but Miranda suspected that they all grew up to have sex with each other, and she was not about to raise a couple of gays. Not that she considered herself homophobic. Most of the best pageant coaches were homosexual, and she genuinely enjoyed their company, even considered them friends, but spending a few hours with one on the weekend was different from having one as a son.

"Is that what you want, Ray? A couple of gay boys?"

"I don't think that's how it works," he replied, genuinely concerned.

But Miranda wouldn't hear him. She knew her boys would be better off if she just let them be, so that's exactly what she did.

The sign on the bank downtown said it was already eighty-six degrees, and Miranda's pregnancy hemorrhoids felt like she was smuggling fried grapes. Bailey was slouched in the passenger seat scrolling through the pink iPod she'd won at the Miles of Smiles Perfect Face Invitational (Hendersonville, Tennessee). Pageant weekends were always stressful for Bailey, but something about this one felt heavy. Not only was she relinquishing her title of Junior Miss Beautiful, but her mother had decided to take a risk and enter her in the Most Beautiful Princess division, fudging her birthdate by three months to meet the age requirement.

"Isn't that cheating?" Bailey asked when Miranda informed her of the scheme the day before.

"I like to think of it more like a *gamble,*" her mother said.

A gamble that if unsuccessful could get them both banished from the Southeastern Pageant Association for life, but Miranda believed it was worth the risk. The SPA sponsored only four pageants a year, and two of them weren't much better than dog shows.

"And sometimes gambles pay off big time," Miranda said with a wink.

"But why?"

"What do you mean?"

Bailey looked her mother in the eye, knowing the answer before she asked. "Why are we lying about my age?"

"Well," Miranda tiptoed, "I was thinking about your diet, and how we could turn what has become a negative into a positive."

Bailey crossed her arms. "Explain, please."

Miranda looked at her daughter. Recently, she had started to think that Bailey was saying things just to mess with her, asking questions she already knew the answer to just to study Miranda's reaction, as if Bailey was a scientist conducting an experiment and Miranda was a rat. She would never say it out loud, but it kind of creeped her out a little.

"Princess contestants are older, ten to fourteen." Miranda explained. "In your regular category, you'll be one of the oldest, so you'll look big, bigger than you even are in real life. So next to the girls in the princess group, you'll look normal size. Smaller even, which is better!"

Bailey stared at her. She was thinking about the five Cadbury Creme Eggs she'd eaten during that morning's "elliptical workout."

"So . . . it *is* cheating."

"I'm trying to help you," Miranda said, confounded by her daughter's reluctance to endorse her deceitful, yet sensible plan. "Just . . . trust me. It'll work."

The warm purr of a lawn mower sputtered to life in the distance. Miranda laid on the horn again, inciting a dirty look from a portly neighbor on a Rascal using a grabber to jerk obscenely large underwear from a clothesline.

"Hey there, Emma." Miranda waved, then honked again. "Mom, hurry up! We're late!" She honked again. "I'm gonna leave these boys on the porch if you don't get out here!"

Drumming her fingers on the steering wheel, Miranda saw her old, battered swing set slouching like an elderly nanny in the corner of the yard. Her father, Roger, had built it from found materials when Miranda was five. It quickly became Miranda's second home and her only needed source of entertainment. There were two swings, a tube slide, a rope bridge, a pole to slide down, and a set of monkey bars. The design made it versatile enough to be whatever her imagination wanted it to be. When she wanted to be a princess, it was a castle. When she wanted to be a pirate princess, it was a pirate ship. When she wanted to be Princess Leia, it was the Millennium Falcon. Now, weather-beaten and rusted through, it was a monument to tetanus. Her boys loved it.

Finally, Miranda's mother, Joan (pronounced "Jo-Ann"), unlatched the screen door and waved.

"Jesus, it's about time," Miranda said under her breath. The sliding door of the minivan moaned and sputtered open like a huge mouth deciding whether or not it wanted to vomit. It was the boys' cue to get out.

"Listen to Grandma!" Miranda yelled at their backs as they ran toward the house. "I'll see you Sunday!" And then added, "Wish your sister and me good luck!"

"Hang on!" Joan yelled as she laboriously inched her way down the worn wooden steps of the screened-in back patio. Miranda felt the increasingly frequent anxiety of a blown schedule and rubbed Brixton for comfort.

"Come on, dammit," Miranda said quietly, cursing the

woman who gave her life. "I don't have time for this crap right now." She turned to Bailey, "I love your grandmother very much."

Joan's knees were swollen from arthritis and stiff from the rain that would start in about four hours. Her left meniscus had ground to powder, leaving her bones to rub against one another like a mortar and pestle. Sometimes they would vibrate on contact, and Joan could feel her soul shudder, that nails-on-a-chalkboard feeling emanating from deep inside her being. Wearing her best smile, and third-best housecoat, Joan finally made her way to the minivan and leaned in the window.

"You off?"

"We're late. Heading to Knoxville."

"Okay." Joan nodded knowingly several times. "In Tennessee?"

"Is there another one?"

"I don't know. Probably." She put her hand on Miranda's belly. "Hello, sweetie."

Miranda put the minivan in reverse, "We need to go, Mom."

"What time should I put the boys to bed?"

"Just let 'em fall asleep in front of the TV. Ray should be by around ten or so to pick them up."

"Okay, then." Joan waved to Bailey and smiled. "Hey, hon. You gonna win this weekend?"

Bailey looked up from her iPod, smiled at her grandmother, and gestured toward her mother. "Mom thinks so."

"Good. Good for you." Joan smiled.

Miranda blushed and let her foot off the brake a little. The car creeped backward. "Mom, we really need to go."

"Okay, well, y'all have a nice time. Be careful." She called in to her granddaughter, "Bring back a crown, sweetheart! Or just have fun. Remember, you don't have to win to have fun!"

Miranda slammed on the brakes and shot her mother a look of grave disappointment. "Dammit, Mom. We talked about this."

That was exactly the kind of so-called encouragement that had forced Miranda to ban Joan from being a pageant chaperone. For some reason, Joan just could not get her mind around what was at stake, and trying to explain it to her was like trying to explain a card trick to a cat. She would never understand. Few did. Pageants were like wars: expensive, cruel, and necessary. Casualties were inevitable, and Bailey needed a warrior's motivation to foster not only survival but victory. To Joan, it was all about having fun, looking pretty, and doing your best, which Miranda thought was sentimental horseshit. Everyone knew the girls who had the most fun rarely took home a crown.

"Sorry," Joan said, raising her hands in defeat. "I'll let you go."

"We'll be back Sunday night," Miranda said through her closing window.

"Okay, then. Bye. Y'all be careful now."

The Town & Country kicked up a cloud of dust as Miranda tore out onto the road. Joan watched her daughter and granddaughter drive away and felt her smile turn sour. She knew how stupid Miranda thought she was, but Joan disagreed. She was a smart cookie. She watched the news. She knew things. Big things. Joan kept her eye on Miranda until she drove through a rarely observed stop sign at the end of the street next to the big, empty parking lot. Some people said it was the biggest parking lot in the state, but Joan thought that seemed unlikely.

Shaking her head, she erased the negative thoughts of her daughter like an Etch A Sketch and pulled herself back up the steps of her porch. Stopping to rest, she asked Jesus if he had a few seconds to talk.

I always have time for you, Joan. How are your knees?

She grinned and shook her head in astonishment. "That is exactly what I wanted to talk to you about."

Entering the kitchen from her back patio, Joan found J.J. and Junior sitting at the table shoving handfuls of homemade cherry pie into their laughing faces.

"Boys! That pie was for your supper," she yelled. "I've got a good mind to send you outside and pull a switch off the tree."

But she knew if she let them outside she'd never get them off Miranda's old swing set. They looked up at her with big, worried eyes, cherry pie filling ringing their mouths like clown makeup. Joan shook her head. *These boys need discipline,* she thought, and Joan was not one to spare the rod.

No child ever turned out worse because he got his backside tanned every now and again.

The Bible was pretty clear on that. Then again, they looked so happy, full to bursting on something she'd lovingly made with her own hands. What was the harm, really? They were just being boys. Maybe instead she should be flattered that they loved her pie, the same recipe *her* mother made, and her mother before her. She couldn't give the boys much, but she could give them pie. Besides, what's a grandmother for if it's not to spoil her grandchildren? The boys rarely ate something homemade. It was nice to be the person who provides them with something healthy for a change. When she thought about it, if she punished them for eating that pie, she would *really* be punishing them for loving her so much. And that didn't make any sense at all.

"Okay." She smiled. "When you finish up, go wash your faces, then it's time for your lessons."

For a little over a year, Joan had been homeschooling J.J. and Junior. Of all the roles she'd had in her life, teacher was probably the one that made her proudest.

"Only in America," she once said to Jesus, "could someone who never finished high school be allowed to have the same educational influence as those so-called professionals."

It really is a great country, said Jesus.

After seventh grade, Joan's father made her drop out of school to work full-time on the family farm. "But that didn't mean I stopped learning," she told the boys in one of her many diversions. "I've read near seventy-five books in my life, and those were *not* books I would have read if I'd stayed in school. So do with that what you will."

Joan believed that her life experiences and personal opinions *had* to be more relevant than anything the boys would learn in a classroom. Public schools had become nothing more than godless reeducation camps created for the sole purpose of indoctrinating children into accepting and perpetuating the liberal agenda. The 700 Club had alerted Joan to the nefarious plot of the public education system to brainwash an entire generation of young people, and she refused to stand idly by while her grandsons were exposed to dangerous subject matter like evolution, global warming, and the performing arts. She would rather the boys forgo education altogether than become hippie theater majors who believed their people came from apes.

With Jesus's guidance, Joan worked up a tight eight-minute presentation for Miranda, who was skeptical at best.

"Homeschooled kids are ignorant and weird," Miranda said. "I got enough problems with those boys. I don't need them to be weird, too."

"But," Joan countered with the deftness of a TV lawyer, "think about how much more time you'll have to focus on Bailey's pageants."

Miranda hadn't thought of that. Smart cookie, indeed.

Joan adored the boys and wanted nothing but the best for them. They were pretty much her only human contact. Her knees prevented her from leaving the house very often, and when she did venture out it was usually only for Sunday service at the Pleasant Ridge Church of Christ or the occasional Mel Gibson movie. God knew she could use the company.

The boys finished their pie, and Joan shuffled over to the stove. Since 1975, an endless pot of pinto beans had warmed on the back burner. It was about all Roger would eat, and the smell reminded her of him. Plus, it was nice to have hot food to offer if anyone stopped by for a visit. She ate a spoonful and made her way to an open door on the other side of the room. Feeling her way across the wall, she flipped a switch and flooded a cramped utility room with light. Jars of canned peaches lined a wall in perfect, uniform rows like three-dimensional wallpaper. Generations of winter coats hung over each other in pregnant bulges above the washer and dryer, and half a dozen dusty fishing rods rested in the corner with Roger's old squirrel rifle. Joan shook her head. She really did need to clean this room up.

It would make a wonderful study.

Carefully maneuvering the deliberate piles of clothes (some to be washed, some to be donated, some to be ignored), Joan made her way to the home computer nestled in the back corner. For her first semester as a teacher, Joan had relied primarily on Wikipedia for her lesson plans. It was easy, free, and allowed her to fix some of the more egregious errors made by the ignorant know-it-alls who posted the information in the first place. However, when she stumbled upon the simple brilliance of Conservapedia it was like getting an honorary doctorate in common sense. Joan felt as if she could have written those articles herself, which was high praise indeed. Pages spit from the Lexmark ink-jet printer Bailey won at the Rebel Belles Glamboree (Huntsville, Alabama), and Joan felt a blush of self-righteous pride. "*This* is what they should be teaching in schools."

Classes began with an hour of Christian apologetics, followed by American history (*real* American history), Bible study, penmanship, recess, a healthy lunch, social studies (the evils of Hollywood values), and if there was time left over before *Wheel,* math.

Joan thumbed through her lesson plan and took her seat at the kitchen table. Through the open toe of her support hose, she felt a wide crack in the linoleum and ran her toe along the length of it. Installed in 1966, the dark brown wood-grain flooring had faded to the burnt yellow of a tobacco chewer's teeth. A distinct path had been worn from the refrigerator to the sink to the stove to the table. In the corner by the window, a small rag rug covered the cigarette burns near the legs of Roger's old secretary desk where, at the end of the day, he would read the evening edition as Joan hurried about making his dinner. Seventy percent of Joan's adult life had been spent in this room, and she was grateful for every imperfection: the discolored flower basket wallpaper, the stove's permanently grease-covered backsplash, the warped cabinet doors, the stained porcelain of the sink. It was warm, like wrapping herself in her father's tattered cardigan.

The old stuff is the best stuff, Joan.

She laughed. "Yes, I suppose that's true," she agreed, and slid her big toe along the crack until her knee told her to stop.

The boys had started licking the pie pan clean, and a look of pity crossed her face.

"You boys need haircuts." She sighed. "Why can't your mother see how beautiful you are?"

Miranda's indifference to the boys didn't make a lick of sense, but there wasn't a lot about her daughter Joan understood. They rarely talked about anything other than schedules, and whenever Joan tried to question her daughter about the time (or lack thereof) she spent with her sons, Miranda would blow up and use terrible words that started with the letters *f* and *s*. Joan would just shake her head.

"Why a pretty girl like you would want to make yourself so ugly by using those words is beyond me. I don't even know where you learned words like that. Certainly not from me." Joan had never said those words, although after three or four beers, Roger would occasionally use profanity. But he worked hard, he deserved those beers.

Roger Sylvester Ford drowned in the shower while brushing his teeth. Time management had become an obsession for

Roger. Insurance didn't just sell itself, and if he was ever going to surpass that pompous ass Brad Souther as the insurance leader of Daviess County, then he needed every spare minute he could find. With his right hand, Roger would brush his teeth while his left used the removable showerhead to rinse the Pert Plus from his hair and mustache. It was so efficient that after a few weeks he had begun shaving and flossing in the shower as well. All told, the new system saved him nearly five and a half minutes a day, time that would later be spent around the Big Table at Gabe's Restaurant bullshitting with other local businessmen who fancied themselves the town's power brokers and brain trust.

As a boy, the sight of his old man's upper plate soaking in a bedside glass of water had given Roger nightmares, and he vowed to never get dentures. Considerable time was spent each morning tending to his healthy yet slightly crooked teeth, primarily his molars. "That's where the cavity monsters hide," he told a terrified five-year-old Miranda, who spent the next three years of her childhood believing tiny, malevolent ogres lived inside her mouth.

Roger had gotten his routine down to a science: Starting in the back and working left to right, he would brush in thirty deliberate circles before moving forward to his bicuspids and repeating the process. He did this top and bottom, front and back, three times a day. Normally, it was more than sufficient, but that morning he felt a tiny sausage remnant stuck behind a back tooth. With precious seconds ticking away, Roger poked at the food, but slipped on some toothpaste he'd just spit out and shoved his toothbrush halfway down his throat. Panicked and gagging, he threw his head back and slammed it against the tile wall, knocking himself unconscious. The removable showerhead swung like a pendulum on a grandfather clock ticking down Roger's final seconds. An arcing stream of water filled his open mouth and drowned him as he sat upright in the tub. Joan discovered the body fifteen minutes later.

Thank God for Jesus. If it weren't for His little pep talks, Joan probably wouldn't have gotten through it.

Don't you worry about a thing, He told her the next morning. *Roger's with me now. And just so you know, he's already the number-one insurance salesman in Heaven.* Joan never asked why angels needed insurance. She didn't have to.

Joan ran her fingers through her grandsons' mops of hair and picked out small sticky pieces of cherries they had flung at each other. "Do you want to start your lessons now, or do you want Nana to give you haircuts?"

"Can we just watch TV today?" Junior asked. "I'm not in the mood to learn anything."

"Yeah," seconded J.J. "No learnin'!"

Gazing into their big angelic eyes, Joan's heart melted like butter over hot grits.

"Of course," she said calmly.

The boys leapt from the table and ran into the living room. Joan called after, "But nothing too violent and none of that Disney Channel garbage! Walt Disney was an anti-Semite, and Israel is our friend! We're gonna need the Jews when Jesus comes back!"

Joan dropped the day's lessons on a growing stack of previously untaught schoolwork and pulled a deck of cards from the junk drawer.

Deal me in.

"Okay," Joan warned, "but I've been practicing."

Jesus laughed. *I'm sure you have. I'll try and stay alert.*

As a wrestling program blared from the living room, Joan slowly lowered herself into the chair and dealt two hands of cards.

chapter five

Miranda and Bailey arrived at the Knoxville Crowne Plaza Hotel a little after 6 P.M., only thirty minutes behind schedule. The parking lot was gridlocked with minivans, SUVS, and overflowing luggage carts. The first real challenge of any pageant weekend was transferring the contents of your vehicle to your hotel room, and whoever parked closest to the entrance could claim the first psychological victory. Miranda just shook her head. "Amateurs." Smiling, she hung a placard she'd lifted from Joan's rearview mirror, and whipped into a handicapped spot.

Bailey was passed out in the backseat. She'd fallen asleep somewhere around Harriman, Tennessee, after inhaling her dinner of McSalad, small fries with no ketchup, and large Diet Coke. On average, Bailey drank six Diet Cokes a day, which was acceptable under the complex meal plan Miranda had put together. Anything with the word "diet" or "fat free" on the label was allowed in unlimited quantities. Everything else had to be approved.

A bellman approached the minivan but was abruptly waved off.

"No! No, thank you! We got it!"

Miranda groaned. She was constantly disappointed by how the host hotels insisted on nickel-and-diming their guests. Everyone expected a tip for doing a job they were presumably already paid to do. It was frustrating and embarrassing, especially when the hotels refused to give a significant discount to pageant attendees.

"Ten percent is not a discount," she'd written to the president of Marriott. "It's a slap in the face. And I'm not the only one who thinks so. With all the publicity these pageants bring your hotels, contestants and families should be asked to stay for *free*."

Slowly lowering herself off the inflatable hemorrhoid donut, Miranda brushed french fry crumbs from her shirt and rubbed her belly just in time to feel Brixton laugh. It was the full, rich laugh of a happy, well-adjusted baby. During the trip, Miranda had told Brixton some of her favorite knock-knock jokes, and the kid could not get enough.

"You're such a smart little girl, Brixton," she cooed. "And funny, too."

Miranda tapped the back window of the minivan with her wedding ring and startled Bailey awake. "We're here, sweetie! Get up and help me with these bags."

Bailey nodded. She knew the drill. She slipped on her shoes and grabbed a luggage cart from one of the bellmen by the front door while Miranda inventoried their bags. Every week there was more stuff: garment bags, makeup kits, hairpieces, photos, résumés, crowns, camcorders, air-brushing system, self-tanner, eyelashes, shoes, back-up shoes, etc. Thank God

Bailey was naturally (for the most part) beautiful, or they'd have to buy a full-size SUV.

Maneuvering the luggage cart through the hardening artery of the loading zone, Bailey thought about Frogger. The game had become one of her favorites since winning a Nintendo DS at some pageant. She couldn't remember which one. Currently, Bailey held twenty-four titles in six states, and she couldn't name half of them. They had all become one big pink blur. She hated to think that her greatest accomplishments had come before she was even a teenager, but it was also difficult to imagine that she would ever do anything else in her life that would earn her a room full of trophies.

When she reached the revolving door, Bailey found her mother, ashen faced, mouth agape, staring at a piece of paper taped to the window. Miranda snatched it from the glass and read it out loud to make sure she was as angry as she should be.

"SHOOTING NOTICE"

> "Welcome! This weekend the Learning Channel (TLC) will be following several contestants from the Little Most Beautiful Princess Pageant for a reality show to air later this year (title TBD). By entering these premises, you are legally agreeing to be videotaped. Your image may be used for the program and/or for any promotion pertaining to the program. Cameras will be in the audience during the pageant as well as many of the backstage areas. Production assistants will be on hand to get signatures for release forms; however, because of the large crowd expected to attend, obtaining signatures from everyone will be im-

possible. Therefore, your attendance at the Little Most Beautiful Princess Pageant, and its surrounding activities, is an implicit agreement to be recorded. Thank you for your cooperation and good luck!!"

"A reality show?" Miranda screamed to no one in particular. "Those filthy sons of bitches! They stole my idea!"

For five years Miranda had been trying to convince a network, any network, that a reality show featuring her and Bailey would be the biggest thing on television. Beauty pageants were made for reality TV: pretty girls, cutthroat competition, and inspirational role models. Entertainment distilled to its purest form.

"Aren't there already a ton of pageant reality shows?" Ray asked one night as Miranda sat up in bed addressing envelopes.

"Not like this one. This is a mother/daughter show. It's called *The Princess and the Queen*." She paused to let him tell her how great it was.

"Cute," he said, sluggish from an old Valium he'd found in a winter coat pocket.

"I just think pageants are so much more interesting than the regular reality show garbage: Oriental people having a bunch of kids, or midgets going to work. I mean, good for them, I guess, but who cares, you know?"

The idea, which came to her fully formed in a dream, was so perfect she had a treatment written before breakfast.

THE PRINCESS AND THE QUEEN®

A reality show by Miranda Miller

"My name is Miranda Miller and I'm Miss Daviess County Fair, 1991!"

Aside from my wedding vows, no words have made me prouder to say than those. I know firsthand what it takes to be a beauty queen, and that's why my daughter, Bailey, has become one of the most successful pageant girls in America! But have you ever wondered what it takes to get there? Well, I'll tell you, it takes *two*—a princess *and* a queen!

And that's why you'll love our new reality show, *The Princess and the Queen*!

Nothing is more American than family, pretty girls, and hard work! And in *The Princess and the Queen,* you'll see all that, plus we'll take you "behind the scenes" to see how pageants really work! Sure, it's easy being pretty, but it's a lot like work to get there! (That would be a great slogan for the show! Another good one might be: "One is glamorous, the other is glamour*stressed*.")

The show itself is genius in its simplicity. Basically, camera crews would follow me (a former beauty queen) and my multiple-award-winning daughter (a Southern Pageant Hall of Fame nominee) as we compete in the competitive world of children's beauty pageants throughout the Southern United States. Cameras don't lie! What you will see is the unvarnished truth of what makes beauty pageants the most popular entertainment events in the history of America!

And if that's not enough, as someone who watches only reality shows, I give you my personal 100% guarantee that this show will be the most entertaining and highest-rated show in your network's history!

Miranda then proceeded to cold-call every talent agency in Hollywood. When none of them called back, she made a solemn vow to never work with anyone who didn't return a phone call. Undeterred, Miranda began contacting the networks directly, starting alphabetically with ABC and giving up when some smug intern at VH1 hung up halfway through her pitch.

And then she remembered Maggie Lester. In third grade, Maggie was Miranda's best friend for about a month. Now living in Los Angeles, Maggie was married to a man who wrote for a popular animated show called *The Stupids*. Miranda friended her with a painstakingly casual, Oh-my-God-I-was-just-poking-around-on-Facebook-and-found-your-name-blah-blah-blah message. A few pleasant exchanges about careers, family, and the past twenty-four years passed before Miranda got to the point.

> *So . . . I feel bad for not saying something sooner, but please tell your husband how much I like his show. Really funny!! Seriously. My kids love it! You know . . . I've been doing some writing, too. I know. Crazy, right? But I have to say . . . I do think it's pretty good. It's a reality show. I don't want to say too much, you know, for legal reasons. Not that I think you would steal it, but someone else might read this. But if you want, I could send you a secure copy (or a fax), and if you like it I wouldn't mind if you gave it to your husband to pass along to his agent or the head of the network his show is on. And don't worry . . . if they want to buy it, I won't forget who helped me out! ;)*

Maggie never responded, and while disappointed, Miranda tried to remain stoic.

"I never would have thought little Maggie Lester would turn into some stuck-up Hollywood phony," she told Ray while sitting in bed updating Bailey's Flickr page. "I guess you never really do know people."

Standing outside the hotel, her hands shaking with rage, Miranda read the Shooting Notice again and tried to figure out whom this fucking show could possibly be about. But in her heart, she knew. She knew it like she knew her own fears. If it wasn't Bailey, there was only one other logical choice: Starr Kennedy and her grosshog bitch bag of a mother, Theresa.

Starr was arguably the greatest child pageant contestant ever. By the age of five, she had broken the record for most consecutive wins (thirty-six), and by seven had entered *Guinness World Records* for "Most Concurrent Beauty Pageant Titles" (fifty-two). Rumors were circulating that Donald Trump himself had been keeping tabs on her for the Miss Teen USA Pageant, rumors undoubtedly started by the publicist Theresa got Starr for her eighth birthday. One of Miranda's greatest failures as a mother was that Bailey had never beaten Starr in competition. She did, however, take Starr's crown for Little Miss Golden Roses when the girl was forced to step down over allegations that Theresa provided sexual favors to one of the judges.

Calling the charges "offensive and calculated," Theresa demanded a hearing of the Golden Roses Council of Elders, two of whom recused themselves citing a conflict of interest. But after hearing the evidence, the council's verdict stood. Bailey was officially named Little Miss Golden Roses while Starr was given the insulting title of Honorary First Runner-up. It was a slap in the face Theresa refused to accept, and she vowed to pull her marquee daughter from all future pageants sponsored by the Golden Roses Organization. However, Theresa's refusal to appeal the elders' decision lent credence to the rumors, which had grown to orgiastic proportions throughout the circuit.

Miranda hated Theresa's liposuctioned guts. Everything about the woman made her want to vomit: her sun-damaged skin, bleached blond hair, the way she stuffed herself into her tight Target jeans and clomped around like a Clydesdale in her Jessica Simpson stilettos. She looked exactly like the aging Florida stripper she was rumored to be. All that being said, Miranda found it hard not to admire Theresa's Machiavellian approach to competition. Nothing short of physically assaulting another contestant was off-limits. Bailey had fallen victim to her psychological warfare many times, most recently at the Sweet Ray of Sunshine Invitational (Pigeon Forge, Tennessee) six months prior.

"Good gracious, Bailey!" Theresa said, seeing Bailey backstage, "look at your feet!"

Bailey had grown immune to Miranda's criticism, but Theresa was a master at finding someone's softest spot and plunging an acrylic nail into it.

"What's wrong with them?" the girl asked softly.

"They're so *big*. Are you wearing clown shoes?"

Theresa laughed at her "joke," then put her arm around Bailey's shoulder to physically sense the peak of the girls' vulnerability and went in for the kill.

"Now, don't you worry about a thing, sweetie. Not everyone thinks big feet are nasty. My granny had big feet, and she could climb a tree like a monkey! Just be careful and don't trip, 'cause that would be *really* embarrassing. Not to mention, you'd definitely lose to Starr again. Anywho, looks like you still need to put your face on, so I'ma go. Good luck."

She then used her bony thumb to wipe an inky black tear from Bailey's cheek, and winked at Miranda, who stood by speechless, in awe of that bitch's game.

Theresa's warning became a self-fulfilling prophecy, and Bailey stumbled during her gymnastics routine, giving Starr the title, her third that week. Across the room, Miranda shot daggers at Theresa, who returned them with a frosty, shit-eating shrug.

Four months later, Miranda sent a gift basket of barbeque from Theresa's brother-in-law's restaurant to the judges of the upcoming Cinderella Model Search and Pageant (Bowling Green, Kentucky). The enclosed card read, "Be sure to suck the bones! Love, T." Miranda then filed an anonymous complaint accusing Theresa of bribing the judges with gifts of food, an offense expressly forbidden in the Cinderella bylaws. Citing lingering questions surrounding Theresa's history of judge tampering and wanting to avoid even a hint of impropriety, the Cinderella Organization banned Starr from competition without so much as a hearing. It turned out to be a wasted effort. While attempting a complicated series of back handsprings in a new gymnastics routine, Bailey snagged her toe on the hem of her skirt and fell, landing her as First Runner-up.

"That effing *skank,*" Miranda muttered. The reality show *had* to be about Starr, who else? Besides Bailey, there weren't many contestants who warranted that level of exposure. Karolynne Simpson was a possibility, but she hadn't been truly competitive since her father ran off to Miami with that Vietnamese lady-boy he met on Craigslist. Cashburn Tinsley? Surely that wonky eye prevented her from being on TV since it consistently prevented her from winning a title. Maybe it was just Starr.

Miranda wiped her eyes with her sleeve. "Dammit," she whispered. "Why can't something good ever happen to *me*?" She turned to Bailey, who'd been staring into space, thinking about food. "Take the bags inside, baby. I'll be right there."

As Bailey pushed the luggage cart through the busy hotel lobby, Miranda stood outside ripping the Shooting Notice into hundreds of tiny pieces, imagining it was Theresa's stupid face.

chapter six

In a dark living room that reeked of old man's pajamas and impending death, Ray slumped in a tattered easy chair and fought to keep his eyes open. His hospice patient, Marvin Daye, lay unconscious in the rented hospital bed next to him, wheezing through what was left of his lung. Marvin had smoked two packs of unfiltered Camels a day for sixty-four years, and for the past sixty-four nights, Ray's job was to sit and watch him die. It was a pretty sweet gig. Every few hours Ray would change the old man's catheter and roll him to prevent bedsores. On the rare occasion Marvin was awake, Ray would read to him or try to persuade the old man to drink some broth, but mostly he just changed his IV and watched ESPN. Marvin's prolonged death also allowed Ray to play grab bag with three shoe boxes overflowing with medications. Ray had been catatonic in the chair for two hours. He was pretty sure it was Dilaudid. Dilaudid was the shit.

Faint music emanated from somewhere. Ray looked around for its source. The air felt like pudding. It was a good fifteen seconds before he recognized it as his ringtone: *Here I am, on the road again. There I am, on the stage. Here I go, playing star again. There I go, turn the page . . .*

He unclipped the phone from his waistband and tried to speak. His tongue was pasty and thick. "This"—he cleared his throat—"this is Ray."

"They stole my show!" Miranda's voice was so loud he almost didn't need the phone to hear her. He slumped a little deeper in his chair.

"What?"

"They stole my show! They just up and stole it!"

Every weekend, Ray got at least one call from Miranda complaining about some perceived slight. The week before she had him paged at the hospital.

"Does Bailey walk like a softball player?"

Ray had just spent an hour in the ER helping remove an arrow from a fourteen-year-old girl's leg.

"I don't even know what that means," he said.

"Yes, you do. They walk with that *stride,* you know? Like they know how to fix a motorcycle."

"Are you drunk?"

Miranda produced the sigh that had become their shorthand for moving on from dead-end conversations. A lot of these calls ended with that sigh.

"Who—what show . . . what are you talking about?" He needed water.

"My pageant show! About me and Bailey? Remember? The one I've been working on for five years? How could you forget about that? Someone stole my idea, and now they're doing *my* show about someone else!"

Oh. *That* show.

"Well . . . I'm really sorry, babe. That really . . . you know, sucks. It sucks. It does. It sucks. Sorry."

There was a long silence before, "That's it? That's all you've got to say?"

"Um. I . . ." He exhaled. "What—what do you want me to say?"

"You could try to be a little more sympathetic. Dammit, Ray, why can't you just support me for once?"

Ray sat up a little straighter. The peaceful, easy feeling of the Dilaudid had vanished, leaving behind a growing haze of impatience and exhaustion—serenity with a hangover.

"You're right, Miranda. I don't support you nearly enough. You know what, how about this . . . what if I quit one of my jobs and only work seventy hours a week so you and Bailey can stay home and we can sit around all weekend and support each other. How's that sound?"

Silence.

" 'Cause I'm happy to try having a family." He breathed. "I'm already paying for one."

After another moment of silence, he heard his wife's small, sad voice cracking through the phone. "I just . . . I just really wanted to be on a TV show. I thought it would be a good opportunity. For us. For all of us."

Ray exhaled the rest of his anger and rubbed his red, tired eyes.

"I know. I'm sorry. I'm just . . . really tired."

"You work so hard, Ray. Don't think I don't notice."

"I know you do. Thanks." He looked over at Marvin and tried to remember the last time his whole family was in the same room together. Easter? What month was this?

"Just"—he cleared his throat again—"just try to not let

it bother you so much, the show. There's nothing you can do about it anyway, right? Maybe this is happening because something better is waiting right around the corner."

She smiled. "Maybe."

"I'm sure of it. So get some rest and make sure Bailey's focused and ready for tomorrow."

There was a sniffle on the other end, then the sigh. "Don't forget to pick up the boys at Mom's. Also, check on her knees if you have time. She can barely walk. I don't think she's taking her medication."

"I'll go by when I'm done here."

"Okay. Good night. Sorry I was so . . ." Her voice trailed off, implying a behavior she'd frequently been accused of but didn't want to validate by saying out loud.

"It's okay. Kiss Bailey for me."

"I will."

"And I'm sorry about your show. I know you really wanted it."

He could hear her smile on the other end.

"Thanks. Love."

"Love." Ray turned off his phone and dropped it on the matted rug at his feet. Letting his head fall back, he focused on a yellow water stain on the ceiling and tried to figure out when his marriage became the most difficult yet least time-consuming of his full-time jobs. Things used to be so much more fun, before the kids, before the pageants. Truth be told, the whole pageant thing didn't even make sense to him. Before Bailey was born, Miranda had only competed in three pageants her whole life.

When Christie introduced them, Miranda was dating an abusive but charming asshole named Phil Hatfield, who explained away his violent behavior by claiming to be a direct descendant of the famous feuding family.

"Violence is in my blood, and I don't know a man alive who can change his blood."

Phil managed a regionally famous restaurant called Mom's that had no menu and took no reservations. The dining room consisted of six four-top tables on the first floor of a massive plantation home on the bank of the river. Velvet flocked gold-and-burgundy wallpaper perfectly absorbed the natural light that streamed in from the floor-to-ceiling leaded-glass windows and gave the room a dim romantic hue even at midday. Dinner started promptly at seven, and the first two dozen people who showed up got to eat whatever Phil's mother chose to cook that night. Leftovers were sent home with the diners free of charge, and latecomers were turned away even if seats were available, no exceptions.

"Nothing makes you feel closer to God than feeding people," Mom liked to say as she raised her glass of Sauvignon Blanc, "and nothing makes you feel closer to the devil than my jam cake."

Phil's job was to greet the customers; tell them what Mom was cooking that night; announce any birthdays, anniversaries, retirements, etc.; then play Jackson Browne songs on his guitar until the food was ready.

Having just graduated from Owensboro Community College with an associate's degree in humanities, Miranda was eager to dive into the workforce, but humanities jobs were scarce.

"I've never waitressed before," she told Phil during her interview, "but I have eaten in a lot of restaurants, and I like talking to people, so I'm pretty sure I could do a good job at it." She smiled in a way that showed all of her teeth and none of herself. If those three pageants had taught her anything, it was how to bullshit her way through an interview question.

Sex was inevitable. They were young, good-looking, and single. In Phil, Miranda saw a dreamy self-starting artist and entrepreneur. In Miranda, Phil saw a hot twenty-one-year-old with a great ass. Their eventual hookup was so unsurprising that when she blew him after her fourth night at work, it was as passionless as the birthday obligation of an old married couple. After he came, Phil dropped a set of keys on the table and grabbed his coat.

"All right, I'm outta here. Marry the ketchups before you lock up. And don't touch the register. I know exactly how much is in there." He pointed at her, "This is a test," then winked.

Joan did not approve. Phil was a full six years older than Miranda, and she thought the whole relationship was obscene.

"He's a full-grown man and you're still a baby," Joan said.

"I am *not* a baby, Mom. I'm a woman! And this is none of your business! I have a college degree and I am perfectly capable of making my own decisions."

"I know, dear, but he just seems so . . . worldly."

"Are you saying I'm not worldly? I've been to Cancún! Twice! I am totally worldly!"

Five weeks on, Miranda wished she'd listened to her mother. Working with her boyfriend was not the lighthearted Meg Ryan rom-com she had envisioned. It was closer to a Tori Spelling Lifetime movie. When *anything* went wrong at the restaurant, Phil blamed Miranda. If the silverware was dirty, she should have "fucking seen it and replaced it." If the food was undercooked, she "should have stayed out of the goddamn kitchen and left Mom alone." If Phil's guitar was out of tune, she "should have been more fucking careful when you put the goddamn thing away!" Phil's abuse, while always verbal, had been escalating. The curt, private reprimands had started to become public admonishments, and Miranda was getting the feeling that he got a perverse thrill out of embarrassing her in front of people.

"Miranda!" he called from across the room. "Could you come here for a minute?"

Her chest tightened as she walked across the creaky wooden floor. "What seems to be the prob—?"

"Taste this." He shoved a drink at her.

"What is it?"

"Well, it's *supposed* to be a Diet Coke, but this customer says it's regular. Taste it."

"Phil, you don't have to—"

"Taste it!" he snarled, thrusting the glass at Miranda and splashing soda across her shirt.

The customer interjected, "It's no big deal. I can drink regular Coke—"

"Sir, please." Phil turned back to Miranda and said calmly, "now."

Trembling from embarrassment, Miranda sipped from the glass. "It is regular Coke. That's my fault," she said, turning to the customer, who was now equally embarrassed. "I am so sorry, sir. I'll bring you another one right away."

"Yes. You will!" Phil said, then shook his head in disgust and mumbled, "stupid twat."

From a table across the room, Ray sat with Christie and watched in stunned silence as the scene played out. Miranda first met Christie in their Global History of 20th-Century

Clothing class at OCC. Christie's dislike of Phil was no secret, and she'd set up this dinner so her nursing school friend, Ray, would see how awesome Miranda was and save her from Phil, the unworthy prick.

Ray was not a confronter. Never had been. If, at a grocery store, he was charged the full price instead of the sale price, he didn't bring it up. If someone cut in front of him in line, he might mumble a passive-aggressive insult under his breath, but he never told the person to get back. It just wasn't worth it. If Ray called everyone an asshole whom he felt truly deserved it, he wouldn't have time for anything else. But this was different. He'd been invited there specifically to meet Miranda, and because of that tenuous connection he felt vaguely responsible for her well-being. It was something akin to a date, albeit with a woman he had never met at a restaurant owned by her boyfriend. So Ray tossed his napkin onto the table, walked over to Phil, and got in his face.

"Excuse me. I think you should apologize."

"Sir, this doesn't concern you. It's an issue between me and my employee, and I will handle it. Why don't you just have a seat and I'll bring you a free dessert. Okay?"

Ray didn't move. "I *will* sit down. After you apologize to her and all these people you offended."

Phil cocked his head and glared at Ray, his eyes turning black with rage. They were the only two people in the world.

"What's your fucking problem?"

"Well, for one, I don't like how you talked to her."

"Is that right?" Phil took a step closer. "Well, I don't give a shit what you like. How I talk to her is none of your goddamned business."

Ray felt a warm rush of adrenaline tear through his body. *Holy shit, I'm going to have to fight this guy!* He took a deep, nervous breath but tried to disguise it by drawing it in slowly through his nose and squinting like Clint Eastwood. Diners rose from their chairs and moved to the other side of the restaurant where they secretly hoped the argument would escalate into a full-blown fistfight. Even Mom came out from the kitchen to watch.

Christie went to Miranda who, by this time, was on the floor crying, curled up in a ball by the banister that led to the second floor where Mom lived. Earlier, when Christie first pointed Miranda out, Ray thought she was pretty; now—seeing her whimpering on the cold wooden floor, trying to make herself as small as possible, desperate for someone to protect her—he found her irresistible. No one was going to hurt Miranda Ford ever again. Ray would make sure of that. Nodding to his future wife, Ray tried to tell her this telepathically. She nodded back, pretty sure she'd heard him.

Phil was now snorting hot breath like a cartoon bull. It felt wet on Ray's face, but he ignored it and met Phil's eye.

"It *is* my business because I came here to have a nice dinner with my friend, and you're ruining that by making this young woman cry. Now, either you apologize to her and to everyone else here, or we can go outside and I'll show you what a twat really looks like." Summoning every ounce of testosterone in the room, Ray tilted his head and snarled, "I'll show you *my* twat!" The room went silent.

As soon as the words left his mouth, Ray knew he'd blown it. *I'll show you* my *twat? Jesus, that doesn't even make sense.* He stood his ground and waited for Phil to stomp him into a greasy spot. But surprisingly, nothing happened. Faced with having to confront someone of equal or greater strength, Phil backed down.

Nodding toward Miranda, he barked a cursory "Sorry," then turned to the wildly disappointed diners and brusquely apologized to them as well. Stomping into the kitchen, Phil smashed his guitar on a stack of dishes and stormed out the back door.

Ray grabbed a glass of wine sitting on the nearest table, emptied it in a single gulp, then exhaled for what felt like a full minute.

Getting to her feet, Miranda met Ray in the middle of the room. If it had happened in a movie, everyone else would've faded into darkness as a single spotlight illuminated them from above. Her tear-streaked face beamed at the unexpected savior standing in front of her. They would have stood there forever staring at each other if Christie hadn't finally said something

"Miranda, this is Ray. Ray, Miranda."

That was thirteen years ago yesterday. Neither of them remembered.

Ray looked at his phone sitting on the old rag rug that covered the creaky wooden floor. He remembered the days before cell phones, how nice it was being unavailable. Cell phones had made everyone more accessible, which only made the world smaller. Unfortunately, no one realized that the world was already too small to begin with. Now it felt crowded. Bending over would have required more energy than he was willing to sacrifice, so he forgot about his phone and turned his attention to Marvin's shoe boxes of pills.

"Trouble with the wife?"

Ray jumped. "Jesus Christ. You scared the hell out of me."

Standing in the doorway was Marvin's seventeen-year-old granddaughter, Courtney.

"Didn't anyone ever tell you it's not polite to eavesdrop? How long have you been there?" he asked.

She shrugged.

"Well . . . what's going on with my wife is not any of your business."

"Sorry. I was just trying to make conversation. How's Granddaddy?" she asked, smiling sadly toward Marvin. His shallow breathing rattled like a peach pit in a garbage disposal.

"About the same. Sleeping mostly. Sometimes I think he'll outlive us all."

"I wish he would." Courtney stared at her grandfather for a long time. "He looks so noble. Don't you think he looks noble?"

"Noble" was not the word Ray would have used to describe the shrunken husk of a man in the bed next to him. "Rotting human jerky" was closer. Marvin's dark, sunken eyes and hollow cheeks made his skin cling to his face like a gray ribbed condom had been pulled over his skull. Clumps of white, wispy hair turned sickly yellow at the roots sprouted from his head, chin, and ears. And his toothless mouth hung open as if in the middle of a painful, silent scream. Marvin was the closest thing to a real-life zombie Ray had ever seen.

"Sure. Noble," Ray said unconvincingly. "I can see that."

"Is he awake?"

"No. He's been unconscious since I got here."

Ray pretended not to be bothered by the long silence that followed. Finally, he looked back to Courtney and noticed for the first time that she was wearing a raincoat. "What's with the coat? Is it raining out?"

"No," she said, opening the raincoat, revealing her naked body. "But I am pretty wet."

The coat slid from her shoulders and fell into a pile at her feet just like she'd practiced in the mirror upstairs. Posing against the doorframe, the teenager stared into Ray's eyes with a self-assuredness that terrified him and turned him on in equal measure. He melted into his chair and took in every inch of her body. A bit of baby fat stubbornly clung to her face and belly, which was soft and smooth like a memory foam pillow. But her breasts . . . those things were flawless—the perfect size, the perfect shape, symmetrical, proportional, breathtaking. In California she would've been considered overweight, but in Kentucky she was perfect. Tiptoeing across the room, Courtney placed her hands on the arms of Ray's chair and leaned over him, letting her long blond hair cover his face.

"I've missed you," she whispered.

"I, um"—he cleared his throat—"I've missed you, too," he said. "How was that back-to-school dance? Did you go?"

She shrugged. "Yeah. It was fine, I guess. The DJ only played dance music so I left early and got wasted with some friends, so . . . it was whatever."

Without realizing it, Ray's hands had found their way to her hips. He searched his soul for the strength to stop, but his soul was distracted by the perfect teenage breasts in his face. When their lips met, a quivering numbness swept through his body. His breathing stopped and he felt weightless yet helplessly earthbound, a week-old party balloon blown a few inches into the air by an opening door, then settling again with a gentle, almost imperceptible bounce. Why wasn't there a pill like this?

Okay. This is your last chance, Ray thought. *Stop now before something—uhp, well here we go.*

Courtney slid Ray's pants down below his knees and straddled the married male nurse charged with helping her last living relative die with dignity. It was not an ideal chair for lovemaking—the ancient upholstery chafed Ray's bare ass, and Courtney's long legs barely squeezed through the armrests—but once they got into position, she rocked his world.

It always took a moment for Ray to wrap his mind around the fact that he was having sex with a minor. *I'm smarter than this,* he thought every time, fighting the instinct to run his fingertips down the girl's bare back. But once he was inside her, and the crime had been committed, he figured he might as well go ahead and enjoy himself.

Their eyes locked for a moment. She bit her lip and smiled. "*You* fuck good."

Ray blushed and looked away. Talking during sex embarrassed him, especially if the talk was about the sex currently taking place. It was too present for him. Plus, Courtney was really bad at it. Both her word choice and inflection were odd, making her sound like a horny Scandinavian immigrant.

"In *the* spot," she whispered.

"Mmmmm," Ray moaned flatly, confused and self-conscious, then turned back to her magnificent breasts and fought his sudden urge to come.

Most men thought of baseball or grandmothers to slow

their orgasms, but baseball made Ray think of *Bull Durham,* which made him think of Susan Sarandon, which defeated the purpose. Grandmothers also made him think of Susan Sarandon. So instead, Ray thought about his three hundred sixty-five dead patients. One after the other, their sad, hopeless faces flashed through his head, each one more lust crushing than the last. But not even that was working. Traces of various erectile dysfunction medications were always lurking in his system, making any sustained sexual performance next to impossible.

Ray scanned the room for the least erotic thing he could find: yellowed family photos, a sagging shelf of 1960s encyclopedias, a stack of old *Readers Digest*s piled on the TV, Marvin's service medals, the half-full catheter peeking out from under the sheet. Slowly, Ray's eyes moved up the hospital bed, past the metal side rails, past the IV line . . . until he saw Marvin, wide awake, looking back at him, his mouth still open in that horrible, frozen scream.

"Jesus Christ!" Ray shrieked and bucked hard, trying to stand up, but Courtney had wrapped her legs around the back of the chair for leverage, trapping him in place. Mistaking his sudden horror for passion, Courtney smiled and quickened her pace.

"Okay, *let's* come!"

From his deathbed, Marvin watched helplessly as his trusted caretaker fucked his underage granddaughter in the chair where his late wife used to pray. Ray wanted to look away from the old man, but he couldn't. Using the same telepathy he'd used on Miranda thirteen years earlier, Ray tried to convey to Marvin how immeasurably sorry he was about all this. But the sincerity of his apology was undercut considerably when his face contorted into the unmistakable grimace of an orgasm.

"I'm coming, too!" Courtney squealed as she faked an earth-shattering climax. "Oh, my good sweet *God*! Whooo!"

Exhaling deeply, she untangled her legs from the chair, climbed off, and headed to the kitchen. "That was awesome. You want a beer?"

Pulling up his pants with lightning speed, Ray shot cautious, staccato glances toward Marvin as if they were fingers testing the temperature of a hot stove. The old man was unconscious again—or dead. Either way, Ray was relieved.

"Thank God," he said, falling back into his chair.

Still shamelessly naked, Courtney reentered holding a beer. Her skin was flushed and glistening. "My birthday's in two weeks. Remember?"

"How could I forget?" Ray tore open the beer and drank half of it in one desperate gulp. "You'll be eighteen."

"I know! So we don't have to worry about all that stupid legal stuff anymore. We're still going to Gatlinburg, right?"

Ray wasn't listening. How long had Marvin been awake? How much had he seen? He saw her initiate, right? Dozens of scenarios popped into his head, and most of them ended with him getting raped in prison.

"I'm sorry, what?"

"Gatlinburg! You promised you'd take me to Gatlinburg for my birthday!"

Shit. He sighed. He had. "Right."

A week into their affair, Ray promised Courtney that when she turned eighteen he would take her wherever she wanted for her birthday, naïvely assuming she'd want to do something simple like dinner and a movie. Instead, she shouted, "Gatlinburg!" with such childlike enthusiasm Ray assumed she was joking and laughed. Proving just how serious she was, Courtney immediately stopped the blow job she was in the middle of and locked herself in the bathroom until he agreed to take her.

"Yeah. We can go," he said, eyeing Marvin's boxes of medication. "If you still want to."

"Hells yeah, I still want to! It's all I've been thinking about."

"Mm-hm. Me, too." His voice was hollow and distant like he was speaking from the bottom of his own grave.

The naked teenager took a sip of Ray's beer, made a *yuck* face, and gave it back.

"Lite beer is gross. Okay, I gotta go finish my homework. I got a killer test tomorrow. Hey, do you know anything about algebra?"

Ray shook his head. "No, sorry," he said, then gestured to Marvin with his chin. "I should probably get back to work."

Courtney let out a small laugh through her nose and rolled her eyes.

"Yeah, whatever. Thanks for the sex, Nurse Miller." Giggling, she kissed his forehead, then flitted out of the room, snatching up her raincoat as she went.

When she was gone, Ray blindly grabbed three pills and washed them down with the last of his beer. Taking a deep breath, he leaned in to the elderly gentleman he'd been preparing to reunite with his wife in heaven and whispered, "I am so sorry, Marvin."

The old man opened his eyes and turned to Ray. For a

moment Ray caught a glimpse of his own conscience—a withered, terminal relic.

"You sure are." Marvin's voice was stronger and clearer than Ray had ever heard it. "You're the sorriest son of a bitch I've ever met in my life."

Then turning back to the ceiling, the old man opened his mouth into that horrible scream and drifted off back to sleep.

chapter seven

Courtney Ellen Daye was eleven years old when her parents were killed coming home from an Offspring concert. The police report said that Courtney's father had fallen asleep at the wheel, sending their car into a ravine just outside Evansville, Indiana. The impact of the air bag had broken Courtney's mother's neck as she slept in her husband's lap. Marvin blamed himself for their deaths. He had selfishly suggested the parents' night out, knowing Courtney was fast approaching the age where spending the night with her grandparents would segue from being a gleeful adventure to an embarrassing chore. To compensate, Marvin and his wife, Zola, cared for their orphaned granddaughter as if she were an antique Bible. If possible, they would have placed her on a shelf in a church out of reach of the entire world.

When Zola dropped dead from a heart attack picking tomatoes in their garden, Marvin was left as the then fourteen-year-old girl's only living relative. Two years later, diabetes required the amputation of both his legs, which unfortunately did little to alter his already sedentary life. A spinal fracture from sliding off a barstool had prevented him from walking for the previous sixteen months. Doctors at the Bluegrass Baptist Spinal Center decided that surgery to alleviate the pain was not an option since Marvin's COPD had grown so severe doctors feared he wouldn't survive the procedure. However, repeated surgeries to remove large chunks of tumor-ravaged lung—and the occasional inch or two of leg—took place every couple months for the next year.

"The spinal fracture, well, that's just pain," the surgeon explained to an increasingly confused Courtney. "People live with pain every day. But those tumors, they could kill him."

Marvin's final surgery left him with thirty-two percent of a single lung. His left leg was eleven inches long; his right was just over seven. When his primary care physician gave him less than seventy-two hours to live, Ray was assigned to be his hospice nurse. He assumed Marvin would be a quick job—five days tops. Ten weeks later, Ray looked into the old man's eyes as he came inside his granddaughter.

Courtney's small-town naïveté was tempered with just enough personal tragedy to make her endlessly fascinating to a bored married man approaching middle age. The time she and Ray spent together—playing board games at the kitchen table, sharing frozen pizzas, laughing as they scrolled through each other's iPods—soon became the highlight of his week. For a cute teenage girl, Courtney was surprisingly easy to talk to. Her father had left behind an impressive DVD collection, and in an effort to stay connected to him she had watched every one of them. They talked about movies for hours.

"I think people are just afraid to say Wes Anderson movies are dumb," she said. "But, dude, they're like superdumb.

They're like cartoons for people who think they're smarter than they really are."

But what Ray liked most about Courtney was that she made him feel interesting at a time in his life when he was starting to believe he'd become anything but. She soon became his closest friend. Then out of nowhere, she blew him.

One unfortunate side effect of Marvin's growing list of medications was that he would often involuntarily pick at the stitches of his leg stump.

"Marvin!" the doctor shouted, during a rare housecall apparently believing that losing one's legs causes deafness. "If you keep picking at these, they're going to get infected and then you're going to be in *real* trouble!"

Marvin looked at the doctor and winked. Ray couldn't tell if the old man was acknowledging this as a problem or as his ultimate plan. Wrist restraints were ordered, and then, curious to see what the old man's body was capable of, the doctor prescribed an experimental blood clotter that ultimately didn't mix well with Marvin's twenty-one other daily medications. The resulting vomit was prodigious and unpredictable.

"I hate those wrist restraint things," Courtney said. "They're so cruel. It's like he's an animal or something."

"Yeah, well . . ." Ray replied.

"What if he throws up and chokes on it because he can't move?"

"That shouldn't happen, but if it does, I'll handle it. Don't worry."

"What if there's a fire? How will he escape?"

"There's not going to be a fire," Ray answered.

"But what if there is?"

"Then I'll remove the restraints and carry him out."

"What if you're in the bathroom?"

"Then I'll stop what I'm doing and come get him."

"You can stop in the middle of going to the bathroom? I didn't think guys could do that because it hurt."

She continued on like that until Ray relented and removed Marvin's restraints. An hour later, while kneeling beside the bed to change a catheter bag, Ray felt Marvin's hot, watery vomit rain down on the back of his neck.

"Oh, my God, that is so nasty!" Courtney screamed as she ran from the room covering her own mouth. "It's in your ears!"

"Don't worry, Marvin," Ray whispered as he cleaned the old man up. "It's not the first time I've been thrown up on. I'm sure it's not the last."

The old man smiled, then strained to speak. "I vomited once . . . on a dead . . . Korean boy. He was . . . our translator. I killed him . . . by mistake. I'm . . . sorry." The things people confessed to Ray before they died never ceased to surprise him.

By the time Ray had him cleaned up, the vomit had turned cold and made its way down to Ray's feet, saturating his socks and punctuating each step with a nauseating squish. Climbing into the shower, Ray closed his eyes as hot water pulsed from the removable showerhead, a device forbidden in his house out of respect for Miranda's late father. It was so peaceful he didn't hear Courtney slide open the shower door.

"I brought you a clean towel."

"Ah!" Ray jumped and instinctively covered his genitals. "Jesus Christ!"

She smiled. "I'll just put it on the toilet seat."

"Oh. Okay. Great." He nodded frantically and backed into the corner. "Awesome. I will use it. Thank you. Thanks."

When the girl smiled again, Ray felt the early stirrings of an erection and turned his attention to the numerous bottles lining the shelves. "That's, um . . . that's a lot of shampoo," he said desperately. "I used the green bottle, I think. I don't remember."

"Okay." Her lips pursed into a mischievous smirk, and she scrunched her eyebrows into the face girls use to simultaneously flirt and deride. "Weirdo." Then she giggled and slid the door closed.

Reluctant to move, Ray watched through the frosted glass as Courtney casually took off her jeans and kicked them across the floor. His mouth turned pasty and thick, and he felt his penis move beneath the increasingly inadequate cover of his hands. It was entirely possible he blacked out for a moment, because before he could comprehend what was happening, Courtney had joined him in the shower, naked as a newborn—which she was when Ray was a senior in high school. His heart constricted into a panicked fist pounding a desperate warning against the wall of his chest. Ray grabbed a pink washcloth and covered his penis.

"What are you doing?"

Courtney just giggled and shrugged. "I thought I'd help you get cleaned up."

Steam clouded the near perfection of Courtney's body, but her lack of inhibition was clear. Without another word, she sat on the plastic bench Marvin used back when he had legs, and blew the married nurse as warm water rained down on her head. When Ray came, Courtney stepped out of the shower, grabbed her clothes, and left the bathroom. It was never discussed—until the next night when she did it again.

Acutely aware that their relationship was not only immoral but probably illegal, Ray spent many sleepless nights envisioning himself being passed from cell to cell, traded for a pack of cigarettes or a stick of Juicy Fruit—a nickname he also imagined would become his. At the very least he was sure his disheveled mug shot would wind up on a sex offender Web site with a scarlet dot over his house, assuming he'd still be allowed to live there, which he wouldn't. The Internet said the age of consent in Kentucky was sixteen, but that gave him little solace. He was old enough to be the girl's father, and he couldn't imagine any rational judge giving him a mere slap on the wrist. However, despite the very real consequences, Ray couldn't bring himself to end it. And not just because of the sex. In much the same way he'd felt compelled to rescue Miranda from the abusive Phil, Ray saw himself as Courtney's savior. With her eighteenth birthday just two weeks away, his goal was to keep Marvin alive so Courtney could inherit his house without the courts getting involved. How fucking her accomplished any of that was the part of the plan he hadn't yet figured out.

Staring at the textured ceiling of his bedroom, Ray pulled the sheets up to his chin and tried not to think about his behavior. Instead, he focused on his plans for the next day. Pop Warner football tryouts were coming up and he had taken the day off to help Junior and J.J. prepare. Both boys were small for their ages, and homeschooling had made them socially awkward, but Ray wasn't worried. Organized sports would give them exactly what they needed. Whatever the hell that was.

During his weekly trek to Walmart to pick up the groceries he liked but Miranda refused to buy, Ray also bought a new football, some mouth guards, and two top-of-the-line pairs of cleats. They'd been in a closet for several days, and Ray was pretty pleased with himself for keeping it a secret. His plan was to surprise the boys when they came down for breakfas—

"Holy shit! The boys!" Ray leapt from the bed, dug his phone from his pants, and turned it on. There were nine missed calls from Joan. He looked at the clock on the nightstand: 11:46.

"Motherfucker!"

Snatching some sweatpants off the top of a pile of dirty clothes and an old Mötley Crüe T-shirt he'd masturbated into a few days before, Ray grabbed his keys and shot out the front door.

Fishtailing into Joan's backyard driveway, Ray's Jeep narrowly missed the rusty old barrel where his mother-in-law still illegally burned her trash. Bounding up the patio steps, he banged on the screen door and waited. After a few seconds, he knocked again, then cupped his eyes and peered into the inky blackness of the kitchen. All he could see was the blinking 12:00 of the microwave clock and the glowing burner of the stove Joan had forgotten to shut off. After his third knock, the porch light flashed on, and Joan, wearing Roger's old bathrobe and carrying a broken pool cue, cracked the door.

"Hey, Joan. Sorry if I woke you. The boys still up?"

"No, Ray. It's after midnight. They fell asleep in front of

the TV about an hour ago. I tried calling you, but it kept going to messages so I stopped."

"Yeah, my battery just . . ." He let out an exasperated sigh and let her fill in the rest. He then moved to go inside, but Joan shifted her body and blocked his path.

"They're already asleep, Ray. Why don't you just let them stay over and I'll bring them by in the morning on my way to the market."

Joan referred to every establishment that sold goods and/or services as "the market." It was one of the many things about Joan that bugged the living shit out of him.

"I appreciate that, but I took tomorrow off so the boys and I could practice some football. Tryouts are next week, and they need a little extra coaching."

Joan winced at the word "tryouts." The very idea of her boys having to prove themselves to a bunch of strangers was the height of insult. Who were *they* to pass judgment on *her* sterling young men of God?

"So . . . can I get them? Please?"

Joan stared at Ray for a long time without saying anything. Why was he so jumpy? And why did he look so out of sorts? Was he on drugs? Was he having an affair? She realized she couldn't possibly know the answers, but Jesus would.

He responded immediately.

Oh Joan, you are truly one of my favorites. Ray's not a bad man. He's just a mess because he works so hard. Now, go get those boys and we'll talk tomorrow.

Joan chuckled at her own silliness. Of course, Ray wasn't bad. How could she even think such a thing? He was the father of her grandchildren, for Pete's sake. *Good heavens, what is wrong with me?* she thought.

Not a thing, Joan. Not one single thing.

Opening the door, Joan let Ray into her house, then looked up at the heavens and gave Jesus a quick wink. Try as she might, it was impossible not to blush when He winked back.

chapter eight

The corridors of the Knoxville Crowne Plaza were teeming with little girls wearing enough makeup to offend a South Beach prostitute. Mothers, grandmothers, coaches, and a few bored fathers herded half-naked contestants in and out of hotel rooms while highly paid teams of consultants gave their final opinions on hair, clothes, poise, makeup, and coquettish expressions. "You go, girl!" was heard from every room, often sounding more like a command than an encouragement.

With her hair set in massive three-inch curlers, Bailey weaved through the mayhem, licking peanut butter off a plastic spoon. She was allowed to have peanut butter on pageant days because it was a good source of protein, and Miranda had heard an Olympic swimmer say that protein was good for a body in training.

"Pageanting takes just as much energy as swimming," Miranda said. "More, probably, if you count the mental part."

Cradling a bucket under her arm, Bailey searched for the ice machine. If memory served, it was at the end of the hall near the housekeeping station. Most hotels, the decent ones, anyway, did that now, put their ice and vending machines out of earshot of their guests. Bailey had become very familiar with hotels. Most of them were exactly the same: bright patterned carpeting, drab textured wallpaper, Art Deco wall sconces, flowers by the elevators. Bailey liked it, the similarity. At least if she had to spend every weekend in a new place, she could count on a few things being the same.

Miranda had been up all night crying about someone stealing her TV show, and Bailey had been sent to get ice for the swelling under her mother's eyes. Any excuse to get out of the room was a welcome one, so Bailey grabbed the bucket and—when Miranda wasn't looking—slipped a dollar from her purse.

Bailey's interest in pageanting had dwindled to the point of nonexistence. Aside from the fact that all the pageants felt exactly the same, Bailey had grown increasingly tired of being judged by people who had probably never read a book that didn't have beach chairs on the cover. There wasn't a specific incident that soured her on competing, but standing backstage at the Dixie Dolls Spectacular (Jackson, Mississippi), she realized she didn't really like any of the other girls, or their mothers. Especially their mothers.

"Everyone's so two-faced and mean," she told Miranda. "All they do is smile and wish me good luck, then go off and pray for me to make a mistake. Why do we spend so much time with them?"

"Because you love pageants, Bailey. You have since you were a baby."

"Fine, but . . ." Bailey chose her words carefully. "I think I might like to try something else."

Miranda inhaled deeply. "Like what?"

The true answer was "nothing." Bailey wanted to do nothing. For as long as she could remember, every spare moment of her life had been scheduled: after-school dance classes or vocal lessons, gymnastics, dress fittings, yoga classes, photography sittings, nutrition classes, spin classes, kickboxing. Then every weekend they would pack up the minivan and drive to some random town where Bailey would make herself unrecognizable and perform like a trained chimp. She was tired of it.

"I think maybe I'd be happier spending weekends at home with my friends. I never get to see them because we're always running around doing pageants. And I think it would be fun to just, you know, hang out. Play games, ride my bike, read books . . ."

Miranda looked at her daughter like she'd farted a curse word in church. "Wait. Where is this coming from? Did something happen?" Her tone turned dark. "Did Theresa *do* something to you?"

"No, Mom. No one did anything to me. It's just . . ." Bailey shrugged, "It's just something I've been thinking about for a while now. I think it might be time to retire."

Miranda shook her head. "Nine-year-olds don't retire, Bailey. And you've worked too hard to just quit. Besides, a lot of famous and successful women owe their careers to pageants. Diane Sawyer was America's Junior Miss; Sarah Palin was Second Runner-up in Miss Alaska; Halle Berry was Miss Teen All American; Oprah Winfrey was Miss Fire Prevention; Sandra Bullock was Miss Congeniality—"

"That was a movie, Mom."

"Yes, but I think they based that on a true story, so . . ." Miranda gave a knowing smile. "Besides, you name me one attractive, famous woman who sat around all day reading books."

Bailey nodded. "Yeah, that's a really good point, but I just thought it might be nice to go out on top, you know? People love that."

"No one loves a quitter, baby. They love winners. And you're a winner, not a quitter."

Bailey wasn't surprised by her mother's response. Miranda was defined by Bailey's success as much as, if not more than, she was. If Bailey quit, then Miranda's life would no longer have purpose. For Bailey to stop competing there would need to be a good reason, and since there *was* no good reason—at least not one Miranda would accept—Bailey devised a plan: She would compete for one more season, never complaining and never giving her mother reason to suspect she was unhappy. Meanwhile, she would try to gain so much weight that in the end Miranda would be begging her to retire. Bailey knew her mother couldn't stand fat girls in pageants, and she was more than happy to sabotage her own body as long as it took her career down with it. It had been a difficult year, especially after Miranda started monitoring her food and making her work out like Madonna. But if pageants had taught her anything, it was patience and determination.

After twelve months of surreptitious binge eating, it looked as if Bailey's plan was going to work. She was getting too big to win her age division, and Miranda would either have to let her quit or live with the shame of having a fat pageant daughter. But desperation breeds creativity, and what was more creative (or desperate) than cheating?

"Mom, I think this is a bad idea," Bailey said again, protesting her mother's birthdate scheme. "Everyone knows how old I am. These moms know more about their competition than they do their own husbands."

"You're just being dramatic," Miranda said dismissively.

"886-98-0093."

"What is that?"

"Starr's Social Security number. Please don't do this."

But Miranda would not listen. So Bailey dropped it. She'd once spent six months dancing to Tom Jones' "What's New, Pussycat?" while dressed as a cat princess. At this point she was immune to embarrassment. It was just one more part of her life that was out of her control.

The ice machine was tucked away in a dimly lit alcove by the emergency exit. When her bucket was full, Bailey fed the stolen dollar into the adjacent vending machine and freed a Baby Ruth from its corkscrew restraint. It landed with a satisfying thud. Tearing off the wrapper, Bailey devoured the candy in three quick bites. Retrieving her change, she found a small treasure in the form of an extra seventy-five cents forgotten by a traveling businessman.

"Sweet," Bailey said, her tongue thick with chocolate and caramel.

Staring at the drink machine, she considered her options, then selected a Mountain Dew, something she'd never tried but had heard good things about. She popped open the can and drained it in one stretch. The belch was deep and resonant, and Bailey smiled for the first time all weekend. In the last two minutes she had consumed more calories than Miranda allowed her in a day. It felt like Christmas. Stashing the candy wrapper and soda can in a nearby housekeeping cart, she skipped happily back to her room, ice bucket in tow, feeling more alive than she had in weeks.

Miranda, meanwhile, stood in front of the bathroom mirror rubbing hemorrhoid cream under her red, swollen eyes. It was a trick she picked up from a veteran pageant mom.

"That stuff was made to reduce swollen tissue," she'd said. "How does it know if the tissue is on your face or your butt?"

Wise people fascinated her.

Miranda inhaled deeply and watched the door, wondering what was taking Bailey so long. Her stomach burned. Brixton had been up all night tossing and turning, trying to soothe her mother's tears, and Miranda was sick about it.

"My happiness isn't your responsibility, sweetheart," Miranda whispered as she rubbed her belly. "Your job is just to be beautiful and perfect."

Having her daughter's future mapped out made pregnancy so much more enjoyable. Bailey and J.J. had both been dream pregnancies despite their respective thirty-five and forty-two hours of labor. Junior, on the other hand, had been a demon fetus. Miranda spent every morning of the first trimester spewing vomit and curse words into the toilet. She lost six pounds, which she couldn't even enjoy because the rest of her looked so haggard. Making matters worse, persistent night terrors—including a recurring one about Santa Claus slicing off her toes with a scalpel—prevented her from getting any rest. A mild sedative was prescribed, but she lost the bottle and was too embarrassed to ask for a refill. The truth was, Ray had snuck a couple of the pills and accidentally spilled the rest down the sink.

At nineteen weeks, Miranda briefly considered terminating

the pregnancy and telling people she'd miscarried. It was an appalling idea for someone so staunchly pro-life as Miranda, who in high school once had to disinvite an exchange student to a church lock-in after rumors surfaced that the girl had had an abortion back in Russia.

"It's just so awful," Miranda eventually confessed to the anonymous voice at the other end of the pregnancy hotline. "I believe every life is precious, but I totally understand why some people choose to kill their babies."

In the delivery room, her new son made up for nine months of agony by sliding out without so much as a push. The doctor, a young Indian fellow whose name Miranda never learned to pronounce—Prajapati or something—was a last-minute replacement for her regular OB-GYN, who ironically was a patient in the same hospital undergoing surgery for what turned out to be inoperable prostate cancer. Dr. P, as Ray called him, snatched the newborn's leg just millimeters before hitting the floor. The young doctor laughed and said something in Hindi, or maybe it was heavily accented English, Miranda couldn't tell. Either way, it seemed rude. But Miranda didn't dwell on it. The important thing was that Junior was finally, mercifully out of her body. It was still the thing she liked most about her youngest son.

Just before dawn, Miranda had given up on sleep and moved to a chair by the window. She'd hoped to watch the sunrise, but her eyes felt fat and heavy like overfull water balloons. The stillness was suffocating. Hotel room silence was different from regular silence. Five A.M. anywhere is abnormally quiet, but five A.M. in a hotel room is outer space.

After everything she'd accomplished, the idea that Bailey wasn't worthy of being on a reality show was painful and insulting. Yes, Starr was thinner and had won more titles, but so what? Bailey was a better *person*. Shouldn't that count for something?

When her last fingernail had been chewed to the quick, Miranda started devising a plan to get Bailey noticed by the reality show producers. Relinquishing her Little Miss crown guaranteed *some* attention, but giving up a title wasn't as sexy as winning one. She had a real shot in the Princess category provided no one discovered she'd cheated; but even that wasn't going to be enough. The producers needed to see that Bailey was a superstar, and that meant she had to steal the focus from Starr Kennedy. Superior Miss was their best and only chance. If Bailey beat Starr in the best overall category, essentially being named the prettiest, most talented girl in the whole pageant, it would be the greatest upset in the history of regional children's pageanting and worthy of TV attention. It was a long shot, but not impossible.

"Maybe the other mothers could even help us out," she whispered to Brixton.

Rumors spread like viruses at pageants, and Miranda was going to start the Ebola of rumors. At breakfast she would tell Joanna Lawson "in strictest confidence" that Bailey's weight gain was the result of precocious puberty and early menstruation, *not* frivolous overeating. Miranda figured if she told Joanna by eight o'clock, the judges would know by eleven. At the very least it would be worth a few sympathy points from each of them, and that could make all the difference. Then she remembered another ace up her sleeve: Bailey's sexy new photographs. Miranda had expected the pics to be controversial, but now if some uptight prig grumbled about inappropriateness, she could simply say, "We are talking about a girl who has just received her color and become a woman. What exactly is the problem here?"

Miranda looked at herself in the bathroom mirror and sighed. She was now as old as her mother was when Miranda was Bailey's age, and that made her feel ancient. The thin smile lines around her mouth and eyes seemed to be reaching out to each other like desperate lovers, straining to meet and deepen their bond. She made a silent vow to smile less. Her hair was dry and brittle, so she wrapped it into a loose bun, but the yellow highlights made it look like a Thanksgiving centerpiece. The tube of hemorrhoid ointment was empty, and the swelling around Miranda's eyes was barely noticeable. Her actual hemorrhoids, however, were bulging and stung like she was getting a tattoo on her butthole. She hated the sensation because it reminded her of the tattoo she got on her nineteenth birthday.

After drinking too many banana daiquiris, Miranda staggered into a beachside tattoo parlor in Gulf Shores, Alabama, and got the Chinese symbols for "peace" and "harmony" tattooed on her ankle. Years later she discovered the symbols actually translated to "rabbit nephew," and she cried for three days.

Using the heel of her hand against the countertop, Miranda managed to force a dime-sized dollop of Wal-rhoid from the tube.

"Thank Jesus," she said as she hoisted her foot up onto the toilet and massaged the ointment into her fiery anus. The relief was sublime. As she rubbed, Miranda was hit with another brilliant idea. While it was obviously against pageant rules to bribe judges, as far as she knew there was no rule against bribing cameramen of third-party reality shows. Wiping her greasy finger on the Shania Twain T-shirt she'd slept in, Miranda rushed to her purse and found twenty-one dollars in her wallet. In the front pouch of her suitcase she discovered a crumpled five and added it to the few emergency bills pulled from the zippered purse pocket where she usually kept her tampons and lighter.

"Forty-seven dollars?" she said after counting it. "What am I supposed to do with forty-seven dollars?"

Three seconds passed between the moment she noticed Bailey's purse sitting on the dresser and when she casually knocked it onto the floor. Its contents—the pink iPod, three different colors of lip gloss, a picture of Mark Ruffalo torn from a magazine, and a dog-eared paperback of *The Lovely Bones*—spilled across the carpet. Miranda nudged the purse with her foot until she saw the *iCarly* wallet Ray got Bailey for her eighth birthday. Miranda casually opened the wallet, pretending to just be curious. Another picture of Mark Ruffalo looked back at her, and Miranda made a mental note to keep better track of what Bailey watched on TV. There were a few phone numbers scribbled on pieces of notebook paper and a school picture of a nerdy boy in glasses who, according to the handwritten note on the back, was named Dashiell and "hearted" Bailey. Then, hidden in a side pocket, Miranda found what she was looking for: a neatly folded, obviously revered twenty-dollar bill. Where had she gotten so much money? Probably from her father. Ray was always spending more than he made. It was one of the reasons they were in so much debt. Money was the thing they argued about most. Money and pageants. Holding the bill between her fingers, Miranda considered the difference it would make to a cameraman. Sixty-seven dollars sounded a lot better than forty-seven, but she still didn't think it would be enough to bribe someone from Hollywood.

The doorknob rattled, and Miranda let out a small canine-like yelp.

"Mom! Open up, I forgot my key!"

Miranda quickly closed her fist around the money and scooped Bailey's belongings up off the floor, stuffing them hastily back into her purse.

"Hurry up, this ice is freezing my hands off!"

Miranda opened the door, pausing briefly at a mirror to see if she looked guilty.

"I just saw like three guys with cameras coming out of Starr Kennedy's room," Bailey said as she entered, "and another bunch of people following Bethenea Jackson around. Do you think it's about the show?" Bailey asked her mother, knowing full well it was about the show.

"Oh, my God, Bethenea Jackson! Of course!" Miranda wanted to kick herself for not thinking of Bethenea. It made perfect sense that she would be the other one, what with black people being so popular now.

The wad of bills had become damp in her tightly clenched fist, either from perspiration or squeezing ink from the paper. After a series of deep breaths, she turned to Bailey and tried to sound casual.

"So . . . put on your eyelashes and airbrush your knees. They look a little splotchy." She slipped on a pair of ratty flip-flops and flew out the door. "Mommy'll be back in a minute."

"What about your ice?" Bailey called after, but Miranda was already halfway down the hall, their future clutched firmly in her hand.

As a girl, whenever Miranda was in public she would play a game called Civilization. The object was to imagine that there had been an apocalyptic event where the only survivors were the people in that room. She would look around and imagine the society that would establish from the people present. Who would become the leader? Who would pair up as couples? Who would be the problem citizens that would need to be dealt with? Regardless of who was in the room, Miranda always saw herself becoming the leader. There were often others more qualified for the job, but eventually she knew everyone would see things her way. She gave thoughtful, impassioned, commonsense speeches that turned her most fervent critics into her most emphatic supporters. Miranda was a fair and capable leader who brought peace to the universe. She kicked ass at Civilization. If she could rebuild society from the ground up, she could certainly get her daughter on a reality show.

At the end of the hall opposite the vending machines, Miranda spotted a young man squatting over an open duffel bag and obsessively cleaning the lens of an expensive-looking camera. He was alone, removed from the chaos. She couldn't see his face, but his long hair and wardrobe—jeans, hiking boots, and a back brace over a Panavision T-shirt—screamed "Hollywood hippie." And hippies smoked pot and pot cost money and she had sixty-seven dollars.

"What's going on here?" she asked, casually leaning against the wall.

"Making a TV show," he responded without looking up.

"Oh, about the pageant?" she asked, trying to sound surprised. "Neat!"

"Mm-hm."

"You know, now that you mention it, I think I remember hearing something about a TV show being made here this weekend. That's very exciting."

He continued cleaning his lens. Her heart beat a little faster.

"You know, my daughter's competing today."

"Cool."

"Yes. Her name is Bailey Miller. She's the reigning Little Miss and she'll be competing in the Princess category as well."

"Cool."

His lack of interest was irritating. Obviously, he didn't understand what was happening here, or perhaps he had become so jaded from years of Hollywood cocaine parties that aloofness was his default setting.

Miranda looked around again—her heart pounding against Brixton's tiny head—and opened her hand. The wad of cash fell into the bag as if the cameraman was a street musician and Miranda was his biggest fan.

"What's this?" He stopped cleaning his lens.

She forced a casual shrug and said, "I don't know. Maybe it's yours."

"It's not mine."

"Maybe it could be. Would you like that?"

The man looked up, and their eyes met for the first time. She wasn't expecting his beard. His voice sounded too soft for facial hair, especially so much of it. Miranda shifted nervously as her red, puffy eyes scanned the hall, for what exactly she wasn't sure—the police, perhaps, maybe her dignity. He picked up the money and counted it.

"Sixty-six dollars?"

"Sixty-seven."

"Sixty-seven dollars. Okay. For what exactly?"

"Well," she said, clearing her throat, "maybe when you see Bailey Miller onstage or walking around the halls, you could shoot some extra footage of her and make sure she ends up on the show. Would that be worth sixty-seven dollars to you?"

He tilted his head, genuinely confused. "Are you bribing me?"

Miranda feigned shock, but her delicate façade was cracking quickly. "Bribing? That's . . . that's not a word I would use."

"Look, I don't have anything to do with what makes it onto the show. I just shoot what they tell me to shoot. You'd need to talk to the producer. She'd probably take your money." He held the crumpled bills out to her. "Here. Sorry."

Miranda's entire body started to perspire at once. Her mouth was a desert. Her hands shook. She felt dizzy. And then she remembered she still had hemorrhoid cream on her face. She literally felt like an asshole.

"Can I just have the twenty back, please?" she managed to squeak out.

"You can have it *all* back—"

"No! Just the twenty. Please."

The cameraman shrugged and pulled a twenty-dollar bill from the wad of cash. "Here you go."

Looking at the bill, she felt her eyes start to burn. "I'm sorry," she said, forcing words around the sour lump expanding in her throat, "but . . . can I have the one that's folded up? It belongs to my daughter. She's competing here this weekend. Bailey Miller. I said that already I'm sure she'd like to have it back."

The man put down his camera and stood up. Miranda took a step back. He was at least a foot taller than she'd expected, and the tattoo on his arm—a half-naked hula girl riding on the back of the devil's motorcycle—had, until this moment, gone completely unnoticed. Had she seen him upright, she would never have spoken to him. In fact, she probably would have turned around, run back to her room, and called security. He took her hand, sending a tense shiver through her body. Is this how she would die? Should she scream for help? How would Ray be told of her murder? How would he tell the kids?

Dear God, please don't let anyone think I was having an affair with this man! she thought.

Then, pressing all sixty-seven dollars into her palm, the cameraman closed her fist around the money.

"Are you okay?" His dark green eyes projected genuine concern.

It was all too much. Miranda expelled a burst of raw emotion, launching a perfect stream of snot to the tip of her chin. Without judgment, the cameraman reached into his pocket and handed her a clean handkerchief, which she used to wipe off the snot and then the hemorrhoid medication. Surprising them both, Miranda then threw her arms around the man's neck and forced from him a small, involuntary, "ah!"

Through a series of heaving sobs, Miranda whispered, "Thank you, thank you, thank you."

Not sure what to do, the cameraman awkwardly laced his fingers behind his head and held his breath until, mercifully, he heard a tinny voice squawking through his walkie-talkie.

"Hey, Freddy, you fall down a well? We need that camera. ASAP."

Freddy the cameraman grabbed the handset clipped to

his collar, "Flying in." He then said to Miranda, still clinging to his neck, "Um, lady . . . ? I gotta go to work."

Miranda let out a huge sigh and attempted to regain her composure. "Thank you, Freddy." Forcing a smile, she released his neck and handed him the handkerchief.

"Keep it," he said. "I'm betting you'll probably need it again."

She smiled. After everything they'd been through, Miranda felt like she owed him an explanation. Forcing a chuckle, she shrugged and said, "Pageants, you know?" hoping he would understand.

"I reckon," he said, then picked up his camera and walked away.

When she was sure he'd reached the elevators, Miranda ran back to her room as fast as her gravid body would allow.

Backstage at the 29th Annual Little Most Beautiful Princess Pageant was a dollhouse of grown women playing with smaller versions of their ideal selves. Fifty scantily clad prepubescent girls scampered about like the main attraction in a Bangkok coffee shop: sexy children marketed as wholesome family entertainment. The room reeked of anxiety, self-tanner, and schadenfreude.

This year's pageant had gotten off to a controversial start, to say the least. Three days earlier, the ballroom had served as the venue for an amateur MMA fight. The hotel's cleaning crew had not been able to find welterweight challenger Duane "Triple Threat" Triplett's tooth. But Tiffany-Chanel Teich found it.

"That's why she messed up her choreography!" Tabitha

Teich screamed at the judges. "I mean, come on! Finding a man's tooth would distract anyone!" She teemed with genuine outrage. "It's only fair that Tiffany-Chanel be given extra points to compensate. Or at least the other girls should have to hold the tooth."

Aerosol cans of hair spray hissed and rattled throughout the room, making it sound like the snake pit it was. When the EPA forced hair spray manufacturers to replace chlorofluorocarbons with a more ecofriendly propellant, many pageant mothers were outraged. The new stuff, while arguably good for the planet, just didn't have sufficient hold.

"I know the environment is important and all, but how is Bonjosie supposed to win a crown with limp hair?" complained one mother, desperate to blame her daughter's lack of winning on *something*.

"That global-warming stuff is all just liberal BS, anyway," said another, puffing away on a Marlboro Ultra Light as she applied fake eyelashes to her squirming five-year-old. "I'm *so sure* BreeDonna's hair spray is destroying the planet. I mean, how dumb do they think we are?"

Some mothers flatly refused to give it up. Tina Stinnet had her Marine Corps brother ship her a case of Final Net from the Philippines, where it could still be purchased. This infuriated the mothers whose military connections were limited to the Middle East. During a trip to Tijuana to get her ten-year-old daughter McKaty, a bottle of Cal-Ban diet pills (also banned in the United States), Marcie Krawinkel found a beauty supply shop that sold CFC-propelled hair spray for next to nothing. She returned with thirty cases, which she sold to desperate moms for upward of fifteen dollars a can.

Adding to the thick clouds of mist and envy was the steady

increase of personal airbrushing systems. Resentment was growing among the mothers who could not afford such systems—especially since those who had the systems refused to share them. Each burst of air was a mocking whisper: *Psssst. Psssst. Psssst.* "I have an airbrushing system and you don't." *Psssst.* The systemless mothers grumbled among themselves that the machines were elitist at best and cheating at worst, essentially allowing rich families to buy their children smoother-looking skin. But despite their complaints, everyone was saving up for her own system, and when she got one she wasn't going to share it, either.

One corner of the dressing room was buzzing significantly louder than the rest. Bright lights and a throng of cameras surrounded Starr Kennedy, a stunning eight-year-old who looked exactly like Catherine Zeta-Jones. Her full lips were tinted with an original color created specifically for her by a former Revlon color engineer to complement her flawlessly airbrushed olive skin. Her eyebrows were immaculately crafted fermatas commanding you to linger on her infinite amber eyes. If a human being could be Photoshopped, she would look like Starr Kennedy. As Starr practiced her talent—a precise reenactment of Britney Spears's 2001 VMA performance, complete with live albino python—Theresa spoke a little too loudly into a camera, leaning forward to make sure the lights picked up the glitter she'd applied to her sun-battered cleavage.

"Starr's just got that something special, that indefinable thing movie producers call 'it.' I don't know where she gets 'it' from, but she's got 'it' in spades!"

Catching herself, she quickly turned to the African American sound engineer. "No offense."

Bailey's dressing area was directly across from this bullshit.

Starr took a seat in front of her makeup mirror, swaying back and forth to the music blasting through her earbuds. Her every movement, down to the slightest facial tic, was a conscious choice. For a child, Starr was incredibly *aware* of her surroundings, especially the cameras. She knew where they were, if they were on or off, and if they were trained on her or someone else. When they were off, she was an average eight-year-old girl—playing with her American Girl doll, whining to her mother for a candy bar, even picking her nose. But Starr had the senses of a bat, and whenever a photographer attempted to steal one of those "real" moments, she would effortlessly slip back into glamour mode. It confounded the producers and infuriated the mothers, who were desperate for the world to see Starr for what she truly was: a little phony.

"Pageants are a great stepping-stone," Starr said as if she were sitting on Oprah's couch, "but they're only one small part of what I'm capable of. God has given me many gifts. And I believe it would be a sin not to explore every single possibility. I mean, not to sound . . . whatever, but I'm talented. I'm not ashamed of it. If you're good at something, you should share it with people. And that's what I want to do."

Miranda could see Theresa mouthing along to her daughter's words, making sure the girl got them exactly right. But she needn't worry. Starr was a pro. Since the age of four, she had been the Kennedy family's primary source of income, and Theresa worked tirelessly to expand her empire. The reality show was a godsend. It paid for the next three months of pageants and gave the family enough money to trick the bank into approving a second mortgage. The Kennedys needed their lives to change in a big way, and Starr was going to be the catalyst for that change. Theresa had never been more certain of anything in her life.

"We've also been having real success in print modeling," Theresa said, raising her voice just enough to make sure everyone could hear, "but Starr's modeling career might have to go on the back burner because of all the TV work. And not just this show. I'm not supposed to say anything yet, but . . . last week, Starr booked her first commercial!"

Theresa smiled broadly, pausing to make sure Miranda heard her.

Was that a wink? Did she just fucking wink at me?

Theresa continued, "She's going to be a beautiful angel for Dillard's department stores' Christmas campaign! Can you believe it?" She forced a laugh as fake as her breasts. "We are just so blessed." A perfectly calibrated sigh was followed by a piercing scream, "Next stop, Hollywood!"

Miranda wanted to throw up in Theresa's whore mouth. Instead, she took a deep breath and listened to her gut.

"You're right, Brixton," Miranda said, rubbing her belly. "Mommy *is* better than that." She felt a small kick from her baby and smiled. "Everything's going to be okay. We're going to show that skank who she's messing with."

chapter nine

Ray woke up every morning at five thirty, an unfortunate remnant of med school when his body learned to reject anything that gave him comfort. No matter how late he worked, how exhausted he was, or how many pills he took, he was never able to sleep more than three consecutive hours. Over time, Ray had grown to appreciate his quict mornings alone in his small kitchen. Those dark, wordless hours—standing over the sink overflowing with dishes; drinking his coffee, staring out the window onto his perpetually overgrown backyard, wondering if the rotting tree house built by the previous owners would collapse on its own or if he would have to pay someone to remove it; hoping to catch a glimpse of Cindy Ellis, his big-breasted neighbor who occasionally worked her core in her underwear on her back patio—had become the only time he could truly call his own.

Ray fiddled with his morning erection but quickly lost interest and slipped on a frayed Miami Hilton bathrobe, a present from his father for his twenty-first birthday. He padded down the hall and looked in on Junior and J.J., both asleep in the top bunk of their bunk beds. When they were younger, the boys had shared a much larger queen bed that had once belonged to Joan and Roger. After Roger's violent death, Joan refused to get anywhere near it, afraid her husband's ghost would haunt her dreams. It had been Ray and Miranda's marital bed until Bailey won their current king size Tempur-Pedic at the Cherokee Heritage Pageant and Pow Wow (Cherokee, North Carolina).

The boys didn't care about their grandmother's haunted mattress. They wanted bunk beds, and when Miranda ignored their request, J.J. went over her head and wrote a letter to Santa. A week later he received a response.

"So last night Santa texted me a list of chores," Miranda said, handing them her phone as proof. "He said if you really want bunk beds, you have to earn them."

The boys scrolled through the extensive list, presumably typed by fat jolly thumbs.

"And he said he might call every now and then and add to it, if he thinks of something else." Much to her disbelief, the boys did every chore on the list.

When they saw their new beds on Christmas morning they laughed and screamed and wailed, then spent the next four days arguing over who should get the top bunk. J.J. said he should get it because he was older, and Junior said he should get it because he was a Jedi. After a threat to text Santa to have him take the beds back, the boys agreed to share the top bunk, giving them each half the space they'd enjoyed in Joan's old queen. At least once a month, one of them would fall over the side, plummeting five feet onto a pile of toys and dirty clothes.

They were both still tucked in when Ray tiptoed into their

room and placed the new football in the small space between them. Figuring he had at least two hours before they woke up, he closed their door and went to make hotel reservations for his girlfriend's eighteenth birthday in Gatlinburg, Tennessee.

The last time Ray was in Gatlinburg he was a junior in high school. The wholesome, family-friendly tourist attractions made it *the* vacation destination for every church youth group within a four-hundred-mile radius. Ray's youth group had spent six months selling crates of oranges to raise money for a choir tour that would send them on a spiritual sojourn through the Great Smoky Mountains National Park. While the word "tour" implied chartered buses and rock star escapades, the word "choir" promised something else entirely. Eleven teenagers, quivering with earnest Christian entitlement, traveled to sparsely attended churches and dilapidated campgrounds to perform sign language versions of contemporary Christian songs and speak sagely about how empty and sinful their young middle-class lives were without Christ. The only vaguely rock star moment was when a freshman girl let Ray feel her boobs (under the shirt, over the bra) in the back row of the van.

Ray's most lasting memory of Gatlinburg was watching endless rows of outlet stores, souvenir stands, ironic Christian T-shirt kiosks, and overpriced novelty yard art carved out of tree trunks with chain saws zip past his window.

"Gatlinburg is so boring," Ray told Courtney, trying to talk her out of the trip. "The whole place just needs to get hate-fucked by Las Vegas. Actually, that's more Branson, Missouri."

"That's rude. What's hate-fuck?"

Ray had since amended his opinion: Branson was like Vegas's born-again younger brother. Gatlinburg was their paste-eating cousin.

The Miller family's living room was never what Ray would consider "clean." However, sometimes the room was what Miranda called "straightened," meaning that everything was in its corresponding pile: gowns, toys, shoes, trophies, etc. This morning the room was not straightened. It looked like it had been ransacked by government agents searching for hidden microfiche. Ray did his best to not step on anything that looked important or expensive and settled at the small desk in the corner of the room. He turned on the Miller family computer—a primeval Dell that must have weighed fifty pounds, thirty of which Ray assumed was porn. After checking his e-mail, which was empty, he checked the Gmail account Miranda didn't know about and saw three e-mails from Courtney: two forwards regarding some dancing reality show she kept insisting he watch, and a cringe-worthy poem she'd written about their sex in the chair the night before. He deleted them all, then read his joke of the day (Q: Why don't orphans play baseball? A: They don't know where home is.), considered a quick visit to RedTube but decided to give his penis a rest and instead Googled "Gatlinburg Tennessee."

The city's official Web site immediately depressed him. Gatlinburg had obviously gotten bigger in the last decade and a half, but it didn't appear to have grown. Every activity seemed geared toward the elderly or mentally disabled: trolley rides; chair-making demonstrations; self-guided Segway tours of the city; Cooter's Place, a museum dedicated exclusively to *The Dukes of Hazzard;* and "the most photographed attraction in Gatlinburg," Christ in the Smokies, a six-ton marble carving of Jesus's face with eyes that follow you around the room.

"Fucking creepy," he muttered.

Clicking "accommodations," Ray found a company inexplicably named Safari Leasing that rented log cabins guaranteeing "beautiful mountain views with speedy access to restaurants and attractions."

Good enough, he thought and opened the bottom drawer of the desk. Under a pile of old tax returns and current overdraft notices, Ray dug around until he found a three-inch stack of business cards bound with a rubber band. Tucked deep inside was a Visa card in the name of Walter Beddow.

Walter Beddow had been one of Ray's favorite hospice patients. A lifelong travel writer, Walter circled the globe several times before pancreatic cancer forced him home. Ray sat for hours as the man gave him a tour of the world he knew he'd never get to see: the azure water of Plitvice Lakes in Croatia, the remnants of the orchard at the Killing Fields, Japan's Bridge to Heaven.

"I've seen the whole world, Ray," Walter said between small sips of water. "I don't know what the next world is going to be, but I'm dying to get there."

The hospice had very strict rules regarding caregivers receiving gifts from patients, but Walter—who'd never settled in one place long enough to start a family—insisted Ray take some of his most cherished possessions: travel journals, photographs, and a Pulitzer Prize he won for a series of articles about Polish concentration camps reopening as tourist attractions.

"It was the damnedest thing I'd ever seen. Normal families smiling for pictures in front of a walk-in furnace. What the hell is wrong with people?"

Walter did not give Ray his social security number, but after hearing stories of the man's escapades in countries where seventeen was considered over the hill, Ray was pretty sure Walter wouldn't have minded.

Besides, Ray *needed* a credit card. Miranda had maxed out their others—all fourteen of them. It had also come in handy with his new girlfriend. Recently he'd been keeping iTunes gift cards in his pockets like dog treats. And while effective at keeping Courtney pacified, it had done nothing to help him end the relationship. Ray's role in his own extramarital affair had largely been a passive one. It was just something that repeatedly happened to him while he was at work. He never initiated, asked for, or expected sex. That, to his way of thinking, somehow made him less of a criminal. Ray had never studied the law, but he could only imagine "She touched me first, Your Honor" would be a slightly more tenable defense when he inevitably went to trial. Arguably, his biggest mistake had been assuming the teenager would get bored with him and leave him alone. That had not happened, and Ray believed the time had come to find a more active solution.

Perusing the Web site for Gatlinburg's Salt and Pepper Shaker Museum, Ray heard Courtney's text tone calling from his phone: *She's my cherry pie, cool drink of water such a sweet surprise . . .*

"It's fucking six-thirty in the morning," he mumbled while scolding himself for not turning his phone off.

The text read: NEED 2 TALK 2 U ASAP

Ray sighed. He liked texting for the most part. Generally,

he was a big fan of anything impersonal and succinct, but the shorthand of texting disappointed him. It was as if the world had finally figured out the perfect way to communicate, then decided to do so using only Prince lyrics.

He responded: WHAT ABOUT? IS MARVIN OKAY?

She's my cherry pie, cool drink—

He set his phone to Vibrate.

HES GOOD I JUST TOOK P TEST! POS!!

"What?" He needed coffee. Dragging himself into the kitchen, Ray thumb-typed: I DON'T UNDERSTAND. USE YOUR WORDS.

He tossed his phone on the yellow Formica table and flipped on the radio. Pretentious nonsense from Coldplay whined from the speaker, and Ray immediately switched it off. The rising sun was just starting to peek through the window, casting the room in an amber glow like a photograph from the '70s. His favorite mug was at the bottom of the sink under a stack of plates, and pulling it out would have triggered an avalanche of chores, so he opened the dishwasher and grabbed Miranda's Kentucky Wildcats travel mug. He plugged in the expensive cappuccino machine Bailey won at the Miss World Illinois Pageant (Carbondale, Illinois) and glanced out the window to see if Cindy Ellis was exercising. When he didn't see her, he scanned the magnetic poetry on the fridge: i hate stupid people

Ray removed the word "stupid." Then the word "people." Then "hate," until "i" was left all by itself.

His phone buzzed.

The screen read: DON'T B MEAN—IM PREGNUNT!! :(

Ray stared at it for a long time. Mr. B, his sophomore American history teacher, once told him that when the colonists first arrived in the New World, the Native Americans literally could not see the ships approaching because their minds were not capable of processing the enormity of the situation. That was happening to Ray.

"Don't be mean. I'm pregnunt," he read aloud and immediately felt the cold hand of providence reach down his throat, pull out his lungs, tie them into a balloon animal, and stuff them back into his chest. "Fuck me."

Had Ray's life been a movie, shrieking violins would've played as a spiraling red background accompanied his short drop to the chair.

This has to be a joke, he thought. Courtney's sense of humor was questionable at best, and this was just the kind of fucked-up thing she would find hilarious.

He texted back: ARE YOU KIDDING?

After a few seconds she replied: NO! NOT FUNY!!

Maybe she misread the test, he thought, hoped, prayed.

He texted: ARE YOU SURE?

YES VERY 4 TESTS!!

He took a deep breath and texted: IS IT MINE?

The moment he hit Send, he wished he hadn't. The question implied she was a slut. Furthermore, it said to a jury that not only was he a pedophile but he was an insensitive one.

She responded: DUH!!

Ray felt like he was being pulled underwater. He needed a plan, something simple and effective, like murder but not murder. Ray wasn't a murderer; he was just an idiot. He pulled his robe tight around his shoulders and felt the rough embroidery of the Miami Hilton logo set against the aged softness of the terry cloth. Ray liked embroidery; he respected its endurance. It never faded, it never shrank, when the robe was threadbare and ready for Goodwill, the embroidery still looked great. Embroidery was a survivor. Ray Miller had always been more robe than embroidery, but that was about to change.

"Florida." Ray whispered, barely recognizing the voice as his own.

From the pocket of his robe, Ray pulled out Walter Beddow's credit card and rubbed it between his fingers as if trying to summon a genie. A plan came into focus. Ray would go to Florida and become Walter Beddow. He had no family there, no ties at all, so there'd be no reason for anyone to look for him. The Visa bill was paid automatically from a bank account also in Walter's name, which eliminated a paper trail. And if he rented a car, no one could trace his plates. Ray Miller could very easily cease to exist. That realization was a bit depressing, but he could tend to his wounded ego on the beach. Plus, with a large percentage of Florida's population being over sixty-five, hospice work would be plentiful.

Ray was now nodding furiously. This was happening. He was going to become a fugitive from his own life. The clock on the wall read six forty-one. If he was out the door by seven, he could watch the sun set in the Gulf. Rummaging through the useless detritus of the junk drawer, Ray managed to find a pencil and starting making a list: clothes, cash, his nursing license—he'd worry about changing it to Walter's name when he got there—his iPod . . .

"What else, what else . . ." he said, pacing furiously until two distant voices paralyzed him.

"A football!

"Cool! Throw it to me!"

"Go long!"

Crash! "Touchdown!"

Giggles in bare feet bounded into the kitchen. When the boys saw their father hunched over the table, they smothered him with hugs motivated by nothing but pure love and appreciation.

"Thanks for the football, Dad! It's awesome!"

"You're welcome, buddy."

"Will you come outside and play with us?"

Ray sighed and smiled. "Of course I will."

"What's wrong, Daddy? Why are you crying?"

"Hm?" Ray touched his cheeks. They were hot and wet. How long had he been crying? Why hadn't he before today? Wiping his face, he smiled at his sons.

"Sometimes grown-ups cry when they're happy."

"That doesn't make any sense."

Ray laughed. "No. I guess it doesn't. I'm fine." He wiped his face dry with the sleeve of his threadbare robe. "Why don't you go get dressed and I'll meet you outside."

"Okay! Can we have pancakes after?"

"Sure."

The boys let out a "wah-hoo!" and ran from the room, stripping off their pajamas, leaving them where they fell. Ray looked around his shitty kitchen at the reminders of the life he'd built with his family: photographs of trips, finger-painted refrigerator art, the shoe box from Bailey's first pair of high heels now filled with hundreds of broken crayons. Everything had a story and Ray knew every one. He thought about his wife and daughter, somewhere in Tennessee doing what they loved most in the world. He thought about his boys, and how much they needed a dad, *their* dad, him, Ray Miller. He thought about Brixton and how much he loved her even though he'd yet to meet her. This certainly wasn't the life Ray had imagined for himself; however, it was the life he'd made for himself. And he would deal with it like the man he was: a lying, pill-popping, adulterer with almost four kids, a forged credit card, and two women pregnant with his children. Ray Miller may not have been a great man, but he certainly wasn't Walter Beddow.

His phone buzzed with a text from Courtney: COM BY 2NITE. WE NEED 2 TALK

"Yes, we do," he mumbled to himself and texted back: C U @ 7

Florida would have to wait. For now, anyway.

chapter ten

Wesley James Veteto checked his veneered teeth in the hand mirror he kept in the breast pocket of his tuxedo and took a seat in front of the camera. An onyx stud the size of an acorn held the banded collar of his Van Heusen shirt in place and perfectly matched the impossibly tasteful ring worn on his left pinkie. The man lovingly known as Uncle Wes had spent the past two and a half decades carving out a niche as master of ceremonies, entertainer, and all-around cheerleader for every notable children's beauty pageant in the Southern United States. Because of his immense popularity, Uncle Wes commanded a yearly salary in the six figures, plus numerous perks: first-class airfare, car service, suite accommodations, and a dog sitter. Many pageant organizers considered him as important to the pageants as the contestants themselves, going so far as to ignore years of tradition and national holidays to fit Wes's increasingly demanding schedule.

As the official Web site of Birmingham's 24th Annual Columbus Day Pageant and Celebration read: "Due to a scheduling conflict, this years festivities will be postponed until the third weekend in October, instead of the second. Just like one can't imagine celebrating Christmas without Santa Claus, we cannot imagine anyone else but our beloved Uncle Wes crowning our 'Nina,' (Little Miss), 'Pinta' (Princess), and 'Santa Maria' (Queen). Thank you for your continued understanding."

A former sergeant in the Marine Corps, Wes left the service after a disciplinary action forced him to pursue a career in the private sector. Third-generation military, Wes's grandfather had served in Patton's army and boasted of once sharing a bottle of whiskey with the general on the newly liberated streets of Palermo. His father, a lieutenant colonel, completed three tours in both Korea and Vietnam before retiring to advise President Reagan on the creeping Communist threat to America and her allies. Hoping that some quality time on the battlefield would finally give him and his father something to talk about, Wes entered Marine Division Recon training at Camp Pendleton. Ten days later he was expelled from the program and the corps.

"The incident," as Wes referred to it, occurred several years before "don't ask, don't tell" was instituted, when official military policy was something more akin to "Don't get caught with another Marine's cock in your mouth." Which he did. Twice. Luckily for Wes (and his father's reputation), his lawyer was able secure an honorable medical discharge, the official condition being listed as a "persistent groin abnormality."

While not keen to discuss his ouster, Wes was always eager to talk about his time *in* the corps, which delighted pageant organizers no end. His military service lent the pageants an air of patriotism, making them feel wholly American, even *necessary*. And in a post-9/11 world, what could be more important than that?

"I've spent time near the Middle East," he once told a group of rapt mothers. "And let me tell you, ladies, they do *not* have beauty pageants there. They don't have the kind of freedoms we enjoy here in this country." He then choked up. "So when you say your prayers tonight, you think about that. About what we're giving those people over there by having these girls up on that stage today."

As emcee, Uncle Wes believed it was his duty to personify America. His wardrobe was exclusively red, white, and blue, and while the more conservative observers did not consider a sequined Old Glory vest to be respectful, Wes could not have disagreed more.

"Oh, that's just silly." He chuckled. "I mean, what's more American than drawing attention to yourself?"

If anyone questioned Uncle Wes's sincerity, he or she needed only to wait until his show-stopping finale during the final "parade of girls." As the contestants strode the stage in their ball gowns for the judges' last looks, Uncle Wes performed his rendition of America's second national anthem, Lee Greenwood's "God Bless the USA." Singing to the contestants, he gave each one a small American flag while a carefully timed slide show—personal pictures of a uniformed Wes as well as pictures of Mount Rushmore, the Statue of Liberty, and Ronald Reagan—played on a screen behind him. Wes milked the moment like Betsy Ross's breasts, extracting every last drop of life-giving patriotism and feeding it to the hungry crowd. It was enough to make a straight man cry. Being on stage gave Wes's life meaning. He wasn't carrying a rifle, or hunting down Muslims, but he *was* serving his country.

And while some might have disagreed, Wes believed it was every bit as important as his time in uniform.

His career also allowed him the flexibility to spend significant time with Paulo, the five-foot-four-inch undocumented Cuban immigrant he'd lived with for the past fourteen years, and their teacup Yorkie, Shirley Temple.

Giving his hand mirror one last look, Uncle Wes double-checked his hair, a carefully crafted Elvis-inspired pompadour with oh-so-subtle highlights that appeared to glow onstage as if flecked with tiny fiber optics. Wes's hair had become something of a celebrity itself. It commanded a full paragraph of his extensive bio, and visitors to unclewes.net were invited to check out a "hilarious interview" the hair had given to the webmaster. There was even a chapter dedicated to it in Wes's self-published autobiography: *Master (Sergeant) of Ceremonies: One Patriot's Journey from Marines to Queens,* which he sold at pageants for $15. Autographed copies ("the perfect Christmas gift for anyone on your list") were a bargain at $20.

Among all the skeletons in Wes's spacious walk-in closet was the potentially career-ending bombshell that his iconic hair was actually a very expensive toupee. It had become such a part of who he was that he rarely, if ever, removed it. Wes's real hair was a series of errant strands and patchy clumps that lay on his lumpy skull like a comatose ferret. Without his toupee, he looked like a crazy old queen instead of the confident, sexually ambiguous semicelebrity he was. Even after fourteen years, Paulo had seen his partner without it only once, and on that day, deep down inside, a small part of his love for Wes died.

Playing up his slight but natural Southern drawl, Wes addressed the camera, "I just feel so blessed to be able to do what

I do, and I just love these girls like they were my own, even the ones who never win anything, because they have worth, too. God has blessed each and every one of them—some more than others, obviously—in terms of money or looks or hair. And believe me, I know about hair!"

He let out a very well-rehearsed laugh to accent the very well-rehearsed line. "But when those girls step foot out on that stage, its not about what kind of house they live in, or who their people are, it's about competition and talent and preparation and most of all . . . glamour!" He smiled and waited for the next question, which had been given to him before he sat down.

"You've been doing this a long time, Wes. Who are some of your favorite girls?"

Grandly rolling his eyes with an exaggerated folksiness that would make Dolly Parton blush, he bellowed, "Oh, my Lord, why don't you just ask me to choose between chocolate and cheese! There are so many exceptional girls: Jonnaleigh Robinson is a doll, Bailey Miller is one of the best *ever,* Bethenea Jackson goes without saying, but"—Wes lowered his voice and leaned in as if revealing nuclear secrets—"between you, me, and the fencepost, there has *never* been a girl like Starr Kennedy. She is a superstar, with two *r*'s." He chuckled. "You mark my words, that girl is gonna win herself an Oscar before she's fifteen. I'd bet my eyes on it."

From the corner of his just-gambled organs, Wes noticed Miranda staring at him and felt his brow burst with perspiration.

"Well, I really should get going," he said to camera. "It's almost time for the glamour!"

Passing Miranda, Uncle Wes gave her a genuine hug and

whispered, "You look beautiful, dear. You're glowing. Good luck today."

As he absorbed her into his massive chest, Miranda thought about the copy of Wes's book she'd bought the year before, and for the first time in her life was proud that she didn't read books.

Backstage took on a renewed sense of urgency as the first contestants (0–6 months) were carried across the stage. Bailey had already been stuffed into her new evening gown: a sleek red, cross-shoulder, strappy number inspired by a gown Miranda had seen some TV actress wear to the Golden Globe Awards. It was a new look for Bailey, and she pretended to share her mother's enthusiasm for the change. Most girls were still wearing knee-length party dresses with stiff, cumbersome crinolines, like they were going to prom in 1987, but ever since Starr won the Little Miss Tennessee Perfect Gala (Franklin, Tennessee) in a breezy but elegant maxidress, everything changed. Regardless of anyone's personal feelings about Starr Kennedy, it was impossible to deny that she was the child pageant world's prevailing trendsetter.

Miranda took a step back and assessed her daughter. For a few months she had been trying an "elegant grad student" vibe on Bailey, even going so far as to have her pose with horn-rimmed glasses and an e-cigarette in one of her new pictures. Unfortunately, the picture was unsuitable for competition because of poor lighting and a hint of nipple. Even with her extra weight, Bailey's appearance was flawless. Her hair sparkled as if it had been rinsed with a mirror, and her skin had the tawny glow of a second-generation Asian American. The girl could have walked into any bar in

America and been served a beer, no questions asked. But Miranda still felt something was missing, the one special thing that would grab not only the judges' attention but the reality show producers' as well. She had been holding on to something for years, a trick she knew, waiting for the perfect time to use it. She'd hoped to wait awhile longer, at least until Bailey was twelve, but this was an emergency.

"What are you doing?" Bailey asked as her mother picked up the airbrush gun.

"Just stand still," Miranda whispered as she quickly airbrushed two arcing shadows on the girl's chest, hoping from a distance it looked like cleavage.

"Perfect," Miranda gushed. "Now . . . show me what you've got."

Bailey took a deep breath, perfected her posture, and tilted her head ever so slightly to convey an otherworldly confidence. "Being possessed by the chic demon" is what Bailey called it. Her lips curled into the perfect smile, a welcoming, mischievous grin that demanded you to just *look*. She seemed to be constantly winking at you, but she wasn't, she just made you feel that way. Bailey grabbed a handful of fabric and sashayed across the floor, deftly controlling the train of her gown with imperceptible kicks from the red sequined Converse All-Stars worn ironically to show that being glamorous doesn't mean you can't also be playful.

"There's no law that says *you* can't be a trendsetter, too," Miranda answered when asked why it was suddenly okay to wear sneakers onstage.

Watching her daughter glide across the room, everything else in Miranda's world fell away. *This* was what she loved. It was the reason she was put on this earth. Brixton kicked her approval, and Miranda rubbed her tummy, totally unaware that she had allowed herself to smile.

"Oh, my goodness, Bailey!" a voice called out. "What a beautiful dress!"

Miranda's Kegel muscles tightened. The air grew cold as the smell of cigarettes and too much perfume filled her nostrils. Theresa Kennedy slithered up, put her arm around Miranda's shoulder, and squeezed.

"Hello, Theresa," Miranda said, afraid to look away for fear the bitch might cut her daughter's face with the Diet Rite can clutched in her bony talons. "Bailey, what do you say to Mrs. Kennedy?"

"Thank you, Mrs. Kennedy."

"You're so welcome, dear." She then lowered her voice to a conspiratorial whisper and leaned in close, "and congratulations on getting your first visit from your monthly friend."

Bailey was not aware that her mother had told everyone she had gotten her first period. She just assumed Theresa was trying to mess with her head, so she nodded.

"Thank you."

"Yes, thank you," Miranda said, implying she should move on.

"You must be very frightened," Theresa said, taking a step toward Bailey, "but it happens to us all. Just remember to always be prepared for it, and *never* discuss it with a boy."

"Okay. I won't," Bailey said, and then surprised herself by flashing a perfect pageant smile right in Theresa's face. "Thank you, Mrs. Kennedy. You're a good friend."

It was a damn good smile, and it wounded Theresa more than if she'd slapped her.

"Well," Theresa said, honeyed venom dripping from her

words, "it does sometimes make you bitchy. You might want to get on top of that, dear. After a while, it's no excuse. Then you're just a bitch."

Bailey stopped smiling. "I left something upstairs. I'll be right back." She grabbed her purse and darted from the room.

Theresa turned to a seething Miranda and arched her tattooed eyebrows as if to say, *Yes? Is there something you would like to say?* But Miranda refused to be drawn into her wicked devilry and the two women glared at each other, each daring the other to blink first. An eternity passed before Brixton kicked, forcing Miranda to concede defeat with a small, involuntary "oof." Theresa smiled. Another victory.

"So . . ." Miranda asked without caring, "how's Starr?"

Theresa chuckled as if it was the stupidest question ever asked.

"You must be kidding. I know you know this whole reality show is about her. I mean, they're following Bethenea around, too, but psssh, come on. You can't even compare the two. It's totally Starr's show."

Theresa gestured to the lights and camera crew. "All this just for my little princess," she said, then paused to savor the tightness of Miranda's expression. "God's just been so good to us this year. Starr shot her first television commercial, and her agent—who we had to get to help us sort through all the offers—has been talking about roles on some Disney Channel shows, or maybe even her *own* show on Nickelodeon. Something like *iCarly,* but more Christian, more *Starr.* It's all such a blessing."

It was an obvious exaggeration, but enough of it was true to annoy the hell out of Miranda, and Theresa knew it.

"So . . . how are you, dear? Still pregnant, I see."

Proud of her little Brixton, Miranda's spine straightened, "Yes, I am. I'm having another girl, and I couldn't be happier."

"Well, when are you due?" Theresa chuckled. "Because you are as big as a house!"

Miranda hoped Theresa didn't see her wince at the comment, but Theresa Kennedy saw everything.

"Six more weeks," Miranda said.

Theresa's eyes widened in mock concern as she dramatically sucked air in through her teeth. "Wow. Well . . . you look . . . fine. Just fine. I'll be praying for you. And tell Bailey I said good luck." She locked eyes with Miranda. "You know, with her *period*."

"I wi—" Miranda cleared her throat. *Fuck!* "I will."

Theresa smiled, her work complete, and moved nimbly on to her next victim, "Oh, my goodness, Bethenea! That scab on your knee looks so painful! Don't worry, dear. I'm sure the judges won't find it disgusting."

Watching Theresa go, Miranda mumbled a word she had only used twice before in her life, the first time in reference to Hillary Clinton and the other while drunkenly repeating a limerick about a man who liked to hunt.

The Summit Ballroom seated three hundred and fifty people, but with only sixty-five in attendance, it was difficult to blend in. Miranda slipped in and looked for a seat as far away from the cameras as possible. Sitting alone in the back of the room was Dorothy Tunes, an overcaffeinated chain-smoker who still clung to the ridiculous notion that her girls—bug-eyed twins named Melody and Harmony, who competed as a pair—would someday win something.

"You gotta have a gimmick!" Dorothy once told Miranda,

laughing stale breath through her dry, yellow lips. "Besides, they're prettier together. Melody's got a nose like a Jew and Harmony's ain't much bigger than a button, so from a distance they even each other out."

Miranda saw Dorothy first, and like everyone fortunate enough to be in that position, she quietly took a seat somewhere else. Onstage, Uncle Wes was finishing his maudlin rendition of "My Heart Will Go On," missing the high note but covering nicely by going on a Christina Aguilera–like run and staying mostly on key. Thunderous applause filled the ballroom. Wes took a deep, gracious bow and crossed to the podium.

"Ladies and gentlemen, moms and dads, friends and family, welcome to the Princess category!"

A blast of nervous energy shot through Miranda. She sat up straight, then stood, sat back down, then stood up again pacing the aisle until she noticed Dorothy Tunes waving at her.

"Dammit," she said through a fake smile and politely returned the wave, pointed to her belly, and made an arggh-I'm-so-pregnant-and-tired-I'm-just-going-to-stay-here face before sitting back down and forcing herself to stay there.

Uncle Wes cleared his throat. "Please welcome to the stage contestant number one, Misa Lee."

Miranda exhaled. Asians were cute and had great skin, but they were too exotic to actually win anything. It seemed almost perverse to have an Asian girl win a pageant. Clapping politely, Miranda dismissed the girl from serious competition.

"Misa is a ten-year-old fourth grader from Hendersonville, Tennessee. She was adopted from China. Her hobbies include playing the violin, cross-country skiing, origami, and helping her mother around the house."

Miranda scanned the crowd again, looking for . . . something. Her gut told her she needed to stay alert.

"Contestant number two, Jinks Cashion."

Miranda shot up out of her seat as if her hemorrhoids had suddenly become rockets. "Who?"

She'd never heard of this girl, and a surprise like this could put her whole plan in jeopardy. However, when she saw the tubby little charity girl waddle across the stage, she couldn't help but laugh at her overreaction.

"Jinks is an eleven-year-old Christian from Montgomery, Alabama. She enjoys painting and lifting weights with her uncle Steve."

Miranda shook her head. What some parents do to their kids. "Two down," she whispered.

"Please welcome contestant number three, Bailey Miller."

Perfect. Miranda thought. *Right after the fat girl.*

When Bailey walked out onstage, Miranda audibly gasped. For the first time in months, her daughter's beauty was on a par with its potential. Airbrushing her chest was a genius move, if Miranda did say so herself. Not only did Bailey look petite compared to the older girls, she was, in a word, sexy.

"Bailey is . . ." Wes hesitated for a second. "Bailey is *ten* years old from Owensboro, Kentucky. Her hobbies include volunteering at the veterans' hospital, singing, helping with her brothers, and writing haiku about the Bible."

Miranda scanned the ballroom to study the stillness of the dads. The better the girls looked, the less the dads moved. When she spied four men, as still as cadavers, staring at her daughter, Miranda jumped up and screamed. "Yes! Go, Bailey, go! Whoooo!"

Bailey fought the urge to scream back. A year of binge

eating had taken its toll both physically and mentally, and now here she was as if she'd done nothing at all. She needed a new plan. Maybe if she tried to mouth-kiss one of the other contestants . . . but that would probably just cause more problems than it would solve. She'd think of something. Until then, Bailey Miller would hold her perfect smile like a pro and take her place at the edge of the stage next to the Asian and the fat girl.

Meanwhile, a storm was brewing on the other side of the room.

As Uncle Wes introduced the fourth contestant(s), the Tunes Twins—"Melody enjoys playing the piano, and Harmony enjoys listening to her . . ."—an unmistakable voice filled the room.

"Hey! Miranda! What do you think you're doing?"

The ballroom came to a paralyzing halt. Miranda's body started to tingle like it did in college when she took diet pills. Closing her eyes, she pretended nothing was happening and prayed that when she opened them, everyone would be gone. Or maybe *she* would be.

"I know you can hear me!"

Clutching her churning belly, Miranda looked across the room and saw Theresa standing on a chair, glaring at her with animalistic rage. Her mouth had hardened into a bitter, puckered sneer, and her brow muscles had managed to overtake her recent Botox treatment and furrow into a pinched mass. Starr wasn't the only member of the Kennedy family who knew how to put on a show. Theresa jumped down from the chair and strode to the judges' table, followed closely by the camera crews. From her seat, Miranda prayed to go into labor, or for a fire drill, or a heart attack. Anything.

The judges motioned for Miranda to join them and Theresa at their table. Feigning surprise and innocence, she pointed to herself with a raised eyebrow as if to say, "Me?"

"Yes, Miranda," one of the judges called across the room. "Could you come up here for a moment please?"

"Um, of course." Calmly, Miranda ambled to the judges' table, exaggerating her pregnant gait as if every tender step was causing the baby to crown. Uncle Wes stood at parade rest, while Bailey tried to hold her smile, preparing for the inevitable humiliation to come.

Every video camera in the room (sixty-two including phones) followed Miranda as she made her way to the judges' table. When she saw her cameraman friend Freddy shooting her, she wished she'd insisted he keep the sixty-seven dollars. Reaching the table, she smiled and asked innocently, "Is there a problem?"

Spitting out words as if they were hairs in her curly fries, Theresa yelled, "Yes, there's a problem. A pretty damn big problem!"

The lead judge, an obese Methodist named Margaret Flagg, raised her hand to Theresa. "If there's a problem, we will deal with it, but let's do without the coarse language, okay? There are children present." She sighed. "Miranda, there are some . . . concerns about Bailey competing in the Princess category."

Miranda nodded for fourteen seconds. When she was sure she wasn't going to cry she said, "I see. What kind of concerns?"

"Well . . . this is partially our fault." Margaret blushed. "We should have caught it before the pageant began, but because of Bailey's history and reputation, it was somewhat . . .

unexpected." She paused, choosing her words carefully. "First of all . . . Bailey's photographs . . ."

Miranda's spine stiffened.

Margaret took a beat and sighed through her nose. "They're . . . what's the word . . . ?"

"Pornographic," blurted Benny Callaghan, a veteran pageant judge who always dressed like the most fashion-forward member of a barbershop quartet.

"Excuse me?" Miranda said, a bit louder than even she expected.

"You heard me. This," Benny said, holding up one of Bailey's gorgeous new photos, "is obscene."

Miranda did not know what to say. Part of her was relieved they just wanted to discuss the pictures, but another part was disappointed that they couldn't tell the difference between art and smut.

"It's art, Benny." She lowered her voice to protect the children. "I thought gay people understood art."

Watching from the relative safety of his podium, Uncle Wes ordered himself at ease and walked the edge of the stage to hear better.

Margaret stepped in. "Okay, let's calm down. 'Pornographic' is an . . . inappropriate word, Benny—"

"Well, they're inappropriate photos. Bare backs, pinup poses, in one of them the poor girl's wearing nothing but black stockings!"

"That picture was inspired by a very famous photo of Ann-Margret, considered by many to be a work of art!" Miranda was practically shouting.

"I don't care what inspired it. If the FBI found these on the Internet, someone would go to prison for a very long time."

"That's crazy!" Miranda said, but she nonetheless made a mental note to update Bailey's Facebook, Twitter, and Tumblr pages as soon as she got back to the room.

"Who cares about some stupid dirty pictures?!" Theresa screeched like a Disney witch. "She cheated!"

Margaret sighed heavily. "Okay. Miranda, Theresa claims that Bailey doesn't meet the age requirement for the Princess category, which is ten years old."

Miranda's anger quickly turned to self-possession. "She's ten. I'm her mother. I know how old she is. She's ten."

"Then when's her birthday?" Theresa barked.

Dammit! With all her plotting, Miranda had forgotten to memorize the fake birthdate she'd put on Bailey's application. A bead of sweat slid down her rib cage. "Excuse me?"

"When is Bailey's birthday!?"

The two women glared at each other until Miranda feared she would be turned to stone. "You know, Theresa . . . I don't have to answer to *you,*" she said, enunciating in a way that implied more hostility and vulgarity than actual profanity ever could.

Theresa let out a sarcastic snort. "Oh, come on! Our girls have been competing against each other for seven years. Do you think I'm stupid or something?"

Miranda shrugged. "That's not the first word I would use to describe you."

The other mothers could barely contain their glee. It had been a long time since there'd been a public dust-up like this, and the first with such marquee names. It was the same feeling their husbands got watching their least-favorite Nascar drivers smash into the wall.

Theresa's anger could have fueled an army. "Fine. If that's how you want to play it, fine."

Storming to the edge of the stage, she stuck her macilent finger in Bailey's face and shouted, "When's your birthday?"

Misa and Jinks ran screaming for their parents.

"What's wrong?" Theresa sneered. "Period got your tongue?"

Bailey did not want to get involved. This was *not* her fight. So she held her perfect smile, ignored the crazy woman screaming at her from the edge of the stage and prayed for an adult to step in.

"I'm talking to you, you fat little pig! When is your goddamn birthday?"

Margaret winced. "Theresa! Language!"

"Hey!" Miranda screamed and grabbed Theresa's shoulder. "Get away from my daughter!"

"Don't you ever put your filthy hands on me, you bitch!" Theresa threw back her arm, intending to shrug off Miranda's hand, but in her rage she misjudged the distance and backhanded the seven-months-pregnant woman hard across the face.

The audience audibly gasped and took one step back, while every member of the camera crew instinctively took one step closer.

Rubbing her cheek, Miranda looked at Theresa and waited for an apology she knew would never come. It had been a long time since she'd been in a fistfight, and pregnant or not she wasn't going to let some spray-tanned ogress hit her in the face and get away with it, even if it *was* an accident.

Without another thought, Miranda leaned in and slapped

Theresa hard across the face. The familiar, resonant *pop* of skin hitting skin echoed through the hall. The crowd gasped again. Miranda covered her mouth, immediately ashamed of herself, but Theresa just smiled like a teenager who'd finally been given permission to drag race the family car and made a fist.

The punch only grazed Miranda's chin, but the intent behind it knocked out everyone in the room. In her thirty-nine years, Theresa Kennedy had done a lot of things she wasn't proud of, but punching a pregnant woman—even one she despised—was arguably the worst. None of that mattered now. The genie was out of the bottle, and she was pretty sure that genie was going to hit her back.

Rubbing her chin, Miranda recalled the words of her late father: "If you can avoid a fight, do it. But if you can't, then find your opponent's most vulnerable spot and hit them there hard, fast, and often. The worst thing you can do is let a fight escalate. Shut it down as soon as you can. And remember, there is no such thing as fighting dirty. You either kick their ass, or have yours handed to you."

So Miranda took a step forward and kicked Theresa in the vagina.

The room became a vacuum. There was no air, no sound, no past, no future. There was only that moment.

"Are we done?" Miranda went to Theresa, who was now bent over, gasping for breath. "Theresa?"

"Ahhhh!" Theresa screamed and lunged at Miranda, who reflexively snatched two handfuls of Theresa's brittle, faded hair. With her left hand, Miranda yanked hard, tearing out a handful of extensions and leaving a noticeable bald spot. Her right hand, meanwhile, worked itself into a fist at Theresa's scalp, lacing the hair between her fingers, attaching to her head like a tumor.

The other adults jockeyed for better angles, standing on chairs or holding their cameras high over their heads. Whether it was fear of getting involved or just a base desire to see two unlikable women beat on each other, no one even considered stopping them. Contestants pushed their way out onstage to get a peek. Even Benny and Margaret couldn't help but gawk. No one, however, was more engaged than the producer of the reality show, who stood several yards away thinking about the new BMW this footage was going to buy her.

Theresa had never considered the complexities of fistfighting a pregnant woman. Aside from the obvious tackiness of it all, practically there weren't many viable targets. Yes, she hated Miranda, but her baby shouldn't be forced to pay for her mother's bitchiness. Body blows were off-limits, as was anything that could cause Miranda to fall and hurt the baby: tripping, shoving, or tackling. The only acceptable mark was the face, but with Theresa unable to control her own head, all she could do was blindly swipe at it with her open hand. She connected only once, leaving three perfect scratches down Miranda's cheek, making her look like she'd been attacked by an angry French-tipped cat.

"Let go of my hair, goddammit!" Theresa screamed.

Miranda turned Theresa's head so they were eye to eye. "Are you going to stop?"

"Fuck you!" Theresa spat and kept swinging.

Again, Miranda thought of her father's advice, and with her free hand began punching Theresa repeatedly in her fake breasts, not too hard but enough to get her attention. It was a good strategy. After only a few punches, Theresa started to panic, screaming any excuse she could think of for the fight to stop.

"That's not fair! You're going to burst them! This is a sexual assault!"

Theresa thought about kicking Miranda in *her* vagina but worried that also might harm the baby. After two more direct blows to her now permanently misshapen breasts, Theresa decided to sacrifice what remained of her dignity and began wildly flailing her arms, hoping one of them eventually connected. Much like Bailey, she hoped that an adult would step in, but surprisingly (or not), not one did.

Bailey watched from the edge of the stage, knowing her beauty pageant days were finally over. No one was going to let her, or her mother, within twenty miles of a pageant for a very long time. It was an odd feeling. Bailey had been dreaming of retirement, but a part of her never thought it would actually happen. And now that it was here, she felt unprepared, like a test she hadn't sufficiently studied for. Black, glitter-flecked tears ran down her face as she watched her pregnant mother repeatedly punch a horrible woman in the boobs, and even though the fight was technically about her, Bailey felt no responsibility. She was a civilian now. It was someone else's job to get worked up over this nonsense. That being said, pageants had defined her entire existence since she was six weeks old. A part of her—albeit a very small part—would miss it. Any little girl can call herself a princess, but very few have the crowns to back it up.

As the host of the event, Uncle Wes figured it was probably his responsibility to restore order. Twenty years of vacationing in the Florida Keys had taught him a little something about breaking up hair-pulling catfights. Jumping from the stage, he planted himself firmly between the two women and attempted to hold them each at arm's length.

"Miranda! Theresa! Come on, now! The girls are watching! You're embarrassing yourselves!"

Grateful someone was finally putting an end to this—and satisfied she'd kicked Theresa's bony ass—Miranda released Theresa's hair and staggered backward into the crowd. Theresa, however, was too panicked to understand the fight was over and interpreted her freed hair as an opportunity to regroup.

"Aaarrrrrrrrrggggghhhhhhhh!" she screamed and flailed her arms with twice the intensity.

"Theresa! Stop it, now, sweetie! Everything's okay! It's over!" Wes took a step closer, trying to grab her arms, but he misjudged the distance and received a close-fisted blow to the top of the head.

"Oh, my Lord!" He doubled over just as Theresa's other arm came down and snagged his hairpiece on her wedding ring, ripping it from the double-sided tape that anchored it to his grotesque pate. "My hair!"

Theresa finally opened her eyes when she felt what she believed to be some kind of animal attached to her hand.

"Ahhhhh! Get it off me!"

Again, Theresa flailed her arms, sending Wes's precious trademark soaring over the heads of the onlookers and onto the stage, where it landed under the incriminating glare of the spotlight.

Seeing Wes without his hair, Theresa screamed again, believing she had scalped the child pageant icon.

"Oh, my God, Wes, I'm so sorry!" Then, unable to take any more, Theresa Kennedy fainted.

The crowd barely noticed. All they could see was the man who looked like a bizarro version of their beloved Uncle Wes. *This* man appeared to be at least ten years older than Wes claimed to be, and his imposing barrel chest now looked like regular old fat. Sweat had matted the remaining strands of hair to his lumpy head, and the double-sided tape hung down past his ear. The sixty-plus cameras zeroed in on him, and Wes realized *he* was now the focus of everyone's attention. Contestants who didn't immediately start crying looked at him with a morbid fascination usually reserved for burn victims or dead animals. Not since getting caught with Corporal Bowe's phallus in his mouth had he been so overwhelmed with fear and humiliation. Straightening his jacket, the fat old bald man gestured to his hairpiece. "Bailey, dear, do you mind?"

"I don't want to touch it," she said. There was something so creepy and sad about the inanimate pile of hair in front of her. It reminded her of Henry, her dog who got run over by her drunk neighbor.

"Then kick it to me," he snapped, then swallowed hard. "Please."

With the toe of her sequined sneaker, she sent the mound of lifeless hair skittering across the stage. Audible snickers broke the tension, as the crowd started slowly coming back down to earth.

Thanking Bailey with a quick nod, Uncle Wes placed the rug back on his head, and with all the authority a man in a slightly askew toupee could marshal, said: "How about we all take ten minutes?"

chapter eleven

The cabin in Gatlinburg was a ramshackle shit box. "Rustic" was the word Safari Leasing used on their Web site, which apparently in Tennessee was just another word for "shitty." The living room smelled of mildew, menstrual blood, and ashtrays. Staples and duct tape kept the water-damaged wallpaper on the walls, and every surface was mildly sticky, as if the cleaning crew had been instructed to wipe everything down with Diet Sprite. There was a bird's nest in the fireplace and raccoon hair on the pillows. It was not how Courtney imagined spending the most important birthday of her life. She certainly wasn't expecting a luxury hotel, but she also wasn't expecting to step on a snail in the bathroom. The rancid accommodations could have been overlooked, however, had the cabin been anywhere near the city.

"It's like we're not even staying in Gatlinburg at all!" Courtney whined as Ray's Jeep Wrangler wound through a barely paved mountain road that on his GPS looked like a child's first attempt at cursive writing.

She wasn't wrong. Technically, there was "access" to entertainment and restaurants just like technically there was "access" to Alaska. But anything Courtney wanted to do, like putt-putt golfing or designing her own T-shirt or firing a real machine gun, required a twenty-minute drive back down the serpentine road that had made her throw up twice on the way up.

"I'm pregnant, Ray! I throw up all the time anyway. I can't go up and down that road a thousand times a day! I'm not, like, some magic robot or something!"

"I know you're not a magic robot," Ray said, expressionless.

Working two full-time jobs and making sure his pregnant wife didn't find out about his pregnant girlfriend didn't leave Ray much energy to argue about the accessibility of the Appalachian slum dwelling he rented on the Internet with a dead man's credit card.

Agreeing to the trip was the worst idea Ray had had recently, and recently all he'd had were bad ideas. Three days in Gatlinburg was not his ideal getaway, but eventually he grew to see it as an opportunity. How often does a thirty-five-year-old noncelebrity get to spend a weekend in a hotel with an uninhibited, barely legal teenager?

Like most men with an Internet connection, Ray had watched a lot of porn. He'd learned things, and he looked at his weekend as the culmination of his two decades of study, his thesis, a three-day master class dedicated to the power and wisdom of his penis. But he and Courtney weren't going all the way to Christ's asshole to stay inside and have sex. They could do that in Owensboro. Besides, she was now the future mother of his child. Introducing her to reverse cowgirl now just seemed disrespectful. What Ray really needed was a magic pill to make all his problems go away. Thank God for modern pharmaceuticals.

Bee Rock was an underweight drug rep with the sharp features and angry sexuality of a Fox News anchor. Relaxing in the nurses' lounge, Ray snapped out of a Percocet stupor when the pretty blond skeleton handed him a sample pack of pills and a possible way out. The package showed a young woman with a knowing smile hugging her knees while gazing off into a bright future. In a reassuring font, the drug Ceaseocor introduced itself to Ray, and asked, "Why shouldn't the future belong to you?"

"Abortion pills?" Ray asked.

Hearing the "a" word, the young rep's smile broke for an almost imperceptible moment before she answered.

"That's not how I would describe them." The slight edge in her tone made Ray wonder if she was defending the drug from a place of corporate loyalty or personal experience.

"Ceaseocor is a safe and legal solution to a difficult dilemma many women face on a daily basis, unexpected pregnancies. With Ceaseocor there is no stigma and no discomfort. Additionally, it is safe enough to be used at home and has been approved by the FDA, the AMA, NOW, and Planned Parenthood, and is pending government approval in fourteen foreign territories. It's a real lifesaver," she concluded without a hint of irony.

Ray could not believe he hadn't thought of this sooner. It was as if the answer to his problem had been hiding in the shadows waiting for the right moment to jump out and say,

"Hey, Ray, why don't you mash up a bunch of abortion pills and put them in Courtney's Dr Pepper when you take her to Gatlinburg?"

"Occam's razor," Ray mumbled through a faint smile.

"Excuse me?"

He hadn't meant to say it out loud. "Hm? Oh, um . . . nothing. Occam's razor."

The drug rep scrunched her nose to try and look cute but instead looked like a bird smelling a fart. "What's that?"

"It's, uh, basically it's the idea that, all things being equal, the best solution is usually the simplest one."

Bee nodded seriously. It may have been the most profound thing she'd ever understood.

"I like that." She took out a small black notebook and started scribbling while Ray imagined the many ways sex with her would be disappointing. "Can I use that?" she asked.

Ray shrugged. "Sure. I didn't come up with it."

"Who did?"

"Occam."

"Right. And it's a razor?"

"Yes. It's a razor."

"Perfect."

Putting on his most professional nursing face, Ray took a dozen sample packs and slipped them in his pocket.

"Well, Ceaseocor sounds like a real game changer. I'll pass these along to our OB. Thanks for coming by."

Instantly, Nurse Miller felt taller, as if he was standing upright for the first time in weeks. Why shouldn't the future belong to him?

Ray knew this plan was despicable, but he honestly didn't know what else to do. How else was he supposed to protect the family he loved? He wasn't ending a life; he was saving a family.

It's actually the most moral option, he rationalized to himself. Courtney was young and still had twenty quality childbearing years ahead of her—and at least five to ten sketchy ones. More than enough time for her to prepare for the challenges and ravages of motherhood. She was eighteen. Her life had potential, and there was no reason to throw all that away for some partially wanted baby.

If Ray had any lingering questions about whether he was doing the right thing, the drive to Gatlinburg put those to rest.

"I read that boys do better at math than girls because of something about their brains. Is that true?" "Do you know what the Bible says about breast-feeding at, like, a McDonald's?" "Is six months too young for pierced ears?" "Did you know that bacteria from baby poop never, ever comes out of clothes? You can't see it, but it's always there. Something about their intestines or the way they digest food or something. How gross is that?" "Hey, you're a nurse. Is it true that for the first year of their lives, babies can see in 3-D and after that it goes to normal?" "I read on a mommy blog that mothers have something like a million times more chances of skin cancer, and then when the baby turns two everything goes back to the way it was before. Something about hormones or something. The article was real long so I didn't read the whole thing. But isn't that scary?" "How do you feel about the name Miley Dakota if it's a girl and Timberlake for a boy?"

Ray simply could not raise a child with this person.

There would be no easy end to their relationship, no parting as friends, but he believed/hoped the emotional anguish from "miscarrying" would give him the opportunity to say,

"Look, we've both been through something traumatic here, and I think it's probably best if we just take some time apart to pray about everything and sort out our feelings."

Courtney, being emotionally devastated from having been pushed down the stairs by life, would want to separate herself from anything that reminded her of little Miley Timberlake, and Ray would be free as a bird—a vulture, perhaps, but a bird nonetheless.

If all that wasn't enough to justify his actions, somehow Courtney had gotten it into her head that when her grandfather died, Ray would be moving in with her, a belief so immature he wondered if she also thought a fucking stork was going to deliver her baby.

As Marvin's only heir, Courtney stood to inherit his property as well as somewhere in the neighborhood of forty-five thousand dollars in cash and investments. A sum so immense, Courtney's teenage brain could barely comprehend it.

"You know, Ray, pretty soon I'm going to be rich, and that will be nice and all, but I'm still going to need *major* help getting the house ready for the baby. I was thinking Memaw's old sewing room would be, like, the *best* nursery ever. And the bathrooms need to be totally redone, too."

That was just the beginning of her list. The furniture and carpeting, relics of the Eisenhower era, "totally needed to be totally replaced," and the whole house inside and out was at least two decades overdue for new paint. The plumbing leaked under the house, sparks shot from the sockets whenever anything was plugged in, and there was no Wi-Fi.

"How do you expect to get all that work done if you're off living somewhere else?" she asked one night as he came weakly.

Courtney had never asked Ray to leave Miranda, but he could tell it was coming. She'd been asking questions, many of them starting with, "Hey, here's a hypothetical question . . ." and followed by a question that was in no way hypothetical.

"Hey, here's a hypothetical question: If you were going to leave your wife, when do you think you might do that?" Or, "Hey, here's a hypothetical question: Would you have to pay alimony if you quit your jobs and just lived off my inheritance?"

Plans were being made about his life without his permission, and that needed to stop.

"Hey, here's a hypothetical question: Do you want to have more than one child?" she asked on the way to the cabin.

"I already have three. Or five, depending on how you look at it."

"I mean with me."

"Why would you ask me that?" he asked, genuinely baffled.

She shrugged. "I don't know. I was an only child and I always wanted a brother or sister. I think we should think about having another one right away so they're close to the same age and can play together."

Absolutely not. Ray was going to fill Courtney's Dr Pepper with enough Ceaseocor to kill every fetus within a ten-mile radius. Only then would he be free to go back to the overworked, pill-addled life he had once so foolishly taken for granted, and Courtney would go back to doing whatever it was she did before they met. It was win-win.

Ray was exhausted when they returned to Château de Crap after a day of shopping, minigolf, and a fifteen-dollar (per person) chair lift that gave them the same view of the mountains they had from their grimy cabin window. But the night was young. There was work yet to do. Ray made a fire and Courtney curled up on the couch with an *US Weekly* she picked up at the only non-Christian bookstore they could find. Studying the pages as if they were sacred texts, she asked Ray in a tone that indicated she didn't really care about his answer, "How do you feel about the name Gosling? For a girl. Or a boy, too, I guess. It could go either way. I like it."

She tore the page from the magazine and stuffed it in her pocket.

As the sun set over the mountains, the room started to take on a stunningly different character. The golden-hour glow accented the flicker of the fire and transformed their vile little cabin into the romantic sex retreat Ray had fantasized about. *The only difference between pornography and art* is *the lighting,* Ray thought.

Glancing up from her literature, Courtney did a double take.

"Holy shit balls, what did you do? This place looks awesome!"

Ray shrugged, trying to be cool. "What can I say? I'm just good."

"You sure are." She giggled and pulled herself up from the couch. "How about you start dinner and I'll be right back."

She scurried off to the bedroom, where she put on one of Ray's button-down shirts and slipped into a pair of cute little panties she got at cutelittlepanties.com.

As she did this, Ray went to the kitchen and put his plan into action. He took Courtney's mocha vanilla swirl ice cream cake from the freezer and unpacked the rest of the birthday dinner she had requested: a DiGiorno pizza, a two-liter bottle of Diet Dr Pepper, a bag of York Peppermint Patties ("the little ones like they have at Halloween"), and a cantaloupe.

The blister pack of Ceaseocor had been in Ray's pocket all day. He pushed six pink-and-blue tablets from their womb-like bubble and with the back of a spoon crushed them into powder. Sweeping his freedom into a glass, Ray noticed a warning on the back of the package: "Caution! Take with food. Ingesting this product on an empty stomach may result in abdominal discomfort, heartburn, and/or gas."

Ray shook his head. He was very familiar with side effects. And he was very familiar with drug companies. The makers of Ceaseocor didn't care if a woman farted through her chemical abortion. They just didn't want to be sued if she did. The warning was absurd and Ray knew it, but he decided to wait until after they had cake to give Courtney the pills. It was, after all, her eighteenth birthday. Why make it worse than it had to be?

"Ray, could you come in here for a minute?" Courtney called from the living room.

"Can it wait? I'm starting dinner!"

"Please? It's important."

Ray sighed. "All right, just a sec." He stashed the abortion powder in the cupboard behind an ancient box of Bisquick and went to the living room. "What is it?" he asked curtly, then froze when he saw her. "Holy shit."

Courtney was standing in the middle of the room illuminated perfectly by the roaring fire, the setting sun, and a few candles she'd picked up at Ye Olde Candle and Tobacco

Emporium. His shirt was unbuttoned to her navel, which she had gotten pierced earlier in the week, and her cute little panties were bunched up at her knees.

"You know, we haven't had sex since I've been legal."

"Tha—" He cleared his throat. "That's true. We haven't."

"So then why don't you come over here and fuck me?"

In one fluid motion, Courtney undid the last button of his shirt and let it fall open while subtly shifting her weight, causing the panties to fall to her ankles. "I'm a big girl now," she said, and bit her bottom lip.

Having been raised primarily by a conservative, elderly man, Courtney learned everything she knew about female sexuality from popular culture. Reality TV taught her that pretty was more important than smart, pop singers taught her that nothing demonstrated ownership of your sexuality more than pigtails and kneesocks, and the Internet taught her that pubic hair was a bizarre fetish enjoyed only by gross middle-aged perverts.

"Sit down," she ordered.

Without hesitation, Ray crossed to the antediluvian sofa upholstered in a rough burlap-type material patterned with classic symbols of Americana: eagles, eagles holding arrows, the Liberty Bell, the *Mayflower,* and butter churns. Courtney didn't know it, but there would be no better time for her to ask Ray to leave his wife. In spite of her preternatural sexuality and manipulative character, she was still too naïve to realize that if she used these two qualities in tandem, she would be invincible. Ray was just her third boyfriend (and only the second person she'd slept with). Sex to her was still something to be enjoyed instead of something to be bargained.

Kneeling on a faded blue throw pillow, she unbuckled Ray's pants and smiled at him.

"Thank you for my birthday trip."

"Well, you're . . . very welcome. Eighteen is a big one."

She giggled, thinking that was innuendo, and looked at his average-in-every-way penis. "Mmm, it sure is."

Just as her lips made contact, her phone rang. "Ugh. Sorry." With one hand she continued stroking him and grabbed her phone with the other. "Hello?"

Ray whispered, "Just let it go to voice mail."

She shot him a look and put his penis up to her lips like an engorged index finger, "Shhh." She mouthed, "I'm on the phone," and winked at him. Ray put his head back and tried to pretend that this distracted hand job was the sexual smorgasbord he'd dreamed of.

"This is Courtney. Uh-huh. Uh-huh." Her voice started to break. "Oh, my God." She stood up and turned away.

Ray leaned forward. "What's wrong?"

She waved him off and started to cry. "When did he . . . go?"

Fuck, he thought. *Marvin.*

Courtney plopped down on the sofa next to a quickly softening Ray and sobbed into the phone. "But it's my birthday!"

Genuinely sad for her, Ray put his hand on her shoulder, but she brushed it off with an exaggerated sense of drama.

"Can I do anythi—?"

"Shhhhh!" she snapped.

Still naked from the waist down and uncertain of his role, Ray started to pull up his pants, but Courtney snapped her fingers and waved at him to stop.

"Why?" he whispered, but she didn't respond, so he sat quietly, naked and listened as Courtney made some spectacularly uninformed decisions.

She requested an autopsy even though Marvin's body looked like a half-eaten apple on a hot sidewalk.

"He liked medical shows," she told the presumably baffled person on the other end of the phone. "I think he would've enjoyed being autopsied. And can we do both an open and closed casket? Like, open for a while, and then closed if people get uncomfortable or something?"

That was followed by the even more staggering: "Is death covered by insurance?"

Thankfully, Ray heard his own phone ring from across the room and raised an eyebrow to Courtney, asking permission to answer it. To his great relief, she nodded.

Zipping up his pants, Ray pulled his phone from his pocket and saw it was Miranda.

"Hey, what's up?"

"Where are you?" She sounded panicked.

Ray's pulse quickened. He had told so many lies to make this weekend happen, he wasn't sure how to answer. "Oh, well, I'm . . . uh . . . I'm . . . just working, you know. Working. Same old. Not much. How's the pageant?"

Miranda hadn't yet told Ray about the fight the week before. He just assumed she and Bailey were off somewhere competing.

"Oh, well, we didn't make it to the pageant. I'm at the hospital. My water broke about half an hour ago."

Ray gasped so hard he almost inhaled the phone. Of all the scenarios he had anticipated, his eight-months-pregnant wife going into early labor somehow never entered his mind.

Miranda was doing her breathing. "Ray? Are you still there? Ray?!"

"Yeah!" He was suddenly unable to access the vast majority of his vocabulary. "Yes. Yes, I'm here. Yes. I'm right here. I really thought you were at a pageant this weekend. You're not due for another four weeks!"

"Tell that to Brixton!"

Her chuckle was cut short by a sharp, intense pain similar to the one forming behind Ray's left eye.

"Look, I really need you here, like right now. The doctor thinks this could be a quick one. I know you're working, but how soon do you think you can get to the hospital?"

His watch read eight twenty-four. If he walked out the door with only the clothes on his back, leaving his luggage and bypassing checkout, and there was no traffic, and he didn't stop for gas or food or to go to the bathroom, and he drove eighty-five miles an hour, he could possibly, maybe, if he was lucky, be there in five and a half hours.

He emptied his lungs with a lead-heavy sigh. "Here's the thing . . . Marvin just died."

"Oh, my goodness!"

"Yeah."

"That's terrible."

"It is. It really is."

"One life ending and a new one about to begin. It's the circle of life."

Ray closed his eyes and tightly pinched the bridge of his nose. "Yeah. That's—that's one way to look at it."

"How's his granddaughter? That poor thing, she must be devastated. What's her name?"

Ray looked at Courtney, who was off the phone and still

naked. She pretended she wasn't eavesdropping by lazily picking at a tiny scab on her belly button piercing. Her eyes were red from crying and her face was puffy. "Her name is Courtney. She's pretty torn up."

"I'm sure. How long will it take for the coroner to get there?"

"Hard to say. He said he's pretty backed up. There was a . . . fire and an accident, car accident, I think. Separate incidents. Lots of people dead. Burned. Hard to identify."

He lowered the phone and whisper-yelled at Courtney, "Get your stuff packed up! We have to go, like, right now!" To his amazement, she actually got up with acceptable speed, snatched her cute little panties, and ran out of the room. Ray went back to his laboring wife.

"I've got some paperwork I need to fill out, and I should probably stick around until the body is taken and whatnot, make sure Courtney is okay. She's all alone now."

Another contraction hit Miranda, "Ohhhh, that's so sad!"

"Yeah. So . . . I'll be there as soon as I can. Just keep breathing and don't have her until I get there, okay? Don't push! I want to be there."

"Well, you'd better hurry up, because I want to have her tonight. I *cannot* have her tomorrow. I'm serious, okay? Not tomorrow. It can't be tomorrow."

"I'm on my way."

"Be careful. And tell that little girl I'm praying for her."

He paused. "I will."

He heard his wife smile. "We're going to have another little girl, Ray!"

"Yes, we are," he said, unable to hold back a smile of his own.

"I love you."

"I love you, too. I'll be there as soon as I possibly can."

Still smiling, he hung up the phone and turned to see Courtney, now fully dressed staring at him, new tears filling her eyes.

"How come you never tell *me* you love me?"

Are you fucking kidding me? He sighed. "Come here." He took his girlfriend's hand and wrapped her in a genuinely sincere hug. "Marvin loved you very much. Are you okay?"

"I think so. Even though I knew it was going to happen, it still hurts. He was the last of my family."

Reflexively, Ray went into the "grieving family" spiel he'd perfected over the years.

"You know, no matter how much we try, we can never prepare ourselves enough for when death finally comes. But what I've learned from helping so many people cross over is that while his life down here, with us, has come to an end, I truly believe that it's a new beginning for him. And as long as you talk about him and remember him and honor his memory, he'll live forever."

"Do you believe in heaven, Ray?"

"I do," he answered without hesitation. But it was a lie. After witnessing hundreds of people suffer through unendurable pain as their bodies turned against them, Ray had given up on the concept of a benevolent God. What kind of compassionate creator would take the time to craft something as complex and awe-inspiring as the human body and then riddle it with cancer, AIDS, diabetes, Alzheimer's, heart disease, Parkinson's, etc., etc., etc., etc.? It was the equivalent of Leonardo spending a decade completing the *Mona Lisa*, then hastily finger-painting a mustache and devil horns on her. Why would anyone choose to worship a deity that had such obvious contempt for him?

Losing his faith was difficult for Ray both personally and professionally. It had been a useful tool in consoling his patients' families. They wanted to know that their loved ones were in heaven, with Jesus, but Ray knew they weren't. They were just gone. Dust to dust. But he couldn't say that. Eventually, he contacted an old choir tour friend who had become a successful preacher.

"What's heaven like? I mean, what do you *tell* people heaven is like?"

"Well, I think heaven is like the best birthday party you ever had," his old friend said, "but for eternity. Whatever you like to do the most, whether it's riding horses or playing chess or square dancing or flying kites or whatever—Jesus likes it just as much as you do and He can't wait to do it with you! He's the best at everything!"

"Then why would I want to do anything with Him?" Ray asked. "I mean, wouldn't He just be better than me at everything and make me feel bad about myself?"

"Oh, I'm sure He'd probably let you win every now and then," his old friend answered with a wink in his voice.

"How would that be any fun?"

"You'd be with Jesus," he said matter-of-factly, then turned serious. "You think the devil's going to let you win, Ray? Because he's not. The devil doesn't even play fair. He cheats. That's why we call him the devil."

How could he argue with that?

As Courtney continued to cry, Ray pulled her closer and checked the time: eight thirty-six.

"You know," he told her, then paused just long enough to feel the self-loathing seep into every pore of his being. "I think heaven is like the best birthday party you ever had, but for eternity. Whatever you like to do the most, ride horses or square-dance or fly kites or whatever—Jesus likes it just as much as you do and can't wait to do it with you."

He deserved hell.

"That's so beautiful," Courtney said before wiping her nose on his shirt, then snorting what was left back up into her nose. "You're very smart, Ray."

"That's debatable."

She pretended to know what he meant and smiled. "The nurse said Granddaddy left a note for you. He probably just wanted to say thank you."

There were undoubtedly many things Marvin wanted to say to Ray, but "thank you" definitely was not one of them. "Yeah. I'm sure that's probably it."

One problem at a time, he thought, and tossed the dead man's note on the mental pile of other shit he would have to deal with later. For a moment they were both silent. It was eight forty.

"We need to go."

"Okay." She wiped her nose again, this time with her bare hand, and wiped it on her jeans. "Sorry about not finishing your."—she whispered—"BJ. Can we do it another time? Granddaddy's probably looking down to make sure I get home okay, and I'd be embarrassed if he watched me do that from heaven."

He's seen you do a lot worse, Ray thought. "I think that's very . . . respectful."

"Well, he deserves it."

Ray nodded. Eight forty-one. "We *really* need to go."

"Uch, okay. Jesus! My grandfather just died! Let me fucking be sad about it for a minute!" Snatching her bags, Courtney stomped out of the cabin and climbed into the Jeep. Ray rolled his eyes, grabbed his suitcase, and slammed the door behind him.

The melting ice cream cake dripped off the counter into a gray puddle, while the glass of powdered Ceaseocor sat in the cupboard, forgotten like an orphan's birthday.

chapter twelve

"Look at me!" Miranda roared at her doctor. "Do I look like I give a good shit if my husband's here or not?"

Her voice was used sandpaper, raspy and torn. It was just past eleven o'clock, and despite having no clue as to Ray's whereabouts, Miranda was insisting she give birth immediately. "Get this girl out of me before midnight! Cut her out if you have to!"

While not superstitious, Miranda did believe in omens—the bumper sticker that gave Brixton her name, the pregnant police officer who took her statement (and her side) after the fight with Theresa in Knoxville—and there was no way on God's green earth she was going to let her daughter be born on September 11.

"It would be like having your birthday on Christmas," she said to Joan.

"Satan's Christmas, maybe," her mother muttered.

"Your birthday should be special, and I don't want Brixton

waking up every year, turning on the TV, and being reminded of a mass murder. That is *not* a happy birthday."

Miranda and Ray had been married only a few months when she started to feel a little . . . bored. It wasn't a question of happiness. They were both very happy, but they had settled into a routine so quickly that Miranda felt like she must have slept through the exciting part. Ray got a job at the hospital, and she worked as a receptionist for a kindly old dentist whose palsied hands shook so severely his patients often left with bigger problems than when they arrived. Bills were being paid on time, and the young couple had even managed to set some money aside for a cute little starter house that Miranda still hoped to someday leave for Thoroughbred Acres. It was all very comfortable, very pleasant, and very predictable: home by seven, dinner in front of the TV, sex, Letterman, sleep. Miranda was twenty-three.

And then 9/11 changed everything.

Staring at a perpetual loop of plane crashes and crumbling buildings while catatonic on her sofa, newlywed Miranda had the horrific realization that she would *never* be affected by the tragedy in the same way as the people in New York, Washington, or Pennsylvania. It was the most upsetting and isolating thought she'd had all morning. The greatest disaster of her generation was playing out in front of the world, and she had zero personal connection to it.

"I wish I was there," she mumbled as CNN played "exclusive" new footage of the second tower falling. *What's wrong with wanting to be a part of something that changed the world?* she thought. *Shouldn't every American want that?* Miranda sure did. She wanted to feel the heat of the fires as she ran for her life, her lungs burning from the acrid, polluted air. She wanted to be candidly photographed sitting on a curb, covered in ash, drinking from a bottle of water given to her by a stranger. She wanted to tell her story to CNN. But she didn't have a story to tell.

So she made one up.

Miranda had been to New York only once, in high school, when her drama club took a theater trip to the city. In five days she attended six Broadway shows: *Phantom of the Opera* (hated it), *Cats* (loved it), *Les Misérables* (really loved it), *Rent* (didn't get it), another musical, and a very long, very talky play about some old salesman. Citing the kids' good behavior and his own desire to see an old college roommate (ex-boyfriend), Miranda's drama teacher gave everyone three hours to "explore the city" on their own. Bravely ignoring Joan's concerns about "vagrants and sex perverts" traveling beneath the city, Miranda and her friends boarded the subway with a confidence that rivaled that of actual New Yorkers, and made their way down town to the World Trade Center.

"The observatory was on the hundred and seventh floor of the South Tower," Miranda said, "and I remember, when I got off the elevator, I just froze. Everything was so quiet. It was like being in church, or on a spaceship. It felt so peaceful and safe. No one said anything. They just shuffled from window to window like they'd gotten concussions from banging their heads on the sky. It was like, *bam!* They were speechless, and they were right to be. I mean, I can't even describe how amazing the city looked from up there. It was like a model of a city in the window of a massive department store.

"Off to the left was the Statue of Liberty, and when I saw it, for some reason I started thinking about my great-great-great grandfather, who came here from Scotland, and what he must have thought when he saw that for the first time knowing he was about to start a whole new life. How scared he must have been. Then I watched the tiny cars come and go and tried to imagine being one of the millions of people who lived there, what it must feel like to live inside the beating heart of the entire planet, the center of art and culture and music and fashion and food and . . . life. And then I remember I started to feel very, very small. And before I knew what was happening, I was sitting on the floor, crying.

"Now, I'd always gone to church and believed in God and all that, but I was just a kid, you know? I'd never really thought about what any of it *meant*. But sitting there on the floor of . . . heaven, basically, and looking out over what seemed a lot like a miracle, my whole life just fell into perspective." She took a thoughtful pause. "I know this sounds really cheesy, but I think God was waiting for me in the World Trade Center that day. I really do. And that was the first time in my life I truly knew what it meant to *believe*."

That was the story Miranda told people after 9/11, but very little of it was true. She did go to New York with her high school drama club, and she did see six shows in five days. She did *not,* however, spend her three hours of free time discovering God on the observation deck of the World Trade Center. Instead, Miranda went back to her windowless hotel room at the Milford Plaza and made out with her boyfriend, a lanky theater dork named Dustin Ard.

Since seeing *Cats* their first night, Dustin had not stopped pontificating about how Andrew Lloyd Weber represented "the nadir of contemporary musical theater," an opinion he'd read in the *Village Voice* and fiercely adopted as his own.

Miranda sat nervously on the edge of the bed while Dustin took off his shirt, revealing a severe—and in Miranda's opinion, repulsive—farmer's tan. It was the first time she had seen her new boyfriend shirtless, and a part of her hoped it would be the last. Hairless and smooth, Miranda thought he looked like a mannequin that had been outfitted with a darker mannequin's limbs. Thank God he was a good kisser. Firm of lip and sparing of tongue, Dustin's breath was Velamint fresh. Miranda, however, worried her mouth still tasted like Sbarro.

"You smell good," she whispered so as not to break the spell.

"Thanks. Some guy was selling actual bottles of Polo on the sidewalk for, like, five bucks. I got six of them. This city is incredible."

Miranda managed a noncommittal shrug, "Yeah. It's cool. It's so big and loud, though, don't you think? I mean, I'm having an awesome time. But I'll be happy to go home tomorrow."

"Yeah. I just wish we had theater like this in Owensboro. I mean, is there anything more exciting than the unpredictability of live theater?"

Miranda didn't respond. She wanted to kiss some more but didn't want to seem slutty.

More interested in his own voice than the horny teenage girl lying next to him, Dustin rolled onto his back and regurgitated other more informed people's analyses of the shows they'd seen that week.

"Obviously, *Les Miz* has the source material of Hugo's book to back it up, and I suppose the same could be said for *Cats* and *Phantom*." (Dustin referred to *The Phantom of the Opera* simply as *Phantom*. It bugged her.) "But what *Les Miz* has on its side is *history*. The French Revolution *really* happened, you know? And that's what makes it true, and truth is what makes good art, and that's why it is a superior show. *Rent,* on the other hand, is also truthful, but it's a *false* truth . . ."

Dustin's speeches felt longer than that old salesman play, so Miranda stuck her tongue deep inside his mouth to shut him up. For ten minutes they ate each other's faces off, separating only to breathe and wipe slobber from their red, glistening lips. Emboldened by his seminakedness and her unexpected aggression, Dustin made his move. Skipping second base entirely—an area he had only recently been granted very limited access to—he lifted her skirt and attempted a daring head-first slide into third.

"Oh, my God! What are you doing?!" Miranda shot up off the bed.

Through the dim light of the room Miranda saw Dustin's pale, delicate chest flush red.

"I don't know," he said, shrugging. "We're in New York, so I thought maybe—"

"Who cares where we are? Do you think I'm a different person here or something?" She looked at him, genuinely waiting for an answer. " 'Cause I'm not."

"I know." His voice was as weak as his frame.

"I can't believe you would even *want* to do that! It's so gross. I mean."—her voice lowered to an almost whisper—"that's where I go to the bathroom."

They rarely spoke after that.

The next summer, Dustin and his family moved to Boynton Beach, Florida. A year later, on the night of his high school graduation, he got drunk for the first time in his life and fell out of the back of a pickup truck when the driver swerved to miss a skunk. The former theater enthusiast landed on his head at forty-seven miles per hour. Witnesses said it sounded like a watermelon being dropped from a roof. Vegetative and wheelchair-bound, Dustin now lives in Tampa with his aging parents, who rely on his disability checks to make ends meet.

From the safety of her living room, eight hundred miles away from the chaos, Miranda watched the South Tower collapse again and cursed her immaturity. That wasted afternoon was her most vivid memory, her only real connection to an iconic city that was crumbling before her eyes. She thought about Dustin, his brain too broken to even understand what was happening, and cursed him, too. *For a boy,* she thought. *I gave that up for some stupid boy.*

Regret enveloped her like a cloud of ash. What if she *had* gone to the World Trade Center? What would she have seen? Would God have been there, waiting for her? And if so, would that have fundamentally changed her life? Would she be happier now? More content? Less? Or did it even matter? All Miranda could think about was how she had squandered a once-in-alifetime opportunity. She wished that she had seen the world from twelve hundred feet in the air. But more than that, she wished that she had been the kind of person who'd *wanted* to see it. But she wasn't, and for that she was ashamed. A swirling, sickening emptiness opened up in the pit of Miranda's stomach, and she immediately wanted to fill it with a baby.

"Turn this off," she said to Ray, who had become hypnotized by the endless repetition on the screen. He hit Mute and she laid her head in his lap. Starting with what she could truthfully remember—minus Dustin, of course—Miranda told her new husband about the drama club trip: the musicals, the restaurants, the homeless man who tried to sell Steve Quisenberry Ecstasy, Sbarro. And without so much as a stutter, she segued into the first version of her make-believe New York story, a story she would craft like topiary over the following year. Ray sat quietly and stroked his bride's hair, offering nothing but his full attention. When she was finished, Miranda looked up at her husband.

"I'm glad I chose you."

He smiled. "Me, too."

"I want a baby, Ray. I want us to make a baby right now."

It was the most unexpected thing that had happened all day.

"A baby," he said, with an oddly encompassing inflection that made his response sound like a question, an answer, and a surrender. "But"—he gestured to the chaos on TV—"the world's falling apart."

"I know," she said. "But maybe our kid will have the answer."

Ray didn't know what to say. What is the appropriate response when your wife proposes conceiving the Messiah? Then again, what if she was right? Stranger things have happened. He looked back at the TV just in time to see new footage of someone leaping from the burning tower.

"Let's have a baby, Ray."

"Really?"

"I think so, yeah, really."

He nodded. "Okay."

And without another word, Ray and Miranda Miller made a daughter on their couch while the world burned on TV behind them.

• • •

Conceiving a baby on September 11 was one thing, but having one was something else entirely. By ten fifteen, Miranda's contractions had all but stopped and she was starting to worry. Her OB-GYN, Dr. Larry Fales—a doughy middle-aged man with thinning anchorman hair and body odor—had ruled out a C-section.

"Having a baby is the most natural thing in the world." He smiled warmly. "Women have been doing it since the dawn of time. Brixton is not in distress. Her heart rate is strong. She's just not ready to come out yet. Now, I pride myself on listening to mothers, and that's what I'm going to do right now. I'm going to listen to Mother *Nature*." He smiled and gave Miranda a wink that she felt was too familiar under the circumstances. "Now, just relax and think about what you're going to say to your new daughter. I'll be back in a little while to check on you."

"Fucking hippie," Miranda mumbled as he trotted out of the room.

"He's delivered thousands of babies, dear," Joan calmly scolded her. "It is possible he knows more about this than you do. Here." She popped opened a can of room-temperature store-brand diet soda and snatched the bendy straw from the unwanted Styrofoam cup of water. "Drink this. It'll relax you."

Miranda took a sip and recoiled. "Uch, it tastes like burnt medicine."

Joan took a sip and shrugged. "I like it. It was only a quarter at the market."

Miranda sighed and pushed around on her pelvis, hoping to prod Brixton into descending. "I hate hospitals. Where the hell is Ray? It's been two hours!"

"I'm sure he just got hung up, dear," Joan said in her most mothering voice. "There's a lot to deal with when someone dies." She flashed back to the moment she discovered Roger's waterlogged body sitting in the bathtub, eyes wide open, toothbrush sticking straight out of his mouth like a tiny spear. Joan shuddered. She needed to talk to a friend.

"Are you there?" she had to ask in her head so Miranda wouldn't hear.

I'm always here for you, Joan.

What a friend she had in Jesus. "Of course you are."

What can I do you for?

"Miranda's worried she's not going to have her baby before midnight. Ray's not here yet and she's starting to panic. I keep telling her there's nothing to worry about, but she won't listen to me. Is there anything you can think of that might calm her down?"

Jesus exhaled. *Hmm. She's just stressed. It's a big day. Why don't you try singing to her? I know how she loves hearing you sing.*

Joan smiled. He was right again. "You're so good."

Hey, it's my job. She felt the glimmer of his smile and went flush.

Clearing her throat, Joan ran her fingers through her daughter's hair and sang in a full, proud voice.

"Amazing grace, how sweet the sound—"

Miranda immediately cut her off. "Mom! Not now."

Joan removed her hand.

Try something a bit more upbeat.

"Sunday, Monday, Happy Days! Tuesday, Wednesday, Happy Days!—"

"Mom! Please. I don't want to hear any music, okay? I'm

not in the mood. I just want Ray to get here so I can have this baby!"

"Okay. Whatever you want," her mother said, and started softly humming a tune Jesus sometimes hummed to help her sleep. Rolling her eyes, Miranda snatched her phone and called Ray.

"Uch, goddamn voice mail!" She threw the phone across the room. "Where the fuck is my fucking husband?!"

Joan liked to pretend that unpleasant moments like this didn't happen. What was the point? It was best to just move on, and move on quickly.

"Want another sip?" she asked her daughter, offering up the can of soda. "I think it's yum."

"No."

"Okay. Suit yourself." Joan shrugged as she took her daughter's hand and started lightly stroking it. "Dashing through the snow, in a one horse open sleigh . . ."

At that exact moment, Ray and Courtney were just outside of Goodlettesville, Tennessee, barreling north on I-65. In two and a half hours they had managed to travel two hundred twenty four miles. At this rate, Ray would be by his wife's side by one ten A.M., or dead in a fiery crash.

The low-fuel light flashed on the dashboard. "Fuck," he mumbled. It was the first word either had spoken in forty-six minutes.

Ray pulled the Jeep off the highway and counted fourteen fast-food restaurants, two auto parts stores, nine gas stations, and a twenty-four-hour sporting goods superstore in case an interstate basketball emergency arose. A billboard featuring a corn-fed goddess in denim cutoffs reclining on a bale of hay pointed toward a nearby boot warehouse, or perhaps the location of a local barn prostitute. Sandwiched between a Cracker Barrel and a Waffle House was a gas station where Ray decided to fill up. He cut off the engine, and Courtney started to cry again.

"Jesus Christ, what's wrong now?" Ray snapped.

"Granddaddy used to always take me to Cracker Barrel on special occasions." She wiped her cheeks on her sleeve. "And now he'll never do that again!"

Ray was unmoved. Since leaving Gatlinburg, Courtney had cried about everything. They'd pass an eighteen-wheeler and she'd wail, "When I was a little girl, whenever we'd drive by a big truck, Granddaddy would pull up next to them and get them to honk their horn for me."

Outside Gatlinburg she saw a billboard for Dollywood and started bawling, "because 'Hard Candy Christmas' was Granddaddy's favorite song."

Finally, Ray had had enough. "Dry it up!" he yelled after a McDonald's ad on the radio used the word "starvin,"—"which rhymes with 'Marvin!' "

"No more radio!" he screamed, practically tearing off the knob. "We'll just sit in silence for the rest of the trip!"

Ray was being neither reasonable nor compassionate, and he knew it, but his wife was having a baby, probably at that very moment, and he wanted to concentrate on how shitty he felt for not being there.

Courtney, however, did not appreciate her mourning taking second position to Ray's baby. He already had, like, three of them or something. *She,* on the other hand, had just suffered a tremendous loss—granted, she had already suffered, like, three of them or something—but this was the first one she would have to deal with on her own, as a grown-up. Nothing less than fawning sympathy would suffice. Also, it was still her eighteenth birthday, and the tradition in her house was that on your birthday, you got to do whatever you wanted. The death of her grandfather shouldn't change that.

"I want to go over to Cracker Barrel and get one of those little golf tee games."

"We don't have time for that."

"Ugh! You won't let me listen to the radio and you won't talk to me, so what am I supposed to do? Just sit here and think for six hours? If I thought about everything I know, it wouldn't take six hours!"

"Look," he said, forcing civility, "we have to get back on the road. If you need to pee, then go here at the gas station, but make it quick."

Courtney stuck out her bottom lip, crossed her arms, and glared at him.

"Goddammit, what?"

Tears.

Ray sighed loudly through his throat. "Courtney, I'm sorry, but I do not have time for your—"

Before he could finish, she grabbed her purse and stormed off toward the Cracker Barrel.

"Where are you going?"

She flipped him off without turning around.

"Fuck, fuck, fuck, fuck, fuck, fuck, fuck!" Pulling at his hair, Ray shoved the nozzle back in the pump and ran after her. "What the hell is wrong with you?"

She wouldn't look at him.

"Courtney, you *have* to understand how important it is for me to get home."

"You're mean," she said without stopping. "I'm getting a golf tee game."

A thick antitheft cable ran through the legs of the handmade rocking chairs that lined the long wooden porch of the Cracker Barrel, belying the implied folksiness the place served up like a side of buttered grits. An elderly couple in crisp bright orange Tennessee Vols paraphernalia lazily rocked while openly eavesdropping on the apparent father-daughter dispute. The old man smiled and offered Ray a nugget of wisdom he'd picked up over his many years; "Kids, huh?"

"Yeah . . . mind your own fucking business," Ray responded.

The man smiled back and raised his voice, "I said, 'kids, huh?' "

"Yeah, kids!" Ray said loud enough to make sure the old man heard every word. "Don't get 'em pregnant or they turn into fucking crazy people! The Vols suck!"

Twenty years ago, the old man would have kicked Ray's ass all the way to Owensboro and back again. Instead, he ushered his horrified wife into the restaurant and gave Ray a look filled with so much genuine disappointment it could have come from Ray's own father.

Ray resisted the urge to shake Courtney until she fell to pieces, and took a long, deep breath. The girl had the emotional maturity of a pumpkin. Reason would get him nowhere, so he tried something else.

"Courtney, please! My wife is having a baby!" Ray's voice

cracked. Not much, just enough to sound vulnerable. "What if I wasn't there when you were having *our* baby?"

Courtney stopped. "What?" Fresh tears started to fall. "Where would you be? Why wouldn't you be there with me?"

"I *would* be," Ray said, mimicking the cadence of a bad handsome actor he saw on a popular prime time medical drama. "But that's exactly what Miranda's asking herself right now. 'Where's Ray? Why isn't he here with me?' She's expecting me to be there for her just like you're expecting me to be there for you. It's no different, except she's my wife. I need you to help me get to her. Can you please do that for me?"

Courtney wiped her face, now flushed equally from shame and emotion, and nodded.

"Thank you," Ray said gently. Taking her hand, he led her back to the Jeep and buckled her in like a child in a safety seat. "You good?"

She nodded, and he kissed her on the head, just like he would any of his other children.

"I'll be right back."

Inside the gas station's FoodSmart, Ray picked up a book of *Mad Libs*, a bag of Flamin' Hot Cheetos, a heat-shriveled hot dog, and a bottle of Diet Dr Pepper, which reminded him of the glass of mashed up Ceaseocor left in the cabin. Those were the only pills he had, and the thought of getting more made his brain hurt. *One setback at a time.*

The junk food and Mad Libs immediately lifted Courtney's spirits. She was chatty again, which wasn't ideal, but it was better than listening to her cry. Ten minutes later they were back on the road when Courtney spoke near a whisper, "Don't be mad, but . . . I forgot to go to the bathroom back at the gas station and I have to go really bad. Can we stop again?"

After a long, hot silence, Ray got off at the next exit, where Courtney ran in to a Cracker Barrel to pee. Minutes later she walked out clutching one of those little golf tee games.

At one twenty-six A.M., Ray tore through a back entrance of Bluegrass Baptist and sprinted toward the delivery rooms. He'd dumped Courtney off in her driveway the way a Mafioso dumps a body in front of an emergency room.

"I'll call you!" he screamed over the sound of flying gravel. She even thought she heard him say, "Happy birthday," as he sped away.

In the waiting area, Joan sat half asleep watching a staticy rerun of *Everybody Loves Raymond* on an old TV needlessly bolted to the wall. She shot Ray a judgmental smile and wagged her finger, silently scolding him.

"I know, I know," he said, forcing levity and kissed her on the cheek. "I gotta get in there."

Be kind, Joan. He's had a rough day.

Joan smiled and forgave him instantly. Just like Jesus would.

Pulling on a surgical gown, Ray burst into the delivery room to find Miranda in the middle of a contraction. Her eyes looked like she'd been pepper sprayed, and her hair was matted with sweat. Christie stood bedside rubbing her back, fresh scratches from what looked like a feral cat crisscrossed her neck.

"*Where* the *fuck* have *you* been?!" Miranda screamed.

In eleven years of marriage, she'd never cursed at him, not out loud, anyway. It made him feel small. He started to explain but realized he hadn't spent a single moment of the ride home coming up with a story.

"I, um, I am so sorry it took me so long. It was just"—long exhale—"a bad scene, you know? Death and sadness and . . ." He waved his hands to give the impression of utter chaos, then held Miranda's free hand. "How are you?"

"How the fuck do you think I am, Ray? My daughter is going to be born on the worst day in history. I've been in labor for ten hours, and my husband has more important things to do than show up on time for the birth of—OH, FUCKING SHIT!" Another contraction.

"What is she, lighting firecrackers in there?" She squeezed Ray's hand with the force of a robot. Ray knew he could not complain—about anything—for a very long time, but he couldn't help wincing when he heard the deep pop of his knuckles.

"There you go, babe. Just breathe."

"Ha!" Christie laughed and rolled her eyes, prompting a look from Ray that genuinely frightened her. Fifteen of his last twenty-four hours had been spent in a Jeep with a woman whose every word made him feel like human garbage. He didn't have it in him to deal with another one.

"Christie, why don't you go fu—"

"Hello, all!" The door swung open and Dr. Fales entered, cutting Ray off before he had a chance to end his sentence *and* last remaining friendship. "You're here!" he said to Ray as he snapped on a latex glove. "Good."

He crossed to Miranda and casually stuck two fingers in her vagina without even saying hello. Contorting his face, he hummed softly, then gave a satisfied nod. "Nice," he said, peeling off the glove. "That . . . is almost ready." He could have been talking about a Thanksgiving turkey. Then, like a gynecological Fonzie, he gave his patient a wink and a finger-gun "looking good," and strode out the door.

"What the hell was that?" Miranda said. "Reminded me of my prom."

"What?" Ray did a double take as his wife's small, exhausted smile slowly grew into heaving, convulsive laughter.

Perfect, he thought. *She's having mental breakdown.* He was actually jealous. Six months in a nuthouse sounded perfect.

"Are—are you . . . okay?"

"Yes!" Miranda burst. Then, as if that brief moment of amusement was the last of her joy escaping, she immediately burst into tears. "I'm just so glad you're here."

Ray closed his eyes and sighed. He was suddenly aware that he hadn't slept in thirty-three hours. Was Gatlinburg a hallucination? There was no way that could have actually happened. Was he really going to drug Courtney's Dr Pepper? Why did he do *any* of that? Memories of the past couple days started to break apart and drift away like pieces of an iceberg, melting into an ocean of bad ideas. Ray was now exactly where he needed to be, and like Miranda, he was happy he was there. Smiling at his bawling wife, he leaned down and kissed her gently on the forehead.

"Of course I'm here," he replied, pushing a sticky clump of hair out of her eyes. "Where else would I be?"

chapter thirteen

At four fifteen A.M., Brixton Destiny Miller decided she was ready to meet the world. Miranda felt like she'd lost a war. The sweat on her skin had mixed with the lotion she'd asked Ray to rub on her arms to form a viscous paste that stank like brined lavender. She was close to delirious. An hour earlier she'd asked Christie to find a watermelon and put her feet in it.

"Oh, my God, that would feel so good," she purred.

Ray, however, had gotten his second wind thanks to three cans of Mello Yello and a blister pack he found in the nurses' lounge that turned out to be a new chewable ADD medication for toddlers. All things considered, he was holding up remarkably well.

Dr. Fales sat on a stool between Miranda's knees and told her to push, which she wasn't sure she had the strength to do. She'd already cussed out everyone in the room and pooped on the floor, so quitting at that point would have been an embarrassing waste of resources. Miranda pushed.

"One more ought to do it!"

Ray stroked her hair. "You hear that? Just one more push and we get to meet Brixton!"

"Shut up," Miranda said through gritted teeth, then screamed like she slammed a car door on her uterus. Moments later, the room was filled with the joyful cries of a seven-pound-nine-ounce baby.

Dr. Fales smiled and held her up to show the parents. "Well, it's a girl!"

"Oh, thank God." Miranda said, and not flippantly. It was a genuine thank-you to a higher power.

Dr. Fales took another look at little Brixton and his expression changed. Christie had already seen what the doctor was just now noticing. They exchanged nods and carried Brixton to a nearby table. Ray had given hundreds of nods like that over the years. He felt sick.

"What going on, Larry?"

Dr. Fales smiled automatically. "I just want to check her out real quick. It's a doctor thing."

Asshole, Ray thought.

Miranda sat up as straight as she could with her legs still in the stirrups, "What's wrong? Is something wrong?"

Christie cleaned the baby as the doctor pulled his stool around to the side of the bed facing Miranda and took her hand.

"Miranda, when you were pregnant, do you remember us discussing genetic testing?" he asked suddenly, sounding more like a lawyer than a doctor. "Amniocentesis, or CVS, or any of those?"

Her stomach lurched. Miranda had decided that all prenatal testing was unreliable and cruel since her first pregnancy, when after a routine ultrasound her then doctor indicated that Bailey would most likely be born with unnaturally short legs, and Miranda spent the next three sleepless months worrying about how she was going to raise a dwarf baby. "You know now I feel about those tests." Her voice started to break. "What's going on? Is something wrong with Brixton?"

Dr. Fales took a deep breath and thought about the many places he'd rather be.

"Well, I can't say conclusively . . . but it appears, at first sight, and this is based solely on physical characteristics, but it appears that Brixton might, and let me stress that word, *might,* have Down syndrome."

He took a moment to let them absorb the news, but instead it filled the room like water. Miranda felt like she was drowning.

"We'll need to do some tests to know for sure, but . . . I think it would be prudent if the two of you started managing your plans."

Miranda's head split with questions, but when she opened her mouth the only thing that came out was a very small "no." It simply was not possible for Brixton to have Down syndrome. Miranda would have known, she would have felt it. She was her mother, for heaven's sake. Besides, plans had been made, and they would not be *managed.* There had to be some kind of mistake.

"I know it's not what you want to hear right now," Dr. Fales said, "but . . . there's a reason these children are called special."

Miranda wanted to cry, or scream, or vomit, but she was empty.

"Otherwise," the doctor continued, "Brixton appears to be a perfectly healthy little girl, and she needs her mommy and daddy just like any other little girl."

He gave Ray a sympathetic smile, patted him on the shoulder, and crossed to the nurses.

"What happened?" Miranda asked no one in particular. Was it something she'd done? The stress from the pageants? The fight with Theresa? September eleventh?

Miranda turned to Ray, who was staring ashen faced at the table where the nurses were cleaning his wife's insides off his new daughter. "Ray? Did we do something wrong?" Her voice was a ghost.

"No. I don't know," he whispered. But he did know. Ray may not have believed in God, but he did believe in karma, and she was a stone-cold bitch. His affair with Courtney was an admission to the universe that he believed his actions had no real consequences, but that is not how the universe works. This was Ray's fault, and for the rest of his life, whenever he looked at his daughter's face, he would be reminded of his failure as a father and husband.

Miranda took her husband's hand and held it to her face. The bitter knot growing in Ray's throat prevented him from speaking, so he just nodded at her, hoping she knew what it meant: that he loved her more than anything in the world, and he was sorry for what he'd done.

"Would you like to meet your daughter?"

Christie was standing behind him, cradling a mass of white flannel. The parents tightened their grip on each other's hands and exhaled until they were light-headed. Miranda nodded and took the baby from Christie, who then turned to Ray and practically knocked him over with a hug. Surprisingly, he welcomed the human contact and tried to physically transfer some of his guilt onto her.

Brixton Destiny Miller's tiny red face was topped with a shock of black hair. Perhaps Dr. Fales was trying to let them down easy, but tests would only confirm the obvious. Their daughter had Down syndrome. It took all Ray had not to confess everything: the affair with Courtney, the baby they were expecting, the trip to Gatlinburg, the Ceasocor, Walter Beddow's credit card, his pill hobby, how much porn he watched, everything. He wanted to stand in the middle of the room and scream, "This is all *my fault*! I did this! And I want you to hate me for it!"

But before he could say anything, Brixton let out a massive sneeze that surprised all three of them. The newborn's eyes widened and then, in what Miranda would forever describe as a miracle, looked at her parents and said, "Wow." She then closed her eyes and drifted off to sleep, as peaceful and still as an angel. It was only a sneeze, but Miranda chose to see it as much more than that. To her, it was a sign from God that her daughter was going be okay—because that's what she desperately needed it to be.

Ray managed a smile, but his lips looked like they'd shattered and been hastily glued back together. There were cracks, tiny chips that were lost forever, subtle changes that would always remind him of the moment his carelessness destroyed something special. Miranda leaned forward and kissed away one of Ray's tears that had fallen onto the baby's soft head.

"Everything's going to be okay, Ray."

Still unable to speak, Ray wiped another tear from his face and nodded.

"Hey," she said calmly to her husband, "we can do this."

"Can we?" he whispered, his voice thin and scratchy like an old record.

"Of course we can. You and I can do *anything,*" she said, and looked at Brixton. "Do you want to meet your daddy?"

Ray felt unworthy of the title, or the honor of holding her, and stood motionless until Miranda practically forced the girl into his arms. He cradled her a little more delicately than he would have otherwise. He'd already done enough damage.

"I always forget," he said, his voice becoming more unreliable with every word, "how light they are." Staring at the tiny person he'd made with love, and damaged with hubris, he gave her a small kiss on the nose. "She's beautiful," he said, and meant it.

A volcanic sob was bubbling up from deep inside him, but Ray clenched every muscle in his body to force it back down. Crying would make him feel better, and he didn't deserve to feel better. Besides, if he started crying now, he wasn't sure he would ever be able to stop.

chapter fourteen

Standing in her underwear in front of her grandmother's full-length mirror, Courtney rubbed her belly like a crystal ball and tried to imagine what her body would look like when she finally started showing. At seven weeks, her stomach was still pretty flat, but the Internet said it could be anywhere from three to four months before she noticed anything, so whatever. Bumming her out more than anything else was the fact that her boobs hadn't gotten any bigger. The black minidress she'd bought for Marvin's funeral showed—in her opinion—a tasteful amount of cleavage, but it would have been awesome if that cleavage were fuller. But that wasn't going to happen, so she'd just wear something else. On her rapidly growing list of problems, that one was relatively small.

Courtney had spent the day before with Geralton Waxflower III, Marvin's attorney and executor of his will. Mr. Waxflower had been Marvin's attorney since his original lawyer, Geralton Waxflower Jr., died in a parallel-parking accident ten years earlier. Geralton III was a cadaverous, redheaded yawn who had worked out of his immaculate home office since being self-diagnosed with agoraphobia in the late '80s.

His "condition" was more of a reaction to his utter dislike of people than any real fear of leaving his house: But since his insurance didn't cover misanthropy, he convinced one of his clients—a dermatologist whose wages were being garnished for unpaid child support—to make it official. The formal diagnosis allowed him to work from home, which provided a healthy tax deduction. The federal disability check he received on the first of every month further legitimized his condition, at least in the eyes of the U.S. government.

A compulsive nose blower, Mr. Waxflower had strategically placed boxes of tissues on every available surface of his home, ensuring he would never be more than an arm's length away should he feel the urge to blow. His office, which resembled a midcentury New Orleans whorehouse, was spotted with dozens of white, billowy tufts haunting the room like tiny, mentholated ghosts. Additionally, dozens of antique porcelain dolls, a collection his beloved mother willed to him (and that he'd coveted since childhood), populated the dusty shelves.

To prepare for his meeting with Courtney, Mr. Waxflower placed his one and only visitor chair four feet away from the front of his desk. His profession dictated that he often deliver bad news, and the distance provided a much-needed buffer between himself and a client's undignified emotional outbursts. If it were not for his clients, Mr. Waxflower's job would be perfect. He often found himself wishing that porcelain dolls needed attorneys, since their company was infinitely more comforting.

As Mr. Waxflower droned on through the monotonous details of Marvin's last will and testament, Courtney's mind drifted to other things—primarily Ray, to whom she hadn't spoken since returning from Gatlinburg. She had texted him a couple times, and he'd responded promptly enough, which was fine . . . for now. He was busy. Apparently, his baby was retarded or something.

Then Mr. Waxflower said something that jerked her back to the present.

". . . so, it appears you owe the state $12,735.63, which must be paid within the next sixty days to prevent foreclosure on your house."

"Wait, what? What are you talking about?"

Mr. Waxflower cleared his throat and smoothed his soup-stained tie back under his sweater vest. "Well . . . as I was *just* saying, it appears your grandfather owed several thousand dollars in past-due property taxes."

Courtney spit her gum into her hand and dragged the heavy chair up to the edge of her lawyer's desk. At the same time, Mr. Waxflower pushed his chair backward in an attempt to maintain an equal distance. He made a mental note to bolt the visitor chair to the floor.

"But he's dead," Courtney protested, "so he doesn't owe anything anymore to anybody. He can't. It's impossible."

"Yes," Mr. Waxflower said, reaching for a tissue. "But the law states that you cannot take legal possession of the house until the debt is paid in full." He coaxed a tissue from a nearby box and blew his empty nose. "I'm sorry, Miss Daye, but that's how the law works."

"But that's not right. Granddaddy told me he left me the house and a whole bunch of money. So that's what I want."

"Yes, but as I've explained to you, he had not paid taxes on the house in a long time and there is a lien on it."

He delicately pulled another tissue from the box with the grace and flair of a sleight-of-hand magician.

"What's a lien?"

He sighed heavily, making no effort to hide his irritation. Even with clients who understood the law, Mr. Waxflower was not a patient man.

"Again, as I was saying before, when a person doesn't pay his taxes, the government can put what's called a lien on the property, meaning that in lieu of the money, they can keep the house as collateral against the debt."

"And that's legal?" she practically shouted.

"It is, yes. It's actually how our government works."

"Well, that's stupid. What about the money Granddaddy left me? It's, like, fifty grand or something."

Mr. Waxflower cleared his throat. "It was $25,436.87. Minus the $10,000 that's been set aside for funeral expenses—casket, burial, etc.—you're probably looking at around $15,000."

"Okay. So then how do I owe $12,000?"

"The lien on the house and surrounding property is for approximately $27,000. So fifteen minus twenty-seven . . ."

Courtney's eyes moved upward as if she was trying to watch her brain do the math.

Mr. Waxflower sighed again. ". . . is twelve. Miss Daye, you owe the government $12,735.63 or they will take your house."

All those numbers were making her angry and confused. And who the hell was this weird guy to tell her that she owed the government money when she knew better? Marvin had promised that she would get the house and a bunch of money, and this creep was trying to con her out of it. Mr. Waxflower obviously did not know who he was dealing with.

"What are you trying to pull?" she asked.

"Pardon me?"

"You're conning me. I want a second opinion."

"Miss Daye, I can assure you—"

"You heard me, buddy. I want to talk to another lawyer. Is there another lawyer back there somewhere?" Courtney gestured to a closed door that she imagined was hiding smarter, better-looking men who would tell her exactly what she wanted to hear.

"No. This is my house. Miss Daye, please. I don't make the laws, I just study and respect them, and I promise what I've told you is correct. Considering the circumstances, the county has agreed to give you sixty days to come up with the money, but that's it. Do you have family who can help you?"

"Granddaddy was my only family." Courtney's voice was unstable. "He said he was going to take care of me." She put her head down on Mr. Waxflower's desk and burst into tears.

Nothing was as off-putting to Mr. Waxflower as raw human emotion. It was messy and unpredictable, like children or sex, two other things with which the attorney had very limited experience. However, the job—not to mention human decency—dictated that moments like this be acknowledged. Therefore, Mr. Waxflower pulled his chair back up to his desk, reached across, and gingerly patted her twice on the top of her head.

"There, there," he said, so empty and hollow the words practically echoed. It was the first human being he'd touched in thirteen months.

"I'm pregnant!" Courtney screamed.

Mr. Waxflower reflexively withdrew his hand as if she'd just said she was radioactive, or a peanut—one of the many things the attorney claimed an allergy to. He quickly grabbed another tissue and wiped his hands.

"How am I supposed to raise a baby without a house?" The question sounded rhetorical, but Courtney looked at him with her red, puffy eyes and screamed, "*How?*"

Mr. Waxflower sat like a statue before blurting out the first thing that entered his head. "That is none of my business, I'm sure. Please leave my home office. Our business is done for today."

Over the years, Geralton Waxflower III had learned to depend on the comfort that came from setting boundaries. It was considered by many to be a rude and insensitive way to live, but as far as he was concerned his job as Marvin's attorney did not include consoling his hysterical, pregnant granddaughter. If the girl needed a counselor, she could hire one, but their legal business had concluded and it was time for her to leave.

Courtney stood up and tried to compose herself. "You'll be hearing from my lawyer."

"I am your lawyer, Miss Daye."

"I mean, my *new* lawyer. My *good* lawyer."

Courtney snatched her copy of Marvin's will off the desk and stormed out of the room, making a point to slam the door behind her. The lawyer sighed through his lips like an exhausted horse and decided to quit for the day. Rising slowly from his desk, Mr. Waxflower locked his front door, turned out the lights, and hoped his other scheduled appointments would assume they'd made a mistake and go away. Alone in the darkened room, Geralton took a porcelain doll named Laura from a shelf and slowly began brushing her hair.

On the way to the mall to pick up some strappy heels for the funeral, Courtney tried to figure out how to get Mr. Waxflower fired from being a lawyer. Maybe the police could help her, or the Internet. She'd figure that out later. Right now she had to figure out how she was going to get Ray to give her $12,735.63.

Courtney pulled several dresses from her closet that she felt were both respectful and hot. Her two best friends, Britney and Kaitlin sat on her bed dressed in their sexiest church clothes. Overall, Courtney was arguably the best looking of the three, but she wasn't going to take any chances. Just because she was burying her grandfather didn't mean she couldn't still look cute. Actually, as the bereaved, Courtney had an obligation to look better than everyone else.

"I like this one." She shrugged and stepped into her original choice, the cleavage-baring black minidress. She might not have had pregnancy boobs, but she still had perfect ones. Britney, a star volleyball player with long slender legs that made up sixty-five percent of her body, was bare legged in a thigh-high skirt, so Courtney also slipped on a pair of black leggings. She had enough to think about without wondering if people were comparing her legs to Britney's.

Scrolling through her phone, Britney twirled her long red hair and tried to lighten the mood. "I know your grandfather just died, Court, but it's going to be so effing awesome when you start having parties in this house."

Britney didn't swear because of church, so she peppered her conversations with implied vulgarity. She was an R-rated movie edited for an airplane. "I might just move in with you. My stepmother is being a total b lately."

"Dude, I cannot wait! I am *so* ready for a party!" Kaitlin had recently started calling people "dude." It annoyed pretty much everyone, but if someone asked her to stop, she just did it more. Having an affectation that bugged everyone was empowering. Besides, there was something so un-Kaitlin about calling people "dude" that it had become her favorite thing to do. She was also well aware that her effortless beauty allowed her to get away with pretty much anything. Her fresh, freckled skin was a stark contrast to her shiny onyx hair, and her deep blue eyes were the color of a Blue Lightning Blast Slurpee. If it weren't for the arm she lost in a car accident five years earlier, she could have been a model.

Courtney adjusted the tights over her legs and sighed. "Yeah. A party. That sounds fun." Kaitlin and Britney exchanged dramatically concerned looks.

Britney tried again. "I saw Kevin Biggins at the movies last night. He said he was coming to the funeral today. I think he likes you."

"Dude, he is so hot. He talks about you all the time, Court."

"I know he's only a sophomore, but I'd totally give him a handie."

"Britney! Jeez, he likes Courtney!"

"I didn't say I was going to. I'm just saying, he's totally yummy. What do you think, Court?"

"Yeah. He's nice," she said, checking out the dress in the mirror. "But I'm not interested."

"Oh, my God, dude, I so wish I had your boobs."

Britney nodded, "Me, too. Mine are more like boos." She

and Kaitlin cracked up and playfully fell back on the bed as if they were in a commercial for cotton sheets.

Courtney wanted to smile, but her face wouldn't let her. She nodded and went back to checking herself out in the mirror.

"What's wrong, Court? I mean, obvi it's your grandfather, but is it something else, because if it's something else you can totally tell us."

"Yeah, that's why we're here," Britney said sincerely, "to support you. What's going on?"

Fighting tears, Courtney joined them on the bed and wailed. Everything came flooding out in long, breathless chunks. She told them about how she might lose her house because her stupid lawyer is stupid, and how she owes the government $12,735.63, and if she can't get the money she'll be homeless by Christmas. As she spoke, the girls just stared, mouths agape.

"But that's not the worst part."

"Oh, my God, what's the worst part?" Kaitlin asked as if on the verge of orgasm.

Courtney braced herself, unsure if her friends were mature enough to handle her truth, then closed her eyes and said calmly, "I'm pregnant."

There was a silence longer than Britney's legs.

"Dude . . ."

"OMFG."

Neither girl was still a virgin. Well, Britney was technically kind of still a virgin, maybe—but they were smart enough to take precautions despite their school's abstinence-only stance on the unreliability of birth control.

"And I don't know what I'm going to do because the father is older, and . . ."

"And what?"

Her voice got very small, ". . . married."

Kaitlin and Britney almost exploded. They were simultaneously appalled and titillated. "Holy shit!" they said in unison, the magnitude of the situation exempting Britney from her swearing ban.

"Who is it?"

"I'd rather not say right now. His wife just had a baby, like three days ago." Kaitlin's mouth was a tunnel of disbelief. A string of drool slid down her chin, which she wiped on the shoulder of her good arm. Britney, meanwhile, just kind of blinked and twitched as her brain short-circuited. But Courtney felt better than she had in weeks. Just telling someone made the whole situation more manageable. It was now a common problem shared among friends instead of a secret shame. Plus, she loved gossip even if it was about her.

"Cool. Thanks for letting me vent, guys. I feel so much better."

As the girls processed, Courtney crossed to the mirror and gave her friends a quick once-over and determined that she looked better than they did. She was funeral ready. Then, remembering something important, Courtney turned and in her most deadly-serious voice said, "Oh, and you can't tell anyone, okay?"

They nodded like pliant zombies.

"Cool. Now . . ." She adjusted her breasts and did a quick twirl in her new dress. "How do I look?"

chapter fifteen

For the past nine Father's Days, birthdays, and Christmases, Ray's kids had given him ties. Ray never wore ties and, quite frankly, he didn't understand them.

"Why is a man wearing paisleys, or stripes, or the Spider-Man logo around his neck considered more dressed up than a man in, say, a nice sweater?" a teenaged Ray once asked his father over steaks at the club. "It makes *no* sense."

"A tie lets people know you're successful," his father explained, a fork in one hand, a cigarette in the other. "Look around anywhere. You can always tell who's the most successful by who's wearing a tie."

Ray looked around. "Only the waiters are wearing ties."

Dr. Miller tossed his silverware onto the table. "Look, I'm trying to teach you something. If you don't want to learn, fine, just don't be a prick."

If success was judged solely on the *number* of ties a man owned, Ray would, for once, have impressed his father. His collection consisted of two SpongeBob ties, one Darth Vader, four Yodas, three designed by Jerry Garcia, one Harley-Davidson, a green John Deere, a red bow tie, three with medical themes, and six with snowmen—two of which were identical. He also had a skinny tie with a piano keyboard on it given to him by Joan as a joke. What the joke was exactly, he never knew.

His long-out-of-fashion dress clothes were crushed into a tiny corner of the closet he now shared with Bailey's retired gowns. It was hard to believe, with as much death as he was exposed to, that Ray didn't own a single tie appropriate for a funeral.

Eventually, he gave up and grabbed one with tiny snowmen on it. From a distance they kind of looked like polka dots. It didn't match his gray (and only) suit, but it would have to suffice. Checking the pockets of the suit, he found a five-dollar bill, a wedding program from three years earlier he had no memory of attending, and two random pills that he swallowed dry. He slid the mirrored door of the closet until he heard the satisfying *fwoomp* that reminded him of a coffin closing.

In the living room, Miranda was on the sofa breast-feeding Brixton, who was "sleating" (sleeping while eating), a cutsie family term they'd coined when Bailey was an infant. The past three days had been emotional, to say the least, but Ray had fallen in love with his new daughter so effortlessly, that first night at the hospital now seemed like a bad TV show he was only half watching. Brixton was no different from any new baby: fussy, sleepy, wet, groggy, quiet, impossibly difficult, and impossibly easy. Miranda had even joked that maybe it would have been easier if all their kids had been born with Down syndrome, a joke that instantly made her break down into crippling, apologetic sobs. The Millers were well aware of the challenges that lay ahead—Joan's incessant reminders made sure of that—but Miranda was trying to stay positive, and much to Ray's grateful surprise, she had been.

"Hey there, handsome," Miranda said when Ray entered in his suit. "Where are you off to?"

"Marvin's funeral. I told you I needed to go."

"Right. You don't ever go to funerals. You must have really liked that man."

Ray nodded. "He was . . . a good family man."

"How long do you think it'll be?"

"Couple hours, I guess. Funeral length."

"Is it going to be outside?"

"The cemetery part. Why?"

"Well . . . how would you feel if I went with you?"

Ray felt a little bit of pee slip out. "Excuse me?"

"I've been sitting in this room for two days. The doctor said a little exercise would be good, and I'd love to get some fresh air. Then maybe after we can pick up some Moonlite or something for dinner."

"Okay, well, maybe when I get back we can go down to the river, take a walk, have a picnic, I'm sure there's some festival or something going on down there." He smiled, then frowned. "It's a funeral. It'll be depressing."

Suddenly, Ray felt insanely alert and helplessly sleepy. *Shit,* he remembered these pills. Ambiall (a combination Ambien and Adderall), "sleep aids for adults to help turn off their thoughts and focus on rest." They never made it to market, too many side effects. Ray remembered the sensation from the last time he'd taken them. It was like being shot in the adrenal glands with horse tranquilizer.

"I've never met any of your patients before," Miranda said.

"That's because they're all dead," Ray said, wiping his brow and yawning. "And this one will be, too."

"Don't be condescending. I want to get out of this house and I think it would be good for Brixton to get out, too. She's never seen a cemetery."

"She doesn't need to see a . . . cemetery." Ray was thirsty.

Miranda pulled herself up from the sofa, "Just give me ten minutes."

"Miranda . . . I . . ." He trailed off. There was more he wanted to say, a lot more. The words were forming perfectly in his head, a succinct, incontestable justification for her not going to this funeral, but he was just too sleepy to speak them.

Giving Ray the baby, Miranda charged down the hall to change her clothes. The girl melted into Ray's chest as the leather La-Z-Boy recliner Bailey won at the Louisiana Queen of the Levees Pageant and Katrina Fund-Raiser (Baton Rouge, Louisiana) absorbed them both. He studied his daughter's face, tried to memorize it. It was a good little face.

"You want to go to a funeral?" Ray asked his new baby.

She smiled and threw up on his tie.

chapter sixteen

Seated prominently beside the casket, Courtney, Britney, and Kaitlin reigned like a homecoming court while a few dozen others huddled under the small tent, hiding from the sun. The heat index was in the low nineties (a near record for mid September) and Courtney seriously regretted her leggings. She didn't need them, anyway; no hot guys showed up. But that was okay, that's not what the day was about. It was about Courtney's loss—and Marvin's life, of course. When everyone closed their eyes for the Lord's Prayer, Courtney considered slipping off the tights but remembered she hadn't worn underwear. Being pantyless at her grandfather's funeral seemed disrespectful.

When she spotted Ray ambling toward the tent, her breathing relaxed and she smiled for the first time since Gatlinburg. *Thank God,* she thought. *Someone to take care of me.* It took a moment for Courtney to realize that the short, pretty woman with the baby next to him was his wife. *He did* not *bring her!*

Over the sun-kissed corpse of her grandfather, Courtney screamed at him with her eyes: *What the fuck is* she *doing here?*

Ray shrugged and tried to respond in kind. *She wanted to come. What was I supposed to do? I really need some water.*

Miranda whispered in Ray's ear, "Which one is the granddaughter?"

He whispered back, "The, um, the blond one. In the tights."

"She's cute."

"You think so?"

Miranda chuckled. "Like you never noticed."

Ray chuckled, too, but it was way too loud. "Yeah." Shit.

Watching their exchange, Courtney was convinced they were laughing at her and became enraged. As the mourners recited the Twenty-Third Psalm as if it were their own funeral, Courtney leaned in to Britney, whispered in her ear, and pointed at Ray. Britney looked up at him and went slack jawed. She then told Kaitlin, who turned to Courtney and whispered, "Dude, really?"

All of Ray's sweat glands emptied at once. He wanted to sprint to the nearest bed and sleep so fucking hard.

What the fuck? he thought at her across the cemetery. *Did you tell them?*

Crossing her arms, she nodded as if to say, "Yeah, I did. Check and mate." But Courtney didn't understand chess because it was boring. So instead she thought, *Yeah, I did. Suck on that, a-hole!"*

The minister, a humorless, lonely man with a fifty-two-inch waist, closed his tattered Bible. "Let us pray."

With everyone's heads bowed, Miranda took out her breast and began feeding Brixton, who was getting fussy in the heat.

Courtney had never seen anything so appalling in her life. Miranda might as well have climbed on top of Marvin's casket and pooped in it.

"Our most gracious and loving Heavenly Father, we submit to your strong and welcoming arms, our brother Marvin Sylvester Daye . . ."

Courtney and Ray stared at each other, trying to telepathically impart the magnitude and intractability of their individual positions. Ray also thought he was starting to hallucinate. Was that girl next to Courtney missing an arm?

"Amen," the minister proclaimed, and everyone robotically echoed. "Courtney, dear, let me speak for everyone when I say how truly sorry I am for your loss."

Courtney grabbed her friends' hands, and the three girls broke down in a knotted mass of tears and hugs.

The minister continued, "You can take great comfort in knowing that your grandfather is soaring through the heavens on the wings of a golden dove raised by Jesus Himself."

The crowd nodded as if that was the most reasonable thing they'd ever heard.

"I want to thank everyone for coming today. May God bless and keep each and every one of you."

As Brixton tugged on her nipple, Miranda watched Courtney cry. "You know, Ray, she's only like eight years older than Bailey."

"What the fuck is that supposed to mean?" he snapped and tried to focus his eyes.

"Nothing. Jeez, just that . . . I mean, what would happen to Bailey and the kids if something happened to us?"

"Nothing's going to happen to us."

"I know, but still. It makes you think."

Made to think about his orphaned children, Ray stretched his jaw and stared at the grass beneath his feet. It was so beautiful, lush, and green. Six feet below that was a dead person.

"Hello, Ray."

The voice behind him made him jump. He turned quickly and gasped when he saw Courtney standing with Britney and Kaitlin. *Holy shit. How did she sneak up like that?*

Under the circumstances it would have been weird *not* to hug her, but embracing seemed like a bad idea under the other circumstances. Ray hadn't seen Courtney since he'd essentially shoved her out of his moving Jeep on his way to the hospital. And he didn't welcome an audience for their reunion. Instead, he shook her hand and squeezed her forearm like a seasoned politician. "Courtney. Hi. How . . . how are you?"

Her hand tightened in his. "I've been better, Ray. My grandfather died. How are you? How's your new baby?"

Miranda smiled. "She's doing great. Just so, so very great. I'm Ray's wife, Miranda."

Ray snapped to it. "Sorry. Right, Courtney, Miranda. Miranda, Courtney."

When the two women shook hands, Ray half expected something supernatural to happen, a sudden flash like in a sci-fi story where their consciousnesses integrate and they realize they're sleeping with the same man, or a vortex would open and suck them all into another dimension, or at the very least a clap of thunder. But there was none of that, only the brief stopping of his heart.

"Nice to meet you, Miranda. Ray doesn't talk about you a lot, but when he does it's very nice."

"Oh, well, aren't you sweet?"

"I try."

"I'm so sorry for your loss. Your grandfather must have been very special. Ray's never gone to a patient's funeral before."

"Well." Courtney smiled politely. "I'm glad he's here. After everything that's happened, Ray feels like family now."

She took an envelope from her purse and handed it to Ray. "This is from Granddaddy. It's got your name on it. It was next to his bed when he died. But you would know that because you were there."

"Yes, I was. I was there. Sadly." Ray nodded repeatedly, making him light-headed. He put his hand on a grave marker to steady himself.

"I guess he wanted to say thanks or something, I don't know. It's sealed, so I couldn't read it."

Scratched across the envelope in Marvin's almost indecipherable scrawl was the word "RAY." Eyeing it like it was filled with anthrax—which it very well could have been—Ray took the envelope, slid it into the breast pocket of his suit, and managed with his rapidly thickening tongue to choke out, "Thank you."

Britney whispered something to Kaitlin, causing them both to giggle. Ray blushed like a self-conscious boy. Nothing is more emasculating to a man of any age than being laughed at by cute teenage girls. His head started thumping like a balloon with a pulse.

"Well," Courtney said, breaking the silence, "we should probably go. I need to start packing."

Ray snapped back to attention. "Packing? Are you going somewhere?" he asked, a bit too hopeful.

"Yeah, but I'm not sure where yet."

His eyes narrowed. "What are you talking about?"

"Well, Granddaddy's lawyer says I'm probably going to lose my house because there's a lead on it."

"A what?"

The teenager let out an exasperated sigh, "A lead is when the government can take your house whenever they feel like it if you owe them money. It's retarded."

She caught herself and shot an embarrassed glance at Brixton, who was still slurping away on Miranda's partially exposed breast like a domesticated piglet.

"A *lien*?" Ray asked.

"Yeah, a lien, whatever. Anyway, Granddaddy owed, like, a ton of taxes, so I'm probably going to lose my house, and I don't know where I'm going to live."

Miranda touched her arm. "Oh, you poor dear."

Ray just stared. This was news to him: huge, awful, world-fucking news. Courtney living alone in her own house was the cornerstone of the one-year plan he had carefully crafted for his double life. In the mornings, he'd see Miranda and the kids, leave an hour earlier than usual, claiming a shift change at the hospital, and stop by Courtney's on the way to work. Nights not spent working hospice would be divided between both families, and weekends would be spent at Courtney's when Miranda, Bailey, and Brixton were pageanting and the boys were at Joan's. If implemented perfectly, he believed he could keep that up for at least a year. But that strategy was now swirling down the toilet that was his life.

"Wait, hang on," Ray slurred, the Ambiall being amplified by the humid September day. "I thought Marvin set everything up for you. He told me you were taken care of."

"I guess he was wrong, but my lawyer is superdumb so maybe he screwed something up or something. I'm going to try to get a new lawyer to see if maybe he can change the law. It seems totally unfair."

"How much do you owe?"

"Something like twelve thousand dollars."

"Holy shit!"

Miranda slapped his arm. "Ray, not in front of the girls."

Britney and Kaitlin rolled their eyes and laughed. Ray blushed and straightened his posture hoping to counteract how small he suddenly felt.

Brixton had fallen asleep, so Miranda handed her to Ray, fastened her nursing bra, and took Courtney's hand. "What are your plans, dear?"

"I don't have any yet. I can stay with friends or something for a while, I guess." Britney and Kaitlin put their three arms around her in solidarity. "I'll probably have to get a job. But I'll only be able to work for about six months."

"Why's that?" Miranda asked.

Ray felt his asshole pucker.

Courtney whispered, not wanting her grandfather's body to hear, "Because I'm pregnant."

Miranda took Courtney's hand in hers like a pearl in a oystershell.

"Oh, dear." She sighed hard, forcibly expelling all judgment from her body. "Well, what about the father? Can't you move in with him? Are you going to marry him?"

Courtney paused. "That's not really an option right now."

"I see," Miranda said, nodding sympathetically.

"I'd rather not talk about the father, if you don't mind." She leaned in to Miranda and locked eyes with Ray. "We're in a fight."

Warm, salty rivers of sweat flowed down Ray's face. His

head spun and his insides ached. Pretty sure that he was having a heart attack, Ray sat on the headstone of Mr. and Mrs. Grover Shrewsbury. If it *was* a heart attack, Ray was okay with it. They could just toss him in the casket with Marvin and cover him with dirt.

"I understand." Miranda nodded. "When men find out they're going to be fathers, they can turn into such babies themselves."

She placed a hand on Ray's shoulder and continued. "But you need to make sure the father lives up to his responsibilities. You've got legal rights, you know. You can haul that boy up in front of a judge who'll force him to step up and be a man—"

"You are not a lawyer!" Ray screamed, rising off the headstone as if the Shrewsburys commanded it.

"Well, I know that," Miranda said, trying to cover her embarrassment. "But someone needs to help this girl."

Ray's brain was a jumble of disconnected words, magnetic poetry on his refrigerator door, and he lacked the ability to arrange them into useful sentences. "But . . . you, no . . . it's not . . . right. You can't . . . with advice . . ." Ray's heart pounded. "No. Not . . . a problem . . . of you . . . it's . . ." His eyelids drooped. "Fucked . . ." His eyes rolled back in his head, and he started swaying back and forth.

Miranda reached out to steady him. "Ray, are you okay, honey?"

"I'm just . . . I'm saying . . . no . . . happening . . . take baby . . ." His knees buckled and he started to fall. Pushing Brixton toward Courtney, Ray watched helplessly as the top of the Shrewsburys' grave marker rushed toward his face like a granite fist. The chilling image of Ray's teeth powdering like chalk on a sidewalk caused Kaitlin and Britney to immediately throw up. Copious amounts of blood gushed from Ray's mouth, splattering across the BELOVED MOTHER engraved in the tombstone like a horror movie poster.

"Oh, my God, Ray! Ray?" Miranda rolled her unconscious husband over and recoiled when she saw his face. Four of his front teeth, two upper and two lower, were gone. His lips were split everywhere; his nose was broken. "Courtney, call an ambulance!"

Dazed by the sudden violence, Courtney shifted Brixton to her shoulder and dug in her purse until she found her phone. Brixton was the first baby she'd ever held, and it was different from what she'd imagined, less reverent. It was like holding a puppy, or a Precious Moments figurine.

"Ray? Can you hear me? Ray!" Miranda screamed. "Where are your teeth?"

The commotion woke Brixton from her brief nap, and the baby started crying on Courtney's shoulder. The screaming, crying, and vomiting were soon drowned out, however, by the mechanical humming of winches. Turning back to the funeral tent, Courtney whispered a hasty "good-bye" as two burly rednecks drained their Budweiser cans and tossed them into the grave before lowering her grandfather's casket into the cold, dark ground forever.

chapter seventeen

Slumped in a wheelchair, Ray was escorted from Bluegrass Baptist filled with enough painkillers to kill a moose. Multiple bruises (or perhaps one large one) had turned his face the color of a rotting heirloom tomato. His lips were stitched in so many places it looked like he was holding in a mouthful of angry spiders. The ER doctor on duty, an entitled first-year resident Ray couldn't stand, had assured him that the small chips of teeth imbedded in his lips and gums would eventually work their way out naturally.

"Or maybe not. It's hard to tell right now," the young doctor said as he roughly (yet perfectly) reset Ray's broken nose. "Either way, you will have some scars. They'll be small, but visible, especially when you smile." Thus guaranteeing their invisibility.

Miranda and Christie helped Ray into the passenger side of his Jeep and buckled him in. Leaning his head against the window, Ray relished the coolness of the glass on his right ear, one of the few unscathed parts of his face. Several yards of gauze had been stuffed into his cheeks and nostrils, forcing Ray's mouth open and creating a perpetual stream of drool that dripped from his stitched and swollen bottom lip onto his snowman tie, now a gruesome holiday tableau.

An emergency dentist had managed to reattach one of Ray's broken teeth, an upper canine, but the other three were either shattered or swallowed.

"Well," the dentist said with a smile, "that's probably going to come back to bite you in the ass."

After waiting a moment to make sure everyone in the room understood and appreciated his joke, he burst out laughing. He'd used the line before. It was one of his favorites.

"When the swelling goes down, you can get fitted for some prosthetics that can be wired directly into your gums. It's a pretty standard procedure. Hockey players do it all the time. Until then, you should probably stay away from things like apples and corn on the cob. And tombstones." He laughed again.

Ray did not appreciate the man's sense of humor, but the drugs were strong, and his mouth was swollen so he was able to muster only a weak "Phusc kwew" in response.

Speeding down Parish Avenue, Miranda anxiously drummed her fingers on the steering wheel. She hadn't nursed in nearly four hours and her breasts were aching. They sped past Lic's Ice Cream, and Ray remembered the time he drove to Evansville to see an Offspring concert. He'd stopped at Lic's on the way home. The ice cream was incredible, but for some reason he'd never gone back. Maybe some good things were only supposed to be done once.

Miranda made a left on Fredrica toward their little house on Cottage Drive, blowing through a stop sign she had long considered unnecessary. Placing her hand gently on Ray's knee, she smiled.

"You okay?"

Ray wanted to look at her like she was insane, but his head was too heavy to move, so he gave her a weak *so-so* hand gesture.

"I know. What a week, huh?" She sighed again.

Miranda still hadn't told Ray about her fight with Theresa and the humiliating end to Bailey's pageant career, or about the hearing scheduled for next month to discuss banning Miranda from all future pageants on the Dolls circuit. It all seemed so unimportant now, especially since Theresa had agreed not to press criminal charges.

Rolling his head off the window, Ray tried to speak through the gauze and Percocet. "Wheors" *slurp* "Bwiktong?" *Slurp*.

"Mom's got her. Everything's fine. Don't worry about anything, okay?" She sighed heavily, then tried to ease into a different conversation. "You know, you really should drink more water. The doctor said heat stroke can kill you."

Ray shook his head. "Id wushund heed stoke." It was anxiety and stress and Ambiall and adultery and statutory rape and unborn illegitimate children and legitimately born children with Down syndrome and liens and money and debt and on and on and on.

"Don't be embarrassed, baby. It's not unmasculine to faint."

He nodded, giving up, and leaned his head back on the window, watching the quiet homes zip by. They were nice houses, old but gentrified, well maintained. He'd lived in this neighborhood for over a decade, passed these houses every day, and he knew the names of maybe three of his neighbors.

Ray wondered what their lives were like behind those comfortable reclaimed wood doors, and if maybe they would want to trade with him.

"The doctor said you should stay in bed for a few days. Christie said she'd cover your shifts at the hospital, but I'm going to need some help around the house."

Ray tried to speak, but his tongue felt like an uncooked chicken breast, so he shook his head and let out a series of grunts that were intended to mean, *Sweetheart, I will be fine. I can help with Brixton. I don't need to stay in bed.*

"So . . . I did something."

Ray looked at her.

"Mom's knees are *really* bad, and four kids are just way too much for her to keep track of, especially at her age. So I hired a babysitter."

"Okah," Ray said, knowing there was more to the story. "Woo?"

"Courtney."

Bloody cotton shot from one of Ray's nostrils.

"Wha?! No!" Shaking his head, he tried to speak, but his mouth was too full. He reached toward his back teeth and began pulling an endless stream of bloody gauze from his mouth like a clown at the world's worst children's party.

"Ray, stop it. She's so sweet, and I just felt so bad for her losing the last of her family and her house and getting pregnant by some selfish . . . asshole who won't support her. And you should have seen her with Brixton when you fainted. She was so good with her."

Lightning bolts shot through Ray's face as he carefully forced words through his shredded lips. "No. No. Absowutewy not. Cowtney's a cwient. It's not effical. I dow't need hewp."

"Well, I *do* need help, Ray. And I think this a good opportunity for us to do something nice for somebody less fortunate than us. She needs money, and we can help."

"Miwanda. Wook at me. No way."

"Well, I've already asked her and she agreed. So it's happening. There's nothing more to be said about it, so you might as well just put that stuff back in your mouth and be quiet like the doctor told you to."

Ray considered opening the door and jumping.

"And it's not like she's moving in. She'll just stay a few nights a week, tops."

Miranda pulled into their driveway, and Ray's stomach lurched. Standing in front of his house were J.J., Junior, and Joan, who was holding Brixton while Bailey helped Courtney pull a massive suitcase from the trunk of Marvin's 1998 Crown Vic.

Before the Jeep had even stopped, Ray was leaning out the door retching. The remaining gauze, however, blocked the vomit's egress and rerouted it up through his very tender nose, where it shot out of his one unplugged nostril in hot, painful bursts. The backs of Ray's eyes burned, and he managed to pull out the last of his mouth gauze just in time to throw up again. Stomach acid connected with his exposed dental nerves and white-hot electric pain pulsed through his body, causing Ray to piss his pants and fall out of the Jeep into the warm puddle of vomit in the driveway. Rising to his knees, Ray tried to spit the acrid taste of partially digested blood from his mouth, but he dislodged his newly reattached tooth, which shot down the driveway into a storm drain, where it was whisked away to the murky depths of the Ohio River.

chapter eighteen

"I'm sorry the room is so small." Miranda said, moving a pile of sashes off the futon to make room for Courtney's suitcase.

"No, it's awesome. Such a cool space," Courtney said politely. "I don't want to be any trouble, Mrs. Miller. I'm only staying a few days."

"It's no trouble at all. And call me Miranda. I'm not *that* much older than you."

Courtney almost laughed. Wasn't Miranda like thirty five or something?

Before the room became a shrine to Bailey's career, it had been Ray's sanctuary from the house's rising estrogen levels. He'd managed to squeeze in a futon, a Papasan chair, a small TV, and his guitar, which he would lazily strum and try to write songs while getting high on low-quality marijuana. Over the years, Ray's increasingly busy schedule forced him to give up both the pot smoking and the guitar, which limited his time in the room, leaving it vulnerable for a takeover.

After a hard-won trifecta of Princess, Cover Model, and Grand Glitteratti at the Golden Glitz and Glamour Pageant (Memphis, Tennessee), Miranda and Bailey celebrated by taking a tour of the Holy Land of the South: Graceland. Both were fans of Elvis—at the time, Bailey's talent was a heartbreaking interpretive dance set to "In the Ghetto"—but neither was prepared for how inspired they would be, especially by the trophy room. The labyrinth of gold records, Grammys, and humanitarian awards showed them how a true king presented his success. And if *he* could do it, then so could a true queen.

In the early days, Miranda had displayed Bailey's awards on cramped shelves in her room until they spilled out onto the dresser, the nightstand, and eventually the floor. After years of successful competition, Bailey was literally tripping over the spoils of her success.

"Mommy," the girl said, as confident and proud as any six-year-old Miranda had ever heard, "I need an Elvis room, but for me."

It was scary. Sometimes Miranda thought Bailey could read her mind.

Miranda had always thought Ray's "sanctuary" was self-indulgent and temporary, a place for Ray to keep his "guy junk" until they figured out what to do with the room. Well, Miranda had figured it out: She would build a shrine to the career she had built for her daughter. And if Ray felt like he needed a place to be alone, there was always the toolshed in the backyard, which is where Miranda moved his stuff before he got home from work that night.

Ray was not pleased.

"But baby, all this stuff, our crowns and trophies and plaques and sashes, it finally gives this silly room a purpose."

Ray looked at her, furious and baffled and disappointed. Apparently, she had not been listening when he *just* explained how the room's purpose was to be an island of refuge in a sea of crowns and trophies and plaques and sashes. But it didn't matter. He'd lost his room, and his wife's regard. The next morning Ray woke up early and applied for a night job as a hospice nurse.

Unpacking her suitcase—much of the contents still untouched from her aborted Gatlinburg trip—Courtney reevaluated her plan. Moving in with Ray's family was definitely not something she'd considered, but now that she was in the house, it kind of made sense. The closer she was to him, the easier it would be to influence him. It was definitely better than her other plan, which was basically "trust Ray."

Watching Miranda set out clean sheets and towels, Courtney felt bad, but only for a second. Miranda seemed like a nice enough lady, and her kids were really sweet, but Courtney had to think about her own future. With Marvin gone, someone needed to take care of her, and that person was going to be Ray whether he liked it or not.

Crossing to the stack of plastic storage bins that would act as her dresser, Courtney bumped into a six foot trophy from the South Georgia Miss Peach Festival and Car Show (Valdosta, Georgia).

"Careful!" Bailey snapped.

"Oh, my gosh, I'm so sorry. There are just so many of them. It's really impressive. I mean, seriously. These are so awesome, Bailey."

"Thanks," Bailey said, softening a bit. "I've got more at my grandmother's house. There's not really enough room in here to hold them all."

Bailey didn't know why she was bragging, but she couldn't stop herself. The mortifying end to her pageant career had made her surprisingly nostalgic. As unfulfilling as it had been toward the end, she had to admit she did enjoy the attention. Since Brixton's birth, and with no pageants in the foreseeable future, Miranda had barely spoken to her.

"Not many girls have a whole room dedicated to how awesome they are. I know I never did." Courtney took one of the crowns and put it on her head. "I only won one trophy in my whole life. For gymnastics. I won Most Improved, which basically means I was a bad gymnast, but I showed up every week for practice and didn't break my neck, so they had to give me something. Oh!" she said, remembering. "And I took home a spirit stick once at cheerleading camp my freshman year, so I guess that counts."

"Did *you* ever do pageants?" Bailey asked, hoping her tone implied that Courtney should take her crown off her head immediately.

"Me?" She rolled her eyes. "No way. I'm not really the pageant girl type."

"What's that supposed to mean?" Bailey asked curtly.

"Bailey," Miranda reprimanded, "tone." She then turned to Courtney with a look that demanded she explain what that was supposed to mean.

"Nothing. Just . . ." She hesitated. "I'm not really pretty enough, like pageant pretty, you know? And don't you have to answer a bunch of questions about what's going on in the world and stuff? I don't watch the news really, so I wouldn't do very good."

Miranda laughed. "Sweetheart, with that body, you'd be just fine."

Courtney blushed. "Thanks." She bit her thumbnail, looked back at the wall of awards, and wondered if Bailey had any idea how lucky she was. "Granddaddy didn't have a lot of money, so I didn't ask for much. Even my prom dress last year was a hand-me-down from my neighbor, Big Judy. She got it new for her prom when I was in, like, seventh grade, and I just loved it. It was pink and shiny and flowy. It looked like Glinda the Good Witch's dress from *The Wizard of Oz,* but shorter and sexier and it showed off my boobs great."

Both Bailey and Miranda stole quick glances of Courtney's breasts, then glanced down at, then away from, their own less-impressive chests.

"Big Judy let me wear it, and I looked so hot. I mean, I looked *awesome.* Then at the after-party, my stupid date threw up Crown and Coke all over the front and stained it. He was a jerk. Cool car, though. Big Judy was so mad. I mean, she was a real you know what about it, so I didn't feel too bad 'cause she was so mean." She took a breath, realizing she was sharing too much about herself and changed the subject. "So when's your next pageant, Bailey?"

Miranda looked down at her hands, remembering the feel of Theresa's hair between her fingers, and blushed. The shame she felt for wanting to smile made her blush even more.

"I'm retired," Bailey said blithely, as if giving a sound bite to *Access Hollywood*. "It was time."

Miranda nodded for a long time. "I guess so."

The ensuing moment of silence felt heavy, like a tribute to a fallen soldier.

"Well," Bailey said as an *amen*. "I'm gonna go play on the computer." Then taking the crown from Courtney's head, she placed it neatly back on the shelf and left the room.

"Did I say something wrong?" Courtney asked Miranda.

Miranda sighed, giving the question more weight than it called for.

"There was a . . . misunderstanding at Bailey's last pageant. It was more like a fight. She's embarrassed by it." Miranda paused, embarrassed by it. "Actually, I think it's probably for the best." She picked up an armful of trophies from the nightstand and dropped them into the toy chest. "I was hoping Brixton might take her place, but . . . I guess that won't be happening." Miranda inhaled deeply through her nose, trying to force a smile, but her lips wouldn't move.

"Why not?" Courtney asked.

"Well . . . you know." Miranda waved her hand across her face and shrugged. "You know."

"No. What?"

"Brixton has"—her voice dropped to a whisper—"Down syndrome." It was the first time she had said it to someone other than a family member, and she found it strangely cathartic, almost empowering.

Courtney shrugged. "So? I mean, is there some rule that says a girl with Down syndrome can't compete in pageants? Because that would be super-messed-up if there was."

"No. I mean, I don't think so, but—"

"But what? You should totally enter her. They'd have to be superracist not to let her in. She's a really cute baby. And isn't that what matters in a kids' pageant? Who's cutest?"

Miranda looked at this girl, not much older than a child herself, and wondered: Where did all this wisdom come from? *Of course* she could enter Brixton in pageants. Nothing but other people's prejudices was keeping her from it. That, and perhaps good taste, but that had never stopped her before. If

Tesla Maguire could stomp around on stage with that insulin pump hanging from her waist, certainly Brixton could compete. As an altered version of her former plan started to take shape, Miranda noticed a crown among Bailey's awards. She'd seen it a hundred times before, but today it triggered an idea that ranked with one of the best she'd ever had.

"The Chattanooga Christmas Angels Pageant and Winter Spectacular," she mumbled.

"What's that?" Courtney asked.

"Hm?" Miranda said, forgetting for a moment that Courtney was there. "Oh, the Chattanooga Christmas Angels Pageant and Winter Spectacular. It's one of the biggest pageants of the year. It's in Chattanooga, Tennessee, around Christmas." She took the crown off a shelf and handed it to Courtney. "Bailey won Little Miss Snow Angel when she was four and a half, the youngest in the history of the pageant. Historically it's been very lucky for our family. I think Brixton might do well there."

She picked up her phone and started making a list of what she would need: pictures, makeup consulting, hairpieces, three different custom-made outfits. Girls up to a year old didn't compete in talent, but she could try to teach her a bit of a song, "Happy Birthday" or "Twinkle, Twinkle Little Star" or something. Brixton was only four days old, but the pageant was two whole months away, and Miranda could do a *lot* in two months.

"If you need some help, I'm available," Courtney was surprised to hear herself say. She wasn't entirely sure if it was a genuine gesture or a part of her plan. It just felt like the next thing to say, so she went with it.

Miranda put her hand over her heart. "That so sweet, but

you've got so much going on: school and the house and the baby . . . The next few months are not going to be easy for you."

Courtney nodded. "I know, but . . . I was thinking of dropping out of school anyway and just getting my GED. I really don't want to be one of those girls walking down the hall trying to hide my belly in a big sweatshirt. Everyone thinks those girls are sluts, and I'm not a slut. I'm pretty smart. I've got a B average, so I won't have any trouble if I ever want to, like, go to college or something. You can get Brixton ready for Chattanooga and I can be your assistant. It'll be fun!"

Miranda's eyes filled with tears. For the first time, she knew the true purpose of this room. It was never meant to be a sanctuary for her husband, or even a trophy room for her daughter. This room was meant to be the place where Miranda Miller met an angel.

chapter nineteen

Ray awoke in bed unable to open his eyes. They were puffy and tender like fresh blisters. He pried them open with his fingers and winced at the light streaming in from a bedside window. His drug-induced half sleep would have been a welcome respite had it not been riddled with nightmares he sadly recognized as scenes from his actual life.

"Mawanduh!" Ray tried calling, but he choked on a mouthful of fresh gauze. He gingerly started pulling it out, but the drugs had dulled his agility, and he scratched an empty tooth socket, sending fiery pain rippling through his skin as if every hair on his body was hooked up to a car battery.

"Owhh . . . fugh," he moaned, and wiped his watering eyes on the already blood-smeared pillowcase.

Waiting dutifully on his nightstand was an open bottle of Vicodin and a glass of water. He sighed happily then shook six pills into his hand and delicately placed them in the back of his throat.

Across the room, Ray's bloody suit hung limply over the back of a chair. Miranda had thrown out the snowman tie after forcibly prying it away from Junior, who wanted to wear it to church. The letter from Marvin peeked from the inside pocket of the jacket, mocking him. Ray wanted to read it, but on top of everything else, did he really need a dead man calling him an asshole? Suppressing a wave of nausea, he tried again to call for Miranda, but his stitched lips weren't capable of forming anything that sounded like words. Instead, he let out a long, animalistic groan and hoped someone heard him.

Moments later Courtney entered wearing a bathrobe, her hair still wet from the shower. "Do you need something, Ray?"

Ray quickly sat up, ignoring his racing heartbeat he could now feel in the most swollen parts of his face.

"Whah suh fog er ou doeeg her?!"

Putting her finger near his lips, but careful not to touch them because they were gross, Courtney whispered, "Shh. I'm going to take care of you. And then, when you're better, you're going to take care of me."

"Wheow iz Mawanduh?"

"She took the kids to the grocery. Joan is asleep in the living room and I just took a shower." She let her robe fall open a little, revealing just enough to give Ray an unwanted erection. "I'm all clean."

"Yew canno sta hewe! I fowbed it!"

Mocking him, she leaned in close. "Do you? Do you fowbed it? Well, I don't think you're in a position to fowbed anything." She whispered, "I can't lose my house, Ray. I don't have anywhere else to go. Besides, how are you and me supposed to raise a family together without a house?"

Ray forced his eyes open wide and tried to sound authoritative. "Listhen to muh vewy cawfuwy. We wiww wuk it owt, but yew muss go now. I'ww caw yew in a dah ow two and we'w have wunch. Go ho now!"

Courtney cackled, startling Joan from her nap in the living room. Thinking a critter might have snuck in the house—and forgetting completely that Courtney was even there—Joan climbed out of the La-Z-Boy to investigate.

Taking a step back, Courtney let her robe fall open completely. Ray was powerless. Looking away from her perfect teenage breasts would have been as impossible as looking away from a pair of perfect teenage breasts.

"Do you want to feel the baby?" she asked.

Ray shook his head. "No."

"Are you sure?"

Ray nodded, "Yeff. Ah'm suwe."

"I think you do," Courtney said, placing his hand gently on her stomach, still warm and damp from the shower. With the back of her other hand, she lightly stroked her nipples and stared Ray in the eye. Slowly, Courtney moved his hand down, over her pierced navel to her freshly razor-burned pubis. Ray closed his eyes and felt his stomach float like he was in a car going too fast over a hill.

"Do you like this?"

Ray nodded.

"Well, remember it," she said, pushing his hand away and tightly closing her robe. "Because that's the last time you'll see it until I have my house back." She leaned in close and whispered, "You owe me, Ray. I don't want to tell Miranda about us, but I will if I have to. You need to make this right. It's what's best for everyone."

What else could he say? Courtney owned him, at least for now. Conceding defeat, Ray nodded. "Okay."

He rolled over away from her and cursed himself for not running to Florida when he'd had the chance.

It was the first time Courtney had consciously used sex to get what she wanted, and she found it oddly empowering. *That was so easy,* she thought as she breezed down the hallway toward the kitchen. *I wonder what fat girls do to get what* they *want?*

From the door of the darkened bathroom, Joan stepped out into the hall, her eyes filled with the burden of unwanted knowledge. Distance and age prevented Joan from hearing what was *said* between Ray and Courtney, but there was absolutely no mistaking what had just happened. Courtney had tried to seduce him.

Joan's broken heart went out to Ray. Even in his pained, semiconscious state, he was able to thwart the advances of an aggressive, young, naked woman.

"What a good man he is," Joan whispered.

With Miranda out of the house, the responsibility of keeping order fell to Joan, and she did not take that responsibility lightly. She rolled a *Star* magazine into a baton and started toward the kitchen to literally beat the devil out of the young woman, but something stopped her. There must be a reason this harlot had come into her life so unexpectedly, and before Joan confronted her she needed to know what the girl's purpose was. Then, in a moment of perfect clarity, she knew the answer. Ray's "accident" in the cemetery wasn't an accident at all. It was Jesus.

You're right, Joan, she heard Him say. *I am responsible, but don't say anything yet. I'm going to need your help with this, but there's a lot I still need to figure out. Just be ready and stay vigilant. You're my champion, Joan. Remember that.*

Joan nodded and crossed to the bed where Ray had slipped into a blissful Vicodin coma. The room was a mess, as usual. Miranda had always been a slob, and despite Joan's best efforts, nothing much had changed. Mounds of clothes dotted the floor, and Joan nearly tripped over Miranda's breast pump while reaching for a pile of towels. Noticing Ray's bloody suit (but not Marvin's note), she shoved the lot into a dry-cleaning bag and tossed it in the closet.

What would Miranda do without me? she thought, taking a seat on the edge of the bed and gently stroking her son-in-law's graying hair.

"Don't you worry about a thing, Ray. We're working on a plan to save you, Jesus and me. That girl will be out of our lives soon enough. You just rest up. You're going to need your strength."

Joan leaned back and peered down the length of the house into the kitchen, where Courtney was trying to figure out how to use the cappuccino machine.

"Who in the world does that girl think she is?"

It's a problem, Joan, but all problems have solutions.

Giving Ray's hand a final squeeze, Joan went and lowered herself back into the La-Z-Boy and patiently waited for instruction from her Lord.

chapter twenty

The next few weeks were easier than Ray had expected due in large part to Joan's (and Jesus's) tireless efforts to keep Courtney out of the house. Any woman who would attempt to sexually assault an incapacitated married man must be a she-demon, and Joan was not going to sit idly by and let some she-demon destroy her family. She was a warrior and wasn't afraid to fight. Traps were set, but Courtney proved to be a wily one. When Joan sent Courtney to run a series of errands, she immediately contacted the Board of Education to send a truancy officer to arrest the girl. Much to her disappointment, the school system had not employed a truancy officer in nearly two decades. In fact, it had taken her three calls to locate someone at the Board of Education who even knew what a truancy officer was.

"So, am I to understand that you just allow children to skip school whenever they choose?" Joan asked the insufferably pleasant woman on the other end of the phone. "Don't you realize that your failure to educate this girl is threatening the safety of my family?"

"I understand your frustration, ma'am, but there is just no money in the budget for things like that anymore. It's really sad. Last year we had to sell our piano to buy a photocopier. So we don't even have music classes anymore."

"Music classes are not going to send this child back to the fiery pit of hell."

"Well, I reckon not." The woman sighed. "But it's still a shame, don't you think? I really miss our winter musical."

Joan hung up the phone and said a prayer for America.

Keeping Courtney away from Ray and Miranda was difficult, and since she was hired as a babysitter, keeping her away from the kids was impossible. Joan, however, was steadfast in her mission and volunteered to take on as much child care as possible. Taking care of four children isn't easy for anyone, but for an arthritic sixty-year-old it was downright punishing. Joan's knees had become so brittle that every other step crunched like she was walking through a forest on a late-autumn day. But, like Jesus, she accepted the pain because, like Jesus, she knew her suffering would be rewarded.

Ray, however, did not believe his pain came with a reward; his just hurt. After two days in bed, he finally made his way into the kitchen only to find his wife and girlfriend making breakfast while wearing identical pajamas he'd given them each as a gift. They were buy-one-get-one-free at Dillard's, and Ray remembered thinking when he bought them, *Why not? They'll never meet each other.*

Miranda thought their matching outfits was providence. "This just proves that she belongs with our family!"

Courtney, however, wore a scowl that made Ray think he probably shouldn't eat the eggs she put in front of him. An hour later, he was at the hospital reporting for work. Since his face was still a terrifying purple mass, he was relegated to the nurses' lounge, where he popped an abundance of pills and filled out charts. It was mind-numbing work, but he was happy to have it. In fact, the monotony kept him from thinking about how he hadn't slept longer than an hour since face-planting in the cemetery. The added stress of having to "save" Courtney's house and Brixton's late-night feedings had given Ray a bout of insomnia so severe he considered believing in God just so he could pray for death. His stress was exacerbated by a puckering anxiety he felt every time Miranda called him. *Is this it?* He thought. *Is this the call that starts, "I know everything"?*

To settle his nerves, Ray began supplementing his pills with a steady intake of cough syrup with codeine, and while successful in dulling his anxiety (and everything else), it also made him constipated, which did little to improve his overall mood.

When the day finally came for Ray to permanently replace his missing teeth, he decided against it, hoping Courtney would find him so physically repellant she'd lose interest and move on to ruining someone else's life. It was a desperate, wishful ploy, but with so little hope left in his life, Ray clung to wishes like bottles of cough syrup with codeine.

But there was another reason Ray chose not to replace his teeth. Working in the medical field, Ray had never before been treated like an idiot, and he found people's new perception of him to be endlessly entertaining. Coworkers he'd known for years spoke slower, as if he was now incapable of following simple instructions. Women stole glances at his mouth the way men stole glances at cleavage. One guy at a gas station asked if he could bum a dip. Ray was truly fascinated by people's assumptions, especially the ones made by his hospice patients. Bonnie Eskridge insisted he play something on his banjo, and after demanding Ray not smile at him anymore, Bernard Hale asked that he be replaced with another nurse, declaring that no educated man would "walk around looking like an ignorant Mexican."

Ray couldn't remember the last time he'd had so much fun. It was a welcome distraction from the nagging pile of bullshit that had become his life. He even created a persona for his toothless self, a stoic simpleton named Daryl. When not at work, Ray would entertain himself by dressing in overalls purchased at Goodwill and a John Deere cap snatched from a dead patient's hall tree—sometimes forgoing a shirt altogether—and drive around town being Daryl.

Daryl spent his nights at the Brass Ass Saloon, where he'd shoot pool with unemployed coal miners and trumpet bumper sticker politics through a fog of Busch Light and codeine. One night on the way home, he stopped by a tent revival and begged the preacher, a charismatic charlatan in a bolo tie, to cure his dyslexia. As the preacher and his followers laid hands on Daryl, he fell to his knees and pretended to speak in tongues.

"Klaatu barada nikto!"

An elderly man quickly stood up and "translated" Ray's tongues: "I am the Lord Jesus, and I am coming soon!"

Satisfied, Ray thanked the preacher, dropped a handful

of spare change and five unopened blister packs in the collection plate, and went home.

As Daryl, people expected much less from Ray, and it was everything he never knew he'd always wanted. He felt common and anonymous, and it was the most liberating feeling of his life. Finally, he understood why the world was full of so many ambitionless morons. They were the ones who had it all figured it out. *Who's to say that going to college, getting a good job, and working yourself to death is the American dream?* Ray thought. *Maybe the goal is to have people think you're stupid and leave you the fuck alone.*

The worst part about being Daryl was that everyone assumed he could fix their cars. Because of his complete lack of mechanical ability and general misanthropy, Ray had never paid much attention to how many people he encountered every day who needed help with their vehicles. But when a guy who looks like Daryl says he knows nothing about cars, people assume he must be a criminal: the old lady in the Kroger's parking lot who clutched her purse when Daryl said he didn't have any jumper cables; the soccer mom who quickly rolled up the windows of her overheated minivan when he admitted he knew nothing about radiators; the preacher's wife with the flat tire who dialed 911 and held her thumb over the Send button when it became obvious Daryl couldn't operate a jack.

Ray realized it was time to get his teeth fixed after nearly getting several more knocked out for claiming Dale Earnhardt was not a hero.

"He drove into a wall. He didn't die in combat," Daryl said with a smile, exposing his jack-o'-lantern-like grin.

"You take that back, goddammit!" another toothless man screamed at him over the Brass A's pool table, knocking a cup of dip spit onto the already stained felt. "He was America's greatest athlete!"

"He wasn't an athlete. He drove a fucking car in a circle," Daryl argued. "Anything my grandmother can do is not a sport."

When the guy swung a pool cue at Ray's head, barely missing his recently healed lips, Ray sprinted out the door and never went back.

Implanting Ray's new teeth was simple and uneventful, although they were nowhere near the same color as the rest of his teeth. They were the whitest teeth in his head. In fact, they were the whitest teeth Ray had ever seen. They were the color of light. Ray's dentist claimed that over the next few weeks Ray's diet and lifestyle would "naturally yellow" the teeth until they blended in with the rest of his smile. Ray was skeptical.

"How will they know when they're the same color as the other ones?"

The condescending sixty-five-year-old smiled. "What do you mean?"

"I mean, if they start yellowing naturally, how will they know when to stop? What if they just keep yellowing until they're the color of a banana?"

The dentist shook his head. "Because of science, son. That's how it is now. With computers and whatnot."

Ray had spent the last several weeks being thought of as a complete idiot, and he was tired of it, but he was also exhausted.

"Fine." He sighed. "Whatever."

"And," the dentist said, laughing, "if they change too much, maybe you'll look like one of those rappers with the gold teeth." His face turned grave. "I can't stand rap music.

N-word this and f-word that. Black music used to be so respectful. Remember Johnny Mathis? Good stuff."

"I don't know any Johnny Mathis."

"Really?" The dentist's disappointment was practically scolding. "Do yourself a favor. Voice like an angel. And he didn't swear at all. One of the good ones, Johnny Mathis. Anyway, if your teeth don't change, just come back in and we'll whiten the others to make them match. You could use a good teeth whitening anyway."

Surprising absolutely no one, Ray's new teeth did not naturally yellow as the dentist had promised. After repeatedly refusing to take advantage of the old man's "once-in-alifetime deal" on teeth whitening, Ray stormed next door to a younger dentist, who explained, "The old guy probably ordered the wrong teeth on purpose so you'd buy his whitening package. He started doing that after his fourth wife sued him for divorce. I can shade these new teeth, no problem. However," he said, looking in Ray's mouth, "whitening wouldn't be a *completely* bad idea."

Courtney's new schedule didn't give her much alone time with Ray, which was not ideal, but "now is not the time to be thinking long term," she confided to Britney. When she wasn't working for Miranda, she was scouring her attic for anything of value she could sell on eBay. Digging through dusty boxes and Depression-era steamer trunks, Courtney ignored sentimentality and nostalgia and put her grandparents' entire history up for sale. What had taken Marvin and Zola five decades to build together was now being passively fought over by faceless strangers on the Internet. Courtney's grandmother's antique jewelry, including her wedding ring, went for $1,100.

A collector of military paraphernalia from Maryland paid $450 for Marvin's war medals (including two Purple Hearts and a Distinguished Service Medal), his field gear, and the blood-stained uniform of a North Korean soldier Marvin had killed with a hammer (the incident that had earned him the DSM). That money, combined with what she'd earned from Miranda and whatever she could squeeze out of Ray, had lowered her tax debt to just over eight thousand dollars. It might as well have been eight million. Unless Ray left Miranda soon, or a guardian angel came out of the sky and granted her three wishes, Courtney would be homeless by Christmas.

Since becoming pregnant, Courtney had gained fifteen pounds. But instead of it all going to her belly, the weight had equally distributed itself throughout her entire body, making her look like a homesick college freshman. It wasn't surprising considering she'd been consuming somewhere in the neighborhood of four thousand calories a day. Ray might not have been as available as she'd hoped, but Little Debbie was always there for her.

Her second meeting with Mr. Waxflower didn't go much better than the first, ending abruptly when Courtney stormed out screaming she was going to sue him for being "a creepy asshole" and knocked a porcelain doll to the floor.

"Ray," she insisted, "you *have got* to talk to him."

"What the hell am I supposed to do?" he legitimately wanted to know.

"Didn't you go to college?" she asked.

"Well, yeah."

"So, there you go," she said, winning the argument.

Pleased to be dealing with an adult, Mr. Waxflower patiently explained Courtney's situation to Ray.

"The lien holder, in this case the county, has the right to auction off Miss Daye's house and use the proceeds of said sale to pay her grandfather's outstanding tax bill. Miss Daye will then receive the balance of the auction price—after fees, taxes, etc.—and the house will no longer be hers."

"See? I told you!" she shouted at Ray. "He's trying to take my house! Why does he want a second house? He's not even married!" She leaned across the desk and got as close to the attorney as he would allow. "You're not even married!"

"Jesus, Courtney, calm down!"

"How am I supposed to calm down, Ray? I'm eighteen, I'm pregnant, and I'm going to be homeless! Jesus Christ, I dropped out of school to run errands for your fucking wife! I mean, how messed up is that? I just want my house back. That's all. Nothing else matters." Stomping toward the door, she turned back to Mr. Waxflower. "Fuck you, weirdo."

As the door slammed, Mr. Waxflower turned to Ray and cleared his throat. "Well," he said in a voice dripping with insult and pity, "you certainly have *your* hands full."

Ray glared at him for a long beat. "Fuck you, weirdo."

After the meeting, Ray took Courtney to Dairy Queen, the good one out by the bypass, where they shared a Peanut Buster Parfait and tried to discuss their situation like grown-ups. Mindlessly stabbing the sundae with their long red plastic spoons, they just ended up rehashing the same conversations they'd had dozens of times before. She made desperate threats, and he made desperate promises, although this time their voices lacked the passion of conviction. After ten minutes they stopped speaking altogether. There was no point. Neither of them was going to change positions. Not today, anyway. Through the window they watched a group of happy teenagers pile into a beat-up '72 Ford pickup and speed off to do something exciting and impulsive. Ray hated them. Hated their youth, their potential, their happiness. He took their joy as a personal affront. Courtney thought about her friends Britney and Kaitlin. Since dropping out of school she hadn't seen them much. They still texted, but even that was starting to feel impersonal. She wondered if they missed her, or if they even thought about her anymore. She had never loved school, but she truly hated feeling like she was missing out on something. Ray and Courtney looked at each other and hoped one would say exactly what the other one wanted to hear, but neither said anything. After a long, uncomfortable silence, they went back to their ice cream, each secretly wishing they'd never met the other.

chapter twenty-one

"The girls are beauties . . . but their mothers are *beasts*!"

The promos for Starr Kennedy's reality show were the stuff of nightmares: thirty seconds of Miranda's fight with Theresa intercut with shots of Uncle Wes's toupee flying through the air, and not much else. An unethical editor had even added a few unnecessary bleeps implying that in addition to being violent, Miranda was a potty mouth. It was like seeing her worry journal acted out on TV.

Miranda had been working like crazy to get Brixton ready for her debut at the Chattanooga Christmas Angels Pageant and Winter Spectacular. It had been only a few months, but Miranda sorely missed the feeling of accomplishment that came with prepping for a pageant. Items were being checked off her to-do list with satisfying speed, but with only three weeks to go there was still a tremendous amount of work to be done. The last thing she needed was to be humiliated on national television.

Within hours, the promos had gone viral, inspiring dozens of tribute videos. Sorority girls with pillows stuffed under their sweatshirts pretending to be Miranda squared off against other girls wearing too much makeup. Two drag queens slap-fought each other in slow motion as Christina Aguilera's "Beautiful" played over the scene. There was even an auto-tuned version of the actual audio made into a hip-hop song that got six million views on YouTube. The few seconds that didn't feature the fight focused on Theresa screaming and crying and insulting everyone in her path, including Starr. Miranda had heard that the camera adds ten pounds, but in Theresa's case it had the opposite effect, making her look gaunt and hollow like a rotting cigar store Indian. Maybe it was how she was lit, or maybe, Miranda thought, the camera was able to capture Theresa's inner essence, an X-ray of her soul. Regardless of the reason, Theresa came across as a mentally unstable lunatic, and for Miranda that kind of made the whole experience worth it.

Ray first saw the video when Courtney forwarded it to him with the subject line OMFG! WTF! LOL ☹. Three hours earlier he had taken two of what he thought were Xanax but turned out to be an experimental form of nitroglycerin, and his blood pressure had fallen to 80/40. He hid in a corner of the nurses' lounge and watched the video eight times before calling his wife.

"When were you in a fight?"

Miranda sighed. She knew this conversation would happen eventually and she'd composed a brief, rational explanation that went something like, "I was protecting Bailey from a bully, and if you had been there you would have done the same thing." But after Brixton's birth and the new perspective it had given her, Miranda didn't feel like she needed to defend anything. The pregnant woman in that video was a completely different person. "It was a couple months ago. At a pageant."

"Well . . ." He didn't really know what to say next. "Were you going to tell me about it?"

There was a long pause. "I don't know. I mean, eventually, maybe, probably, but if the cameras hadn't been there then, honestly? Probably not."

Ray was surprised by how much this hurt his feelings. "Oh."

"You just work so hard," she said. "I didn't want you to have to deal with anything else . . ." Her voice trailed off. They both knew it was a lie.

"Okay, well . . . thanks, then, I guess." His mouth was suddenly dry as toast.

"I think I was just embarrassed."

"Why? Looks like you got some good shots in there."

She smiled. "You should see the whole thing. It's going to be on TV next month, anyway." Her voice brightened with forced playfulness. "I didn't want to ruin the surprise for you."

"I appreciate that." He adopted a similarly playful tone and smiled. "I'll set my DVR." There was another long silence. "Are you okay?"

"I will be."

"You sure?"

"Pretty sure."

"Okay. You know, I know we're both busy, but you can still tell me things," he said, meaning it.

"I know."

"Especially when you kick some lady in the crotch on TV."

Miranda laughed. "She was no lady, believe me."

He smiled. He missed his wife. "It might sound weird, considering, but . . . I'm proud of you."

"Thanks, but I'd hold off on that until you see the whole episode."

Ray laughed through his nose. "Not just for that. You're just . . . you're handling everything really well."

Miranda started tearing up and nodded. "Thanks. You, too."

"Yeah, well . . . we'll see about that. I'll call you when I'm on my way home."

Ray hung up and noticed four new messages from Courtney. The clock on the wall said he had five more hours left in his shift.

"Fuck," he whispered as he rubbed his tired eyes. His low blood pressure was making him dizzy. He made a quick pass through the ER and grabbed a half-empty glucose bag awaiting incineration. Then making his way to a private room in the ICU, he locked the door, inserted the IV in the back of his hand, and drifted off to sleep as his head filled with hopeful dreams of his wife beating the hell out of his girlfriend.

chapter twenty-two

The Kentuckiana Fresh Faces Extravaganza (Henderson, Kentucky) was part pageant, part trade show, and all madness. Once synonymous with integrity and class, Fresh Faces had bowed to corporate influence and become the most commercialized of all the Southern pageants. Titles were inappropriate and/or meaningless: Pretty Pixie, Miss Tween Hottie (mockingly referred to as "the CILF"), Princess Breathtaking, Junior Princess Breathtaking, and Queen State Farm Ultimate Goddess sponsored by tristate insurance baron and pageant enthusiast T. C. Taylor. The monetary awards barely covered the entrance fees, and attendees had to pay for parking. What kept people coming back was the Fresh Faces ultimate prize known simply as "the Cup." Measuring eight feet four inches, and boasting a volume of eighteen gallons, the Cup was the largest pageant trophy in the continental United States. Its immense size prevented it from standing upright in most homes, and transporting it was such a colossal burden it was the only major award everyone hoped their enemies would win.

Since Fresh Faces was a mere thirty minutes away, Miranda decided to take Brixton on a reconnaissance mission to see what kind of greeting she could expect at the Chattanooga Christmas Angels Pageant and Winter Spectacular.

Despite her Internet infamy, Miranda had met with very little resistance from the organizers of the Chattanooga pageant. In fact, pageant director Lori Bartlett-Rice had personally sent Miranda a gushing e-mail congratulating her on her bravery and predicting that Brixton "would go down in history with the likes of Rosa Parks and Sally Ride. We are proud that you chose the CCAPWS for Brixton's debut, as we strive for inclusion in all things beautiful."

While the e-mail was a welcome relief, it was the reaction of the other mothers that concerned Miranda the most. Their opinions meant nothing to her personally, but these women were hunters, and a lame doe is easier to kill than a healthy one. However, once Miranda entered the convention center, her anxiety dissipated like the twenty-seven different brands of CFC-free hair spray being hawked by various vendors. She and Brixton were treated with something resembling reverence.

Barbara Lamontagne, whose daughter Emilynn held the record for most second Runner-up titles (forty-three), flitted around Brixton like a hummingbird.

"You know, Miranda, you're gonna love this one just as much as you love the other ones. More probably, 'cause you'll be spending so much more time with this one."

Frances Munn burst into tears upon seeing Brixton, and even Vanessa Casebier, who was the most incessantly negative person Miranda had ever met, commented, "Well, I hear they are very affectionate creatures. Good luck to you, Miranda."

Not a single parent voiced any negativity about Brixton competing, at least not to Miranda's face. Several vendors, however, wanted nothing to do with the child, their primary concern being that people would associate their products with handicapped children.

"We're trying to promote glamour, and lightheartedness, and beauty, and hope," explained Doris Nesley, owner of Doris' Wig-Wom. Est. 1942. "And I'm not sure your daughter is . . . in line with our image."

Francil Robinson, an elderly dressmaker who over the years had made dozens of Bailey's dresses, was visibly shaken when Miranda suggested she make something for Brixton.

"Miranda, dear, children like Brixton don't need fancy dresses, just a considerable amount of prayer."

One veteran coach, a fifty-four-year-old man who went by the single name of Carroll, offered his two cents. "Why don't you just tell people you adopted a Chinese baby? Orientals have that full face and those . . . peculiar eyes. People'd probably believe she was foreign until she was about three or four. And by then everybody'd be used to her and no one'd care."

"It just seems so unfair," Miranda said to Ray in bed that night. "If Brixton's going to win, she's gonna have to compete with the other girls on their level, but she's starting from such a different place. I need some way to make sure the judges treat Brixton like the other girls."

He was in the middle of responding to Courtney's text IS A PONY A BABY HORSE and gladly turned off his phone.

"You mean like an affirmative action thing?" he asked.

"What? No, not at all." Like most thinking people she

knew, Miranda did not believe in affirmative action. "I'm not talking about giving something to someone who doesn't deserve it. I'm talking about making sure that someone born at a disadvantage is guaranteed the same opportunities as people born with everything."

"That's what affirmative action is," he said.

"No, Ray, it's not," she said, exasperated by his ignorance. "Affirmative action is when they give minorities scholarships and stuff they don't deserve just because they're minorities. That's not what I'm talking about at all."

Ray rolled over and tried to ignore the influence his girlfriend was having on his wife. "I don't know, honey. But I'm sure you'll figure it out. You always do."

At six thirty the next morning, Miranda shot up in bed and ran to the kitchen. The answer to her problem—like many answers to her many problems—had come to her in a dream. In it, Brixton was older, fourteen or so, and was being presented with the Miss Teen USA crown from Bailey who was the reigning Miss USA. They were standing on the deck of a cruise ship that was docked in the middle of the Las Vegas strip, but it was a dream, so Miranda chose to ignore the unrealistic parts. Flashbulbs went off like strobe lights, and soon Brixton's smiling picture was everywhere: T-shirts, billboards, buses. It was a great picture; flawless, in fact. And that's when Miranda woke up. For better or worse, Miranda had never been afraid to make bold choices regarding Bailey's photographs, and in her mind the most logical way to level the playing field was to do the same with Brixton.

Miranda scheduled an "emergency" sitting with Glamour Time Photography Studio, the people behind Bailey's "sexy" photos, and took the four best shots to Derek Lang, a genial thirty-five-year-old photo retoucher who was Miranda's go-to guy.

Since teaching himself Photoshop while bedridden with mononucleosis, Derek had become a master at shaving extra pounds off of unhappy brides and cleaning up yearbook photos of pizza-faced teenagers. He took a look at Brixton's photos and made a few simple suggestions.

"Well, I can clean up that little rash around her mouth and maybe give her a bit more hair. That shouldn't be a problem. Otherwise, I don't think there's much work to be done. She's really cute, and the photographer did a great job."

"He did, he really did. And thank you." Miranda paused. "But . . . I was wondering . . . is there some way you could do some other work on the pictures? Something a little more . . . advanced?"

"What do you mean?"

Derek's assistant, Mitch, a perpetually stoned twenty-three-year-old in a Bad Religion T-shirt, shuffled over to join the discussion.

Miranda chose her words carefully. "Well, Brixton is going to be competing with a lot of other girls who don't have the same . . . physical disadvantages that she does. And what I need is photographs that elevate her to the same level as the other girls. Do you understand what I'm saying?"

"Um. I don't think I do, no."

Miranda cleared her throat. "These pageants are very competitive, as I'm sure you can imagine, and if Brixton is going to compete with the so-called normal girls, her appearance needs to be more in line with what the judges consider a more traditional idea of beauty." She paused, hoping he understood, but he didn't. "So, she can't look so . . . *unlike* the other girls if she's going to have a chance. Do you understand?"

"I'm sorry, I don't."

Mitch stared at the pictures through his half-lidded eyes and said, "I think she wants you to Photoshop the retarded off the girl's face."

Miranda's spine stiffened. Although she couldn't deny that's what she was asking, she didn't appreciate it coming from some random pothead.

"I wouldn't use *that* word," Miranda scolded, "but, yes, if there is some way you could make her look more like a traditional pageant contestant, then that is what I would like. Can you do that?"

Derek shrugged. "Sure. I can make her look like an eighty-year-old Jewish man if you want."

Miranda smiled at his joke.

"Come by on Friday. I'll have something for you to look at."

She nodded, said "Thank you," and glared at Mitch as she left the shop.

Three days later, Miranda returned and audibly gasped when she saw what Derek had done with the photos. Brixton's eyes had been separated a bit and colored a deep ocean blue. Her face had been thinned, and a smart blond pixie cut sat naturally atop her head. Only a hint of the Downs remained, giving Brixton a unique but mature look. Brushing her fingers across her daughter's digitally altered face, Miranda felt tears welling up in her eyes.

"She looks just like Gwyneth Paltrow."

If nothing else, Brixton had a real shot at Most Photogenic.

• • •

Despite their own personal dramas and Joan's constant scheming, Courtney and Miranda still managed to spend a great deal of time together. Soon Miranda came to look at Courtney as an apprentice and took her responsibility to teach the girl the ins and outs of pageanting very seriously. Not that Courtney was remotely interested in learning. It all kind of seemed like a big waste of time and money. More than a few times Courtney had to bite her tongue as Miranda mindlessly plopped down her credit card to pay for some seemingly unnecessary item (backup hairpiece, infant-sized garment bag, miniature prop tennis racket) that could have made a dent in Courtney's tax bill. After driving to three different stores to locate a pair of infant heels, Courtney started to understand why Ray was always complaining about money.

Their budding friendship notwithstanding, Courtney's conscience was clear. The two weren't friends before she'd started sleeping with Ray—and she certainly hadn't slept with him since meeting Miranda—so why should it be awkward? As a matter of fact, long stretches of time passed when Courtney didn't even think about the fact that she was carrying her new friend's husband's baby, and when she did, she had almost no hard feelings whatsoever. Quite the contrary, Courtney felt tremendous empathy for Miranda. If anyone knew what an enormous pain in the ass Ray was, it would certainly be his wife of eleven years.

"He works so much." Miranda sighed as they stood in line to pick up two pounds of chopped mutton from Moonlite BBQ. "And when he *is* home, he's so tired and needy it's like I've got another child to take care of."

"Tell me about it." Courtney caught herself, then said out loud, "I can see that about him."

Miranda laughed. "I love him, though. And I know he loves me, too."

Puke.

"But . . . he does drive me crazy," Miranda said almost to herself. "Sometimes he'll just go off in his own little world and you don't know what he's thinking. And he won't tell you if you ask, so you just have to wait until he feels like talking again. It's probably my least favorite thing about him."

Courtney nodded and got a gumball from the machine as Miranda paid for their dinner.

Walking back to the minivan, the sweet smell of barbeque pork wafting across the parking lot, Courtney couldn't stop thinking about what Miranda had said. Ray didn't sound like a very good husband or father, which should have concerned her, but it didn't. Courtney was certain that when Ray left his family and moved in with her, he would change. He would stop working so much, and when he walked through the door every night at six o'clock, he would be the engaged and loving husband and father she needed him to be. She would make sure of that.

A song came on the radio that reminded Miranda of her senior prom and the awkward hand job she'd given Jody Parks in the back row of his dad's Ford Aerostar. She switched off the radio and gently placed her hand on Courtney's belly, shaking the girl out of her inexplicable recurring fantasy of being a cross-country flight attendant.

"Have you talked to the father recently?"

Courtney shifted in her seat, putting her belly out of Miranda's reach. "Yeah. The other day he took me to Dairy Queen, but he's so retar—I mean, he's so stupid. He's kind of still in love with his ex. Well, soon-to-be ex. But he'll come around. I'm not worried."

Miranda smiled knowingly and patted the girl's knee. "Well . . . it's good to stay positive. I'm sure it'll all work out." Adding in her most maternal voice, "You're a great girl, Courtney, and you deserve to be happy."

"Thanks." Courtney blushed. "That's really sweet of you to say."

"Well, it's true."

"But," Miranda said cautiously, "have you thought about what you're going to do if the father doesn't . . . come through?"

"I'm not worried about that," Courtney said curtly, picking at the unraveling hem of her jeans. "He will."

"No, I know he will. Of course he will. But have you thought about the possibility of what if he doesn't?"

With those words, Courtney finally understood why Ray cheated on his wife. Miranda didn't understand men. If you gave them too much freedom, they would eventually go off and get themselves in trouble.

It was like her grandma Zola used to say, "Men are like dogs. They need to be trained well, fed often, and kept on a short leash."

Even at eighteen, Courtney already knew that despite what they said, men wanted to be told what to do. They needed it. It was a mother thing. And Ray was no different.

"Trust me," Courtney said calmly as she turned toward the window, "he's not going to have a choice."

chapter twenty-three

"You want me to . . . kill her?" Joan asked in a choked whisper-laugh, assuming Jesus was teasing her. He *did* have a wicked sense of humor.

Unfortunately, yes. He sighed heavily. *As much as it pains me to say it, Courtney is a poison. And what do you do with poison?*

"Leave it alone?" she answered hopefully.

You extract it. Look, this is hard for me, too. She's one of my children, but every parent with multiple children understands that there's always one you want to get rid of—one that makes life miserable for the others. Unfortunately, Courtney is that child to me. You wouldn't understand, Joan, having had only Miranda.

From her kitchen, Joan heard the boys in the other room laughing at a VeggieTales video. She lowered her voice. "I mean, the girl is obviously guided by demons. I can tell that just by looking at her, but . . ."

But what?

"Well"—Joan chose her words carefully—"she's so young."

She is. And that's what scares me. If she's willing to destroy your family at eighteen, who knows what kind of treachery is in her future?

"Well . . . I reckon when you put it like that there really is no other logical choice, is there?"

No. I wish there was, but I'm afraid there's not. Jesus paused. *Do you have any questions?*

"A couple, yes." She struggled with questioning her Lord, but the gravity of the situation kind of demanded it.

I think I know what you're going to ask. I know you're squeamish about blood, and believe me, I get that. I'm no stranger to blood myself. So I'll let you choose how you do it.

"Thank you."

Anything else?

"Yes. Is there, and this might be asking too much, but . . . is there a way to keep this off my permanent record? I mean, I don't want to get to heaven and have to explain to St. Peter what happened."

Absolutely. This is between you and me, totally off the books. No one else will know. But I am going to have to ask that you choose the time and location. Going into that kind of detail wouldn't be Christ-like.

Joan nodded. That made sense. Location was key. She couldn't do it at Miranda's house because Miranda would be considered a suspect, as would Ray, the children, and probably Joan herself.

"I could do it at the girl's house, but those stairs leading up to her porch would destroy my knees before I even got inside." Joan continued to think out loud. "You know, one of the lunch ladies out at the high school is in my Bible study. We're friendly. Maybe she could slip something in the girl's food—" She stopped herself. "But that's no good, either. The little demon dropped out last month to get closer to my family."

A cloud passed in front of the sun, dimming the room, making it feel smaller, quieter, more intimate.

Okay . . . I know I said I wouldn't plan it, but you seem to be having a really difficult time with this. To stand by and watch you struggle seems cruel. So I was thinking . . . have you considered the Chattanooga Christmas Angels Pageant and Winter Spectacular?

She hadn't.

You'll be in a hotel, with literally hundreds of suspects. If Courtney is babysitting the kids, you'll have access to her room, and hotel pillows are usually full and soft, if you wanted to, say, smother her. That's just one option.

Joan smiled. "That's why you're You, and I'm just me."

The room brightened again as Joan inhaled deeply and ambled over to the counter. She dumped half a can of Maxwell House into her Mr. Coffee and switched it on. There was a lot of planning to do, and Jesus liked His coffee strong.

chapter twenty-four

After many sleepless nights and wrenching internal debate, Miranda had finally settled on a Harajuku theme for Brixton's pageant debut. While not consciously playing up the Asian-ness of Brixton's eyes, there was no real reason to run away from it, either. It was a controversial choice, to be sure. Some attendees had family who'd fought in World War II, and anything Japanese could be seen as disrespectful. But the Chattanooga Christmas Angels Pageant and Winter Spectacular was not the place to play it safe, and Miranda was more than willing to offend a few octogenarians if that's what it took to get Brixton noticed.

"It'll be fine," Courtney reassured her. "That war was a long time ago. Plus, isn't Japan our friend now?"

Ray was surly. Miranda had insisted he take the weekend off and go to Chattanooga with the family. Unbeknownst to her, he had already taken the weekend off and was looking forward to having no human contact whatsoever.

"I have to work," he insisted, sweating through his shirt. His plan was to drink beer and masturbate for three days, emerging bleary-eyed and raw on Sunday night wearing nothing but one sock and a half shirt, recharged and ready to reenter his fucked-up life. But after listening to Miranda cry for half an hour about how hard she'd worked to get Brixton ready, and reminding him of his "responsibility as the parent of a special needs child," he gave up.

"Fine! Fuck it. I'll go."

"Thank you," she said, wiping away a tear, then adding so casually it was barely noticeable she'd spent two days rehearsing it, "You know . . . this feels like such a huge event. I think we should rent one of those big passenger vans so everyone can ride together."

"What? Why? Who's going besides us?"

"Everyone's going. You, me, Bailey, Junior, J.J., Brixton, Mom, and Courtney."

Ray exhaled instead of screaming. "Why . . . is Courtney going?"

"Because she's my friend and she's been a big help getting Brixton ready and we're going to need someone to look after the kids. Mom can't do it all. What do you have against that girl, anyway? She's so nice. I think if you spent some alone time with her, you'd actually like her."

"I like her . . . fine. I just don't . . ." He rubbed his eyes and felt a sudden headache he hoped was a large, inoperable tumor. "I just . . . fuck. Fine. I'll rent a goddamn passenger van."

"Thanks, baby," Miranda said, kissing Ray on the forehead and flitting out of the room.

• • •

The Chattanooga Christmas Angels Pageant and Winter Spectacular was only the *second*-most important thing happening to Courtney that weekend. Despite her best efforts, she was still short $7,842.97 on her tax bill, and the county had scheduled the auction of her house. Hoping to sway the tax board on granting another extension, Mr. Waxflower submitted an out-of-focus videotaped request on Courtney's behalf further explaining her situation and requesting another extension: However, the lawyer's naturally off-putting personality combined with the blurry image of him sitting behind his desk adorned with tissue boxes and porcelain dolls made him look like he was transmitting invasion orders from an old lady's alien spacecraft.

Courtney realized that if she was going to get her house back she'd have to do it herself, so she penned an honest, heartfelt plea.

> *Dear County Tax Board,*
>
> *My name is Courtney Daye and this letter is about you're upcoming eviction of me from the house I've lived in for* most of my whole life! *My grandfather (Marvin Sylvester Daye) was a veteran of the United States of America's Army and raised me after my parents died in a terrible car crash. He left that house to me when he died so I would have a place to live and now your taking it away from me! It's not my fault that he couldn't pay his taxes and for you to take my house away is* bullshit!! *Excuse my language, but I'm very angry about this. What kind of people would put another person (especially an unmarried, pregnant, teenage girl who* you *forced*

to drop out of high school and get a job to help pay my tax bill!!) out of her house? Greedy bastards is who. But I don't think that deep down you are. Please prove it to me by giving me an extention to pay off my lean. The ball is in your court. Thank you.

Sincerely,

Courtney Ellen Daye

One week later, Courtney received a response from the tax board.

Dear Miss Daye,
We received your spirited letter regarding your delinquent tax bill and your late grandfather's house located at 4518 Griffith Station Road. Your emotions are understandable; however, the vulgarity was unnecessary. I regret to inform you that despite your efforts, the County Tax Board has decided to move forward with the sale of your grandfather's home. An auction has been scheduled for the morning of Friday, November 19th. You are invited to attend this auction and bid on the house if you so desire. We are sorry for your situation and wish you the best of luck in all future pursuits.

Sincerely,

Margaret Klemmons-Winger
Daviess County Deputy Tax Commissioner

The P.S. was handwritten.

> *P.S. Congratulations on your baby. I have five children and they are my life. FYI, children understand swear words.* ☺

Standing in the middle of the living room, in the very spot where her grandfather died, Courtney squeezed the letter in her fist, trying to choke Margaret Klemmons-Winger to death. The house was nearly empty, and Courtney suddenly felt like an unwelcome guest. Considering how things had worked out, she wished she'd kept more of her grandparents' stuff. Memories were all she had left, and she'd sold most of them to the highest bidder. Bursting into tears, she ripped the letter into confetti and cursed Ray's name. This was his fault. He promised he would leave Miranda, and save her house, and take care of her, but now Courtney was starting to think that maybe Ray was full of shit.

The room suddenly felt very small: the faded wallpaper, the well-worn rag rug, the sagging shelves of books Courtney would never read. Her life was wide open and she was suffocating inside of it. Everything started to close in on her, cover her like an avalanche. The thought crossed her mind to run, just walk out, leave everything behind, move on. But where would she go? Florida? Maybe. And what would she do when she got there? After everything that had happened, all of her planning, Courtney found herself with nothing. But that wasn't entirely true. She did still have one very valuable thing: the truth. Perhaps the time had come to use it. A decision was made, and a new plan was conceived: at the Chattanooga Christmas Angels Pageant and Winter Spectacular, Courtney would tell Miranda everything—after Brixton competed, of course. Why ruin everyone's weekend?

Ray had stopped drinking cough syrup with codeine, letting his colon return to its standard regularity and his outlook to its standard despondency. Being able to shit comfortably was the one genuine bright spot in Ray's life.

"Jesus, are we *moving* to Chattanooga?" Ray asked, exiting the bathroom and seeing the chest-high pile of battered luggage waiting by the front door. "I thought this was just a weekend."

"This is what it takes, baby," Miranda said, and smiled at his baffled look. "Hey, you're the one who wanted everyone to go." She clapped her hands and screamed to the back of the house, "Let's go, everyone, we leave in ten!"

Ray closed his eyes and rubbed the soft spots of his temples, wondering how hard he would have to push to puncture his brain. "I need to finish packing."

In anticipation of the trip, Ray had been hoarding pills. Pink, blue, hexagonal, round, capsules, tablets, whatever. Everything he found went into a red plastic biohazard bag he hid under the seat of his Jeep. Now, standing in his closet, Ray stuffed the bag into the side pocket of his gray suit (the dry cleaners had miraculously been able to get out most of the blood), shoved his dressiest snowman tie into the other pocket, and considered himself packed.

Joan was ready, too. There had been many dramatic firsts in her life, but killing someone was right up there with losing her virginity and getting saved. Her whole body hummed with excitement. She took a seat in the back row of the van to keep a watchful eye over her family and monitor any sudden movements from the harlot Courtney. Just as she settled in, the girl turned to her and smiled like an idiot.

"You okay back there?"

Joan remained stoic. "I am glorious."

"Cool." Courtney thrust a handful of red licorice in Joan's face. "You want a Twizzler?"

"I do not. Thank you."

Courtney shrugged. "Okay, just let me know if you do. I brought a buttload of them."

Courtney then turned to the boys, who were rubbing their dirty socks in each other's faces and laughing.

"Boys! Calm down! Here, eat this candy and be quiet!"

Nice, Joan. Way to keep your cool. You're going to be great.

"Thank you," Joan said out loud.

Courtney turned back to her. "Did you say something?"

"Yes. But I was talking to Jesus."

Courtney looked at Joan as if she were the cutest thing in the world which, incidentally, she thought was a koala bear in a bow tie.

"That's so sweet. Tell him I said 'hey.' "

Hey? Joan thought. *How dare she! Just who in the hell—*

Easy now.

Suppressing an impulse to forcibly cast the demon through the window, Joan bowed her head and began to pray, not speaking again until they arrived in Chattanooga.

On the road, Courtney also became abnormally quiet. Silence was an ability Ray knew the girl possessed, although he had never been around her when she chose to use it. Something was up, and he didn't like it.

The boys had fallen asleep just outside of Nashville, and Bailey (who had effortlessly lost ten pounds upon retirement) drifted off soon after. Brixton sat calmly in her car seat, staring out the window, wanting for nothing, enthralled by the world speeding past her window. And Miranda was deep inside *The Devil Wears Prada* audio book thanks to the noise-canceling headphones Bailey had won at the 173rd Annual Princess of the Confederacy Pageant and Cotillion (Charleston, South Carolina). With everyone sufficiently occupied, Courtney began composing her grand confession, pausing every so often to look up at Ray. Occasionally, they would catch each other's eye in the rearview mirror, and she sensed he was trying to communicate with her. There was an impatient desperation in his stare, followed by a hopeful acknowledgment that she understood what he was trying to say. But it didn't matter what he had to say, not anymore. Soon they would be together and all this childish nonsense would be behind them.

Just then, Miranda let the headphones fall around her neck and took Ray's hand.

"I'm glad you're here."

"Hm?" he said, turning from the rearview mirror.

"I said, 'I'm glad you're here.' "

"Oh. Good. So am I," he said, looking out at the road in front of him. "This is going to be fun."

She squeezed his hand and gave him the knowing smile of a woman who'd been married for a long time.

Courtney took their exchange as a personal affront. *Unbelievable,* she thought. After everything she'd done, how accommodating she'd been of everyone else's feelings, for

Ray to openly mock *her* feelings like this was beyond the pale. Well, she wasn't going to stand for it, not anymore. Angrily, she flipped back several pages of her confession and furiously scratched out the words "I hope we can still be friends."

chapter twenty-five

"Oh, my God, no!" Miranda cried when she entered the parking lot of the Chattanooga Marriott and Convention Center. Parked prominently by the front entrance was a large production truck adorned with the TLC logo. All the hope and optimism she'd been filled with over the past few weeks was instantly forced from her body like air from an end-of-summer beach ball.

Ray let out a sigh that sounded enough like the word "fuck" to make Jr. and J.J. giggle. It was the only word the boys said for the next thirteen and a half minutes.

When Miranda reached the hotel's huge sliding doors and saw the familiar shooting notice taped to the window, her throat tightened into an acidic knot.

"What more do these people want from me?" she asked no one in particular. They weren't content with stealing her show and using it to make her look like a crazy person in front of the entire world. Now they were going to ruin what should be one of the most important events of Brixton's life.

"Haven't I been punished enough?" Miranda asked Ray, who nodded and kicked himself for not keeping that bag of pills closer. Miranda had cried an ocean over this goddamned reality show. So much, in fact, Ray had worked up a speech similar to the one he gave his dead patients' families.

"You know, Miranda, no matter how much we prepare ourselves for disappointment, we're never really ready for it—"

Miranda waved him off. She didn't want to hear it. She closed her eyes and held her breath, hoping to stem the onset—or at least the severity—of her tears. And when she exhaled, there was . . . nothing. Not a single tear. There wasn't any feeling of sadness, only the memory of it. *It's just a silly TV show,* she thought. And as if she had uttered some mystical incantation, all the anger and jealousy and hurt went away, leaving her with a feeling she hadn't known her entire pageant career: perspective. Her shoulders started to burn with relaxation like they did when she drank wine too fast. Miranda didn't want a TV show anymore. She'd been given something greater than fame and fortune. She'd been given an opportunity to reprioritize her life. Miranda Ford Miller was a different person now. She was the mother of a special needs child pageant contestant, and that, in turn, made *her* special. She didn't need some stupid reality show to tell her that.

Clutching Ray's hand, Miranda opened her mouth to tell her husband about what had just happened to her—the epiphany that would forever change the dynamic of their family—when a short-haired woman clutching an iPad marched up and smiled.

"Miranda Miller!"

There was something familiar about her. Miranda checked

her outfit: designer jeans, heels, fleece vest. Obviously, she wasn't a pageant representative, and she wasn't wearing enough makeup to be one of the mothers. She appeared to be some kind of professional woman, triggering Miranda's instinct to be extra cautious.

"Yes?"

"Oh, thank God." the woman said with the exaggerated sense of exhaustion Miranda often noticed in such women. "You are a hard woman to find. I'm Caroline Hayek. I'm a producer from TLC."

"Oh." Miranda took a step back. "Right. That's where I know you from. You were in Knoxville. Have a nice day." Miranda turned and led her family into the lobby of the hotel.

Caroline followed them inside, yelling, "Miranda, wait!"

"What do you want?" Miranda said, snapping back on her heels.

"Well, first of all," Caroline said in a slight Southern accent Miranda hadn't noticed before, "I just want to say that if our promo brought you or your family any unwanted attention, then I sincerely apologize. We had literally two thousand hours of footage to slog through and that thirty seconds was by far the best. When you see the show you'll know what I mean. So I apologize if it embarrassed you, *but* . . . I have to say, the response to it has been unlike anything we've ever seen."

"Well," Miranda said, managing to sound both polite and sarcastic, "congratulations on your success, Ms. Hayek. I'm sure you've earned it. Now, if you'll excuse me, my daughter needs to eat." Miranda gestured to Brixton, who was just beginning to stir in Courtney's arms.

"Oh, my goodness, is this Brixton?"

Miranda instinctively stepped in front of this person and snatched her daughter from Courtney. "It is, and how did you know her name?"

"You're kidding, right? Brixton is all anyone's talking about!"

"*Who's* talking about her?" Miranda asked louder than she meant to.

"Everybody! And that's why I want to talk to you. Can we sit down?"

"No. What do you want?"

Caroline took a deep breath. "Miranda, I don't know if you're aware of this or not, but you've become a role model for mothers all over the world. In thirty seconds you demonstrated how completely unafraid you are to stand up for your kids, even use violence if necessary."

Miranda shifted uncomfortably.

"And now with Brixton you're saying, 'I don't care if she *is* different, my daughter is just as beautiful as your "normal" child!' It's *so* brave, I can't even tell you. *I'm* inspired, and I don't even have kids!" Caroline laughed, as if not having kids wasn't something she thought about a thousand times a day. "And I think if we take that in-your-face, 'mother bear' attitude of yours and combine it with the bravery you've demonstrated with Brixton—and I assume will continue to demonstrate—then I think we've got ourselves a show."

Miranda raised her eyebrows and leaned in closer, assuming she's misheard. "Excuse me?"

Caroline laughed again. A *real* human reaction from a *real* human being. Priceless. *This* was why she produced reality shows!

"Certainly at some point you've thought about what a great show your family would make. A former pageant queen has a daughter who becomes a pageant champion, then gives birth to a special needs baby and enters *her* in pageants, I mean . . . it's the reason reality TV was invented!" Caroline took a breath and gave Miranda her best saleswoman smile. "So, what do you say? Are you interested?"

The words had barely left Caroline's lips before Miranda blurted, "Absolutely! Yes! I'm interested. We're all interested. Aren't we, Ray?"

What? No. He was not interested. The last thing he wanted was for his family's problems to be someone else's disposable entertainment. He was perfectly aware of how fucked-up his life was, and he didn't need someone else distilling it into bite-sized episodes and spoon-feeding it to bored housewives so they could feel better about their own shitty lives. Ray had never seen a reality show that treated its subjects with a shred of dignity, and even though his family was undoubtedly flawed, they still deserved better than to be on television. Hell, if a thirty-second promo could make Miranda cry for six days, what would ten half hours to do her? Ray wanted to tell Caroline Hayek to take her show and shove it up her Pilates'd ass. But when he looked at Miranda, all he could see was the overwhelming joy of someone whose dream had finally come true. It would've been cruel to take that away from her. He'd taken so much from her already. How could he say no?

"Is this what you want?" he asked. "I mean, what you *really* want?"

Miranda considered her recent epiphany, then promptly dismissed it as postpartum hormones.

"I think so. Yes. Yes, I do. It would be so good for Brixton, too. She could be a role model for other girls like her. Don't you want that?"

He sighed. *Not really,* he thought. *I just want her to be normal and happy. But if that's not possible, then at least you should be happy*. He shrugged. "Sure."

Miranda squealed with joy, kissed Ray on the cheek, and whispered in his ear, "Thank you so much. I love you."

"I love you, too."

Caroline felt like she'd finally won the progressive slot jackpot at Mandalay Bay. This kind of stuff made her horny, and in that moment she was one light breeze away from orgasm. After six years writing needless celebrity news for E! ("You can't spell 'tasteless' without E!"), Caroline left to work as an associate producer on several unsuccessful reality shows, including *Famous Stamos* and *Thai the Knot*. *This,* however, was the kind of show she had wanted to do all along: quality, uplifting family programming.

"So, Miranda, if you have some time this evening I've got a contract I'd like you to look over, and if you think everything's okay, we can start shooting tonight. I'm in room five fourteen, come by around eight?"

Miranda was vibrating. "I'll be there."

"Then I'll see you later. Nice to meet you, Ray."

Ray nodded and extended his hand, but Caroline was already darting across the lobby, her face in her iPad.

Barely visible under a crush of hanging bags, pillows, and children, Courtney stood by silently as the Millers were handed a brand-new life. Just like that, Miranda got everything she'd ever wanted. *How is that fair?* she thought. *Why don't good things ever happen to me?* She took a deep breath and allowed

Miranda her moment. Soon enough, Miranda would know how it felt to have something important taken away from her.

"Courtney! Courtney! Is this yours?"

Courtney looked outside and saw a small bare butt pressed up against the window. "J.J., pull your pants up and get in here right now!"

J.J. ran inside, zipping up his pants and laughing. Courtney sighed and pushed the overloaded baggage cart through the hotel lobby completely unaware that Joan was watching her every move, determining the best time to kill her.

chapter twenty-six

For the first time in its storied history, the Chattanooga Christmas Pageant and Winter Spectacular was being held in November. This was to accommodate Uncle Wes, who had finally made good on his promise to Paulo to spend the entire month of December in Rio. Thanksgiving was still a week away, but the lobby of the Chattanooga Marriott already looked like Santa's Village. A dozen fake Christmas trees (one decorated with tiny menorahs and Stars of David) circled the perimeter of the lobby, imposing good cheer on all who entered. Thousands of twinkle lights blinked and flashed in festive synchronization with the generic holiday standards bellowing from hidden speakers. A giant column decorated in red-and-white candy cane stripes rose from behind the reservation desk like Santa Claus's erect penis.

"Happy Holidays from the Chattanooga Marriott and Convention Center," said a bland, oily-skinned woman from behind the desk. "Are you checking in?"

"You bet we are! Miranda Miller and family," Miranda squealed.

The woman ran the Millers' credit card, and Miranda was reminded why the whole family never came to pageants together. "Five hundred and fifty dollars for three rooms?" Her voice rose at the end like a community theater actor instructed to play 'incredulous.' "The arrogance of these hotels charging so much."

"Yes, ma'am," the clerk replied. "Do you still want the rooms?"

Miranda sighed. "I suppose," she said, confident that "the network" would pick up the bill. "I guess if it weren't for you guys we'd have no place to stay, would we?"

"No, ma'am. I don't reckon so."

Miranda chuckled as if she'd made a joke, then happily signed the registration, feeling for the first time in her life the satisfying rush that comes only from spending other people's money.

"Thank you, Mrs. Miller," the clerk responded in a barren monotone.

The twinkle lights reflected off her shiny skin, making her humorless face look almost festive. For longer than he should have, Ray imagined having sex with this woman. In his experience, unattractive women were pretty good in bed. Fat girls came quicker, but they tended to just lie there. Ugly girls, however, were memorable. They tried harder, like they had something to prove. Or maybe it was just gratitude.

"Where is my fucking Carmex?" Courtney barked, rummaging through her purse and snapping Ray out of his fantasy.

"Would you like some help with your bags, Mrs. Miller?" The clerk mumbled.

Miranda considered this for a moment and smiled. "You know . . . I think I would like that very much."

As the bell captain led them to the elevators, Miranda could tell that everyone was talking about her, but in a good way. With a famous daughter, a loving husband, a can't-miss TV show, and a young, white nanny in tow, Miranda finally felt like she had everything she'd ever wanted. And without even taking a breath, she immediately started thinking about what she wanted next.

The three adjoining hotel rooms were barely big enough to keep everyone comfortable. Ray, Miranda, and Brixton took the biggest room on the end. It would serve as the command center: Brixton's dressing room, prep space, and, if needed, press area. Joan and the boys would stay in the room next door, and Courtney would stay in the third room with Bailey, who over the past few months had grown to believe that the pregnant teenager staying at her house was the coolest person alive.

Courtney was like fireworks: a lot of fun to play with but with the very real potential to scar you for life. It was irresistible stuff for a soon-to-be-ten-year-old girl looking to start a new phase of her life. Fascination grew to hero worship when Bailey asked Courtney point-blank what a "BJ" was, something she claimed to have overheard two sixth-grade girls talking about in the restroom.

"Okay," Courtney said, as serious as she'd ever been in her whole, entire life. "I'll tell you, but you can't tell your mom and dad I told you, and you cannot do it for, like, a long, long time, like six or seven years at least, okay?"

Bailey agreed, and Courtney launched into a twenty-minute visually demonstrative, exceedingly graphic answer that went way beyond what Bailey needed, or wanted, to know. She was completely skeeved out, but at the same time had never felt so respected by another living person. A full-grown adult was casually telling her things she wasn't supposed to hear—gross, exciting sex things—as if they were equals.

Soon after, Bailey went out and got her hair cut and colored just like Courtney's. From behind they looked nearly identical, which triggered a sadness inside Ray that felt bottomless and eternal.

However, despite their matching hairstyles and frank discussions of oral sex, Bailey did not envy Courtney's *life*. Not at all. The idea of getting knocked up at seventeen, losing your house, and moving in with a strange family sounded only slightly worse than putting a boy's thing her mouth.

For Joan, the defining moment of her life had arrived. Bailey had gone to visit the few friends she'd actually liked from her pageanting days, and the boys had fallen asleep in front of the TV. Through the door of the adjoining room, she could hear Courtney showering—probably because the girl felt as dirty on the outside as Joan knew she was on the inside.

Be nice.

"Sorry," Joan whispered.

Everything is happening exactly as it should.

Joan nodded and gathered her provisions for the night: a sleeve of saltine crackers, a can of Diet Coke, and her murder weapon—a pillow. She slipped quietly into Courtney's closet, which was surprisingly large for a hotel, and thought how nice it would be to have something like it in her own house.

You pull this off, Joan, and I'll build you your dream closet. I used to be a carpenter, you know. A good one.

Joan blushed and smiled. "I think I read that somewhere."

Wait until she told that holier-than-thou Wanda Gilchrist that Jesus Himself was going to build her a walk-in closet. That'd show her.

Leaning against the wall, Joan slowly lowered herself onto the floor and made her body as small as possible. Her knees popped and burned, but she refused to complain. "Soldiers don't whine," she whispered, and pulled a blanket over her head as camouflage. Jesus would let her know when it was time. Until then, she would stay alert and ready to act at a moment's notice. Settling in, Joan put the pillow behind her head for support and closed her eyes. Three minutes later, she was sound asleep.

Dripping from the shower, Courtney checked the time on her cell phone: 7:18. The auction had ended hours ago, and she was pissed that she hadn't heard from her stupid lawyer. After taking stock of what remained in the house, Courtney decided to just go ahead and auction off everything. This included her grandmother's full-length mirror, wedding dress, and good silverware that *her* mother claimed had once been used by President Zachary Taylor. Courtney didn't need any of it. She was ready to create new memories.

On the nightstand was her grand confession, an epic tale of love, death, budding maturity, and unmarried teen pregnancy. It was quite possibly her favorite piece of writing ever, or at least her favorite that didn't have vampires in it. Lifting passages from her diary and peppered with her own peerless insights on the nature of relationships, the Confession read like a lost text from Nora Roberts, if Roberts couldn't spell well and thought "chester drawers" was a piece of furniture. Nothing was left out, including an apology which, while sincere, felt superfluous since it likely would not be accepted. Courtney considered taking it out, but accepted or not, it seemed rude not to include it. There was also the question of whether she should give the letter to Miranda, read it off the page, or memorize and recite it. Because of their friendship, Courtney thought she owed it to Miranda to look her in the eye and recite it from memory, even though she wasn't great at memorizing. She still couldn't remember her social security number, but that was just some stupid numbers on her driver's license. The Confession was actually important.

Courtney's phone chirped. It was Mr. Waxflower. She rolled her eyes and answered it. "It's been, like, over an hour. What's going on with my house?"

"Miss Daye?"

She let out an exasperated sigh. "Duh. You called *me*. Is the auction over? How'd I do?"

Mr. Waxflower cleared his throat. "Yes, Miss Daye, I am calling to inform you that the auction of your grandfather's property is complete. There are still some details to be worked out—papers to sign and items such as that—but it appears that with everything sold, and after the city collects its share of taxes, and all other fees have been paid—"

"Oh, my God, just tell me how much."

"Somewhere in the neighborhood of ninety-two thousand dollars."

Silence.

"Miss Daye?"

It was more than she'd expected, a shit ton more. "Astonished" was the biggest word she knew to describe how she felt.

In fact, she wouldn't have been more surprised if Mr. Waxflower had called to tell her he was in love with her.

"Are you fucking kidding me?" she asked.

Mr. Waxflower squirmed. "Um. No. I am not."

"Holy shit!"

"Miss Daye, please."

"Sorry, but that's . . . that's a lot of money. I wasn't expecting it to be so much."

"Well, apparently several of your grandfather's neighbors had been trying to purchase the property for years and the bidding escalated quickly. The winner, a Mr. Jim Ed Gaither, is planning to expand his farm, and——"

"I don't care. When can I get a check?"

Again, Mr. Waxflower cleared his throat. "I can have a cashier's check to you probably by the end of next week, provided everything goes smoothly with the sale."

"So, by Friday then?"

"If everything goes smoothly with the sale—"

"Awesome."

Courtney hung up without saying good-bye. Politeness was for the poor. She was rich now, and she wasn't going to waste her time being well mannered to Mr. Waxflower, who technically worked for her. Money changed everything, including what she was going to say to Miranda. Taking out her notebook, she started rewriting the Confession. Forget the apology. Forget the friendship. Ray was hers now and she was going to take him, *buy* him if she had to. If Miranda had a problem with that, then she could kiss Courtney's rich white butt.

Ten minutes before her meeting with Caroline, Miranda was a wreck. She had packed only three outfits for the entire weekend, and two of them were Target maternity dresses. With every change of clothes, Ray insisted she looked great, but Miranda wouldn't hear it.

"You just don't understand television, Ray."

"And you're an expert?"

She thought for a moment. "Yes. Somewhat. I watch a lot of it. And I know that no one is going to take me seriously if I show up dressed like a Southern housewife with four kids."

"But you *are* a Southern housewife with four kids. That's why they want you for the show."

She ignored him. "Do you think the network would buy me a new wardrobe?"

"Probably not." Football was on TV and Ray was having a hard time not being drawn to it even though he didn't really care about it. "You look fine in the clothes you have."

"I don't want to look 'fine,' Ray. I want to look good."

"You *do* look good."

"I look housewife good, but I want to look TV good."

"What's the difference?"

She gave him a withering look as if to say, *You poor, poor ignorant man*.

"Remember when Sarah Palin was picked to run for Vice President? The first thing they did was take her shopping because it is important for a woman to look good in front of the cameras. No one would've taken her seriously dressed like an Alaskan housewife."

"People never took her seriously anyway."

"Don't be mean. She and I have a lot in common."

"How?"

"Well, we're both former pageant queens, we're both from small towns, we've both been persecuted by the media, and we both have a special needs child." Miranda looked over at Brixton, who was sleeping soundly on the other bed, and smiled.

"Well, maybe the two of you could become pen pals or something."

Miranda rolled her eyes. "Yeah, right."

Then again, why not? It wasn't beyond the realm of possibility that someone like Sarah Palin would watch a reality show about beauty pageants, especially one featuring a special needs child. A surge of giddiness rippled through her body, and she made a mental note to ask Caroline if she knew how to get the former governor's e-mail address.

Settling on her one pair of nonmaternity jeans, a black sweater that did a decent job of masking her baby weight, and the pair of sequined Chuck Taylors she found forgotten in one of Bailey's old bags, Miranda gave herself one last look in the mirror and felt as satisfied as she was going to feel.

"Okay . . . do I look like I should be on TV?"

After overreacting to a fumble he cared nothing about, Ray turned from the TV and did a double take.

"Wow. You look fantastic." Not that Miranda didn't normally look great, but there was something different about her tonight, a brightness in her eyes that had been absent for a long time. What was it? Satisfaction? Confidence? Hope? Whatever it was, it suited her. *This* was the woman he'd fallen in love with, and all of a sudden he realized how much he'd missed her. A feeling he hadn't known in a very long time overcame him, warming him like a favorite quilt. If he didn't know any better he'd swear it was happiness, but that couldn't be right, could it? His wife was about to go off and sell her family for a fleeting taste of celebrity. However, seeing her smile somehow made all that other garbage fall away. Ray took her hand, pulled her onto the bed, and kissed her hard.

"I love you, Miranda. I really do."

"Well, I love you, too," she said, thrown by his sudden affection.

"No. I mean I *really* love you. And I'm going to make everything okay. I promise."

She was on her feet like a shot. "What do you mean? What's not okay?"

"Nothing. Nothing's not okay. Everything's . . . fine. I'm just . . . I'm going to work very hard to make our lives better."

Miranda gave him a curious look. "Okay," she said, then caught a glimpse of herself in the mirror. "I do look pretty good, don't I?"

They smiled.

"You look great."

"All right, I'm leaving. Don't eat anything. When I get back, we'll go have a nice dinner somewhere to celebrate. I think I saw a Black Angus down the road."

"Sounds good. Break a leg, or whatever they say in a situation like this."

Halfway out the door, Miranda turned back and carefully picked Brixton up off the bed. "Almost forgot our little meal ticket." She laughed nervously, hoping Ray knew it was a joke, then strapped her sleeping baby daughter into her sling and danced out the door.

With at least an hour to himself, Ray thought about masturbating, but he was completely flaccid and working one up would take too much effort. Instead, he unzipped his garment bag and fished around his suit pockets for his biohazard bag of pills. And that's when he saw it: the wrinkled, bloodstained envelope bearing his name, Marvin's letter, waiting patiently for the perfect time to show up and shit all over his life.

"Goddammit," Ray moaned.

The envelope felt heavy, like it was filled with a lifetime's worth of bad karma. The old bastard always did know how to spoil a mood. Knowing he probably wouldn't be in a better frame of mind anytime soon, Ray popped something he hoped was Lexapro and fell onto the bed. He took a deep breath and opened the envelope, half expecting to hear Marvin's ghostly voice escape. The letter was nearly a page, which was something akin to a miracle considering the old man's condition at the time of its writing. It must have taken him days. Each word was carefully crafted and nearly illegible, as if written by a vibrating child.

> *Ray,*
>
> *Firstly, I want to thank you for taking care of me in the final weeks of my life. You did a good job even though I died anyway. However, that does not excuse what you did to Courtney (intercourse). She is a 17 year old child. A child! How would you feel if a grown man did that to* your *daughter? Shame on you. God will punish you harshly, so I do not feel that I need to. I also wanted to tell you that whatever Courtney tells you, she is not pregnant.*

Ray leapt up off the bed and read that last sentence again. "Holy fucking shit." Ray could barely breathe.

> *I know she told you she was, but it is not true. I heard her talking to a friend on the phone and she was happy to not be*

pregnant. When she thought I was asleep, she told me everything. She said she was afraid of me dying and she wanted someone to take care of her. I think she wants that person to be you. I am not telling you this because I think you are a good person. You are not. I am saying this because my first wife tricked me into marrying her by saying she was pregnant. Thank God for Korea and annulment. No man deserves that even if that man is you and the woman is my granddaughter. I am not proud of her behavior, but she is a scared little girl. You are an adult. I know this gives you reason to push her out of your life forever, but even though she is lying she likes you. She may even love you. Please be kind to her. That is my dying wish. You owe me that. See you in hell.

Marvin

Ray ran to the bathroom and threw up into the toilet, and then with equal enthusiasm he tore open the minibar and downed a tiny bottle of vodka followed by a tiny bottle of Jack Daniel's. After a series of deep breaths, he texted Courtney with the nimbleness and fury of a tween girl. MIRANDA GONE. NEED 2 C U ASAP. COME 2 MY ROOM!!!

Ray could feel what he hoped was Lexapro coursing through his body as he read Marvin's letter again, relishing every misshapen word. Everything started to make sense. This was why Courtney was so anxious all the time, why she'd cut him off from sex even though pregnant women are infuriatingly horny, and why after nearly four months she didn't look fucking pregnant! Because she wasn't fucking pregnant!

His phone sang “Evil Woman” by ELO—Courtney’s newest text tone. I NED TALK 2 U 2. BAILEY SLEEPN. B RITE THER.

Before he could respond, Courtney was standing in his room, an eager smile plastered across her lying face. “I’ve got some great news, Ray!”

“Save it. We have to talk. Sit down.” His coolness was almost sinister. For the first time since she’d known him, he didn’t act afraid of her. If she hadn’t been so freaked out by it she would have found it sexy.

“What’s going on? Are you drunk?”

“That’s my business. Sit down.”

“Okay.” She crossed to an easy chair by the window and tried to be cool as the oversized chair swallowed her up, making her look—and feel—like a child. “So . . . what should we talk about?”

“Let’s start with this.” Ray slammed the letter onto the table in front of her.

“Oh.” The sight of Marvin’s shaky handwriting made her voice crack. “It’s from Granddaddy.”

“Read it.”

“What is—?”

“Read it,” he insisted.

“Okay. Jeez.”

Ray hummed like he’d been freebasing espresso. Every cell in his body wanted to scream, “You lied to me you little bitch!” But that wouldn’t be as satisfying as hurting her. It was important to Ray that Courtney knew her grandfather, the one person she’d loved most in the world, the last person who’d loved her unconditionally, had died disappointed in her. When she got to Ray’s favorite part—the part about her not being pregnant—her face went white.

"Oh, God." she whispered almost imperceptibly.

Ray cackled. "That's right." It was without question one of the top five most satisfying moments of his life.

Courtney's eyes turned pink as she continued to read. Her mouth hardened, turning in on itself into a puckered frown. Her head shook involuntarily as if her body was finally rejecting all of the lies. When she was done reading, Courtney placed the letter neatly on the table, sank deeper into the chair, and cried into her chest.

"So, what the *fuck* is going on?"

Eighteen seconds passed before she was able to speak. "What?"

He jammed his finger at the letter. "What is this? At the very *least* you owe me an explanation."

But there was nothing to explain. He wouldn't have believed her, anyway.

"I don't owe you shit, Ray," she murmured, her embarrassment adding a deeper hue to her already scarlet face.

"Are—are you kidding?" he stuttered. "You've *got* to be kidding. Do you have any fucking idea what you've put me through? Do you even realize what you could've done to my family? Jesus, what the fuck is wrong with you?"

There was a lot she wanted to say: that despite everything she truly loved him and only wanted them to be together; that they could get past this . . . misunderstanding; that they really *could* have a future together. But he wouldn't have heard it. He was done listening, and she was done trying.

"You'd have been a terrible father, anyway," she said quietly. Pulling herself out the chair, she slapped Marvin's letter against Ray's chest and walked out the door. "I'm done."

But Ray was not done. "Come back here, goddammit!

You don't get to just walk away!" He chased her into the hall, slamming the door behind him. "You lied to me! You lied to my family! What the hell were you thinking?!"

She didn't answer.

"Courtney?"

She still didn't answer.

"Courtney!" Fueled by anger, adrenaline, and what he hoped was Lexapro, Ray grabbed the girl by both arms and shook her like Humphrey Bogart would shake women in movies back when that sort of thing was okay. "Answer me!"

"Ray? What's going on?" Turning toward his wife's voice, a bright light hit him in the face like a fist. Next to Caroline and two expressionless cameramen was Miranda with Brixton attached to her breast, mortified that her husband was already embarrassing her in front of her new show business friends.

Throwing on an easy smile, Ray let go of Courtney and casually waved to his audience. "Hey, hon, Caroline. How was your—your meeting?"

But before they had a chance answer, Courtney turned to Ray, and wiping a fresh tear from her cheek asked, "Do you want to tell her, or should I?"

Joan lurched awake when she heard the door slam. For nearly two and a half hours she'd been asleep in the closet and had forgotten where she was. The blanket over her face made her think she had been presumed dead and was lying on a coroner's gurney being prepped for an autopsy.

"I'm alive!" she screamed, pulling off the blanket and finding herself on the floor of a closet.

"Oh, right." She sighed once she's gotten her bearings.

Dazed but ready, Joan quietly opened her Diet Coke and took a long pull. The caffeine and lukewarm sugar substitute gave Joan enough energy to pull herself up off the floor. Her knees cracked like dry bamboo, but she didn't complain. When this was over, Jesus was going to fix her knees *and* build her a closet.

The room was dark except for the TV, which was turned up so loud Joan could feel it in the floor. She inhaled deeply until she made herself dizzy.

You okay?

"I'll be fine."

I know you will. Now, go get 'em, kiddo.

With this final blessing as motivation, Joan tiptoed across the room, clutching the down-filled murder weapon with trembling hands. Mere inches in front of her, the harlot Courtney was asleep on the bed. Her back was to Joan, but even in the ambient glow of the TV the old woman knew it was her. The trampy hairstyle was unmistakable.

Are you ready?

"Yes," she whispered, the pillow shaking more with every step.

Remember, you will be forgiven for what you do here tonight. This kind of evil must be vanquished, and since I can't do it myself, it's up to people like you, Joan. My true believers, my soldiers.

Joan blushed. She thanked Jesus for trusting her with such an important mission and took her position behind the sleeping whore. Marshalling every ounce of strength in her one-hundred-sixty-six-pound body, Joan brought the pillow down with a righteous vigor and held it over the girl's face as tightly as she could.

Nice job! Just a few more seconds and it'll all be over.

There was, however, a complication that Joan had not

considered. The girl was fighting back. The would-be murderer had assumed that when a person was smothered in her sleep, she just stayed asleep until she was dead. But that was not the case, especially since the girl wasn't actually asleep. Joan had also failed to take into account that a healthy eighteen-year-old girl was a lot stronger than a sixty-year-old grandmother. Dodging kicks and fists, the old woman pushed harder as the muffled screams of a familiar voice seeped through the pillow. The voice didn't even sound like Courtney's, but Joan knew that was just the devil trying to trick her.

Scratching and clawing for her life, the girl dug her fingernails into Joan's forearms, tearing her skin like tissue paper.

"Ahhhh!"

Don't let her go! I will heal thy wounds!

Blood ran from the scratches, soaking her fingers and causing the pillow to slip. But Joan was not about to let a little blood prevent her from completing her mission. Jesus bled, too, and He didn't quit. Leaning on the pillow with her forearm, Joan wiped her hands on the bedspread and attempted to get a better grip. However, the shift in position was just enough to give the girl an opening, and she let out an audible scream.

"Grandma, stop! What are you doing?"

"Bailey?!" Turning toward the door, Joan hoped her granddaughter hadn't seen too much. It would be difficult to explain, to be sure, but Bailey was a smart, Christian girl. Ultimately, Joan believed, she would understand. "Where are you?"

"Get off of me!" Bailey kicked hard, hitting her grandmother squarely in the knee. Joan collapsed to the floor like a marionette whose strings had been clipped.

"What the hell is wrong with you?" Bailey jumped out of bed and ran to the door. "Mom! Dad!"

"No! Oh, my goodness! Bailey, wait! I thought you were somebody else!" Joan struggled to lift herself up off the floor and hobbled after Bailey into the hallway.

"Do you want to tell her, or should I?" Courtney asked Ray, who stood in the blinding lights of the cameras.

Just then, Bailey ran from her room screaming, "Mom, Grandma just tried to kill me!"

One camera turned just in time to catch Joan staggering from the room clutching a bloody pillow.

"I wasn't trying to kill you, sweetheart," Joan said. She pointed to Courtney. "I was trying to kill *her*."

"What?" Miranda cried. "Mom, what are you talking about? Why were you trying to kill Courtney?"

"Because Jesus told me to."

A tingle shaped like an Emmy crept up Caroline's spine. She would masturbate tonight for sure.

As far as Courtney knew no one had ever tried to kill her before, and she wasn't sure how to respond. She looked around and noticed everyone staring at her. No one wanted to complicate (or alleviate) the tangled mass of insanity unspooling in front of them, so they stood by and waited for Courtney to advance the story, or at least end the scene. The hallway buzzed as if it had taken a fistful of Ray's pills. Courtney looked into the camera and realized whatever she said next would be on YouTube forever, making whatever she said the absolute truth. Her words would determine the fate of the Miller family as well as the direction of a major television show. They would define her to everyone she'd ever known and everyone she'd ever meet. They would follow her for the rest of her life. She was about to become a character in Miranda's story, and she would undoubtedly be the villain. In a matter of seconds, Courtney had been given complete dominion over the future of many people's lives. And she did not like it. Not one bit.

Courtney looked at Bailey, who was sobbing and clinging to her father's waist as her grandmother—a crazy old woman who had just tried to kill her—stood by in shame, bleeding onto her shoes. She looked at Miranda, rocking her new baby, trying to figure out what the hell was going on and whom exactly she should be mad at. Then she looked down and saw the crumpled letter from her dead grandfather on the floor by her married lover's feet. For the first time in her life, Courtney felt like an adult, and she wanted to behave as such. So she gave Ray a sympathetic smile and slapped him hard across the face.

Everyone gasped.

She then went to Miranda. Ray stopped breathing. Caroline crossed her legs like she was about to pee and prayed for another fistfight; but Courtney was done fighting—for Ray, her house, her past, or even the future she thought she wanted. This part of her life was over. She pulled Miranda into a warm, sincere hug and whispered soft enough so as not to be picked up by the cameras, "Thank you for everything. You've been supercool to me." Smiling now, she leaned down and placed a gentle kiss on Brixton's forehead. "Good luck, sweetie."

Then, as if on cue, Courtney heard the elevator doors open down the hall. Her future was waiting. She took one last look around, waved good-bye to Bailey, and walked out of the Millers' lives forever.

Uncertain of what had just happened, but knowing she

didn't want to know, Miranda pried Bailey from her father's leg and led her back to their room, quietly closing the door so as not to add to the drama. The cameras stayed fixed on Ray for another minute, a starving calf sucking at the teat of a dead cow.

"I think we got it," Caroline said, cueing the cameramen to lower their weapons.

In an instant, Ray felt a clipboard in his hands.

"I'm going to need you to sign this release," Caroline said, smiling.

Ray nodded and signed his name without hesitation, because that's what Miranda would want him to do.

"Thank you," she said, and snatched back the clipboard. "I look forward to working with you over the next several months, Ray. It's going to be a lot of fun." She smiled at him and shook his hand. God, she loved her job.

"Let's go, boys. First round's on me," Caroline said, waving two fingers in the air like a Marine signaling his team back onto the chopper. The cameramen fell in line and followed her down the hall, laughing as if Ray couldn't hear them.

When they were out of sight, Ray pulled the biohazard bag from his pocket and popped two of what he hoped was cyanide. Marvin's letter was still at his feet. He looked at it for a long time, not sure if he should burn it or frame it. He picked it up and read it again, a faint smile forming as he let it sink in one last time, a death row inmate's stay of execution. He didn't even realize Joan was still in the hall with him. It looked like she was staring off into space, but her eyes were closed. Dried blood had caked on her arm, and the skin around the scratches had started to turn purple.

"That could get infected," Ray said as he tore Marvin's

letter into ten thousand pieces. "You want me to take a look at it? I am a nurse, you know."

Joan shook her head and tried hiding her shame by folding her arms in the pillow. "No. I'll be okay. Jesus will take care of me."

Ray sighed. "All right, well, let me know if he doesn't. Make sure you at least wash them before you go to bed."

She nodded. "I thought she was bad, Ray. I really did."

Ray nodded. "Yeah," he said more to himself than to her. "Maybe. I don't know. I think probably she was just young."

He turned and opened the door to his room, which was filled with the cries of his daughter, wife, and infant.

Alone in the hall, Joan looked upward, trying to get through to Jesus.

"What happened?" she asked. "How could we have made such a horrible mistake? Are you disappointed in me?"

After three failed attempts to reach Him, it was clear He was not going to answer.

Limping back to her room, Joan wrapped a clean towel around her mutilated arm and lay on her bed, as the boys dreamed nearby. She tried one more time to contact her Lord and Savior, but again there was no response. She had embarrassed Him, and He was ignoring her. Closing her eyes, the exhausted old woman pulled a pillow tight over her head and wished herself invisible. And as the sound of her granddaughter's muffled screams echoed through her head, Joan wept.

nine months later

Miranda's new Nissan Murano barreled into the parking lot of the Opryland Hotel and stopped with a lurch. She smiled apologetically at the family she nearly ran over, then shook her head as she watched them drag their bags the fifty yards to the hotel. Poor bastards. Nissan had given her the car only a few weeks earlier, and she still wasn't used to the power.

"Murano is the only midsize SUV fit for a queen . . . and maybe a princess or two" is what she said in the commercial, and after driving it for a little while she was actually starting to believe it.

Miranda had been in an exceedingly good mood lately. Her reality show, *A Special Kind of Beautiful,* had debuted to record numbers. "The biggest nonscripted pageant themed debut in women eighteen to forty-nine in the history of the network!" Caroline breathlessly announced in an early-morning phone call the day after the premiere. By the end of the third episode, the Miller girls were a full-blown phenomenon.

Season two was to begin filming this weekend.

Miranda turned to Bailey, who was staring out the window. "You okay, sweetie?"

Bailey nodded, oblivious of her mother's near vehicular homicide. She was focused on remembering her new choreography. The success of the show had made Bailey realize that maybe retirement wasn't what she'd wanted after all.

"How can you just quit competing? Pageants are who you are. If nothing else, you owe it to yourself to see how much farther you could go." At least that was Caroline's convincing argument.

Additionally, Bailey's therapists believed the familiarity of competing might help her overcome her persistent night terrors and fear of being alone. Caroline and the network were in negotiations with Miranda and her lawyers to tape Bailey's therapy sessions for an upcoming holiday special.

Bailey's return to pageanting (and sanity) would be the primary focus of season two, and there was no better venue for her comeback than the Central Tennessee Prettiest Girl in the World Pageant (Nashville, Tennessee). She had been crowned Little Miss Pretty at the age of seven—the second youngest in history—and was going back to reclaim her crown. No one had ever won two nonconsecutive Little Miss Pretty titles before. Not even Starr Kennedy, who had been MIA since Theresa's indictment for kidnapping after trying to move the girl to Los Angeles without her father's consent. But none of that mattered. If anyone could recapture her old glory, it was Bailey Miller. And even if she couldn't, it would make great TV.

"No!" Brixton screamed, throwing her water bottle, which bounced off the back of Miranda's head and rolled under the seat. At thirteen months she was already outearning the rest of the family thanks to her ebullient personality and full-time publicist. Talk shows, magazines, local morning programs—Brixton had done them all. She'd even taken her first steps on *The Tonight Show.* Something about her story had struck a chord with Midwestern Christian housewives: "the demographic G-spot for TLC advertisers," Caroline crowed.

Brixton had become the role model her mother dreamed she'd be. Even Sarah Palin sent a letter "congradulating" Miranda and her family for giving hope to the millions of families touched by special needs children. The letter hung proudly in a gold-plated frame in Brixton's growing corner of Bailey's awards room.

Of course, Miranda was not without her critics: The Family Research Council sent out an e-mail claiming that "this kind of 'tolerance' and 'inclusion' is all well and good, but where does it stop? Does this mean a child who claims to be gay should be allowed to compete? We certainly hope not." Fox News claimed that while they had no problem with Brixton being a role model, they were concerned that publicizing her condition might become a rallying cry for government subsidized health care. And MSNBC called for Child Protective Services to investigate if Brixton's media exposure was a violation of the Americans with Disabilities Act.

"Who cares what those people think?" Miranda told *People* magazine. "It might not be what other families would choose to do, but we're not like other families. Brixton is my daughter, and I can tell you, Down syndrome is *not* the most interesting thing about her. She is special for many, many reasons. No one knows what's better for her than I do. My daughter's transformation from special needs child to self-assured princess is *not* exploitation. It's a miracle straight from God, and I'll fight anyone who says otherwise. Trust me."

• • •

When Joan finally got through to Jesus, He could not have been more apologetic.

I am so sorry, Joan. From that angle Bailey looked just like Courtney. I'm terribly embarrassed. Can you ever forgive me?

Humbled by the request, she instantly forgave the one true Son of God and acted like the whole thing had never happened.

With everything safely behind her, Joan was eager to get back into her routine, especially homeschooling the boys. However, Miranda thought it might be better if the boys were taught by Bailey's on-set tutor.

"The show's paying for it, so it's like they're going to private school," Miranda explained. Joan was disappointed, but she didn't argue. The boys needed structure. And besides, Joan was going to be very busy with her next project: writing a book based on her conversations with Jesus. It seemed like the logical thing to do. No one else on the planet had access like she did. The idea made her dizzy.

"So many stories," she gushed with a smile. "No one's going to believe it!"

That's true, Joan. They probably won't.

Ray sat in the nurses' lounge staring blankly at his locker. Ten minutes passed before he could summon the strength to mutter "Percocet." The success of the reality show, and the myriad endorsements that came along with it, had given the family enough financial freedom for Ray to stop working double shifts, but he chose not to. Season One had almost killed him, and hiding out at the hospital was much more appealing than dealing with the bullshit that came with being a reality-level celebrity, which like it or not he had become.

Just like they did with Starr Kennedy, the network had used its most outrageous footage to promote Miranda's show. Unfortunately for Ray, that footage consisted of him vigorously shaking, then being slapped by a cute teenage girl in front of his wife. He looked like a criminal and a pervert. The *Hollywood Reporter* called him "one of the creepiest TV dads of all time." Every show needs a villain.

Eventually, Miranda summoned the courage to ask Ray if he'd had an affair with Courtney. The question came weeks after Chattanooga, when he was least expecting it—after some unusually spirited sex. His awkward pause before answering told Miranda everything she needed to know. Overcompensating, Ray fiercely denied any wrongdoing, then forced a mocking laugh to imply that his wife's query was both ridiculous and insulting. So she let it go. Knowing the truth wasn't going to make her love Ray any less, or make things any better, so what difference did it make? Besides, it couldn't have been too serious if it hadn't disrupted their lives at all. Although, she thought, openly confronting him *would* make for a pretty great sweeps episode.

Soon after Chattanooga, Ray quit working hospice despite it being the only unselfish thing he had ever done in his life. Rummaging through an elderly patient's medications for something to take his mind off her labored breathing, Ray looked up to find her watching him.

"Are you . . . waiting . . . for me to . . . die?" the old woman wheezed.

He gently took her hand and nodded. "I suppose I am, yes."

Closing her eyes, she painfully exhaled. "How sad for you."

He'd never really thought of it like that before, but she was right. It *was* sad for him. Really fucking sad.

"I spend my nights sitting in strangers' living rooms waiting for them to die. And when they do, I just move on to another living room," he told Miranda later that night. "I really am the Angel of Death. I've got to find a healthier way to spend my time."

The next night on the way home from work, Ray stopped at Walmart and bought a Wii Fit. A week later he exchanged it for an Xbox.

Ray texted Courtney thirty-seven times, but she never responded. It was maddening. Not because he wanted to talk to her, or even know how she was doing. He just didn't want to spend the rest of his life looking over his shoulder like a mob informant in witness protection. He went to see Mr. Waxflower, who agreed to speak to Ray only through his closed front door and claimed to have no knowledge of Courtney's whereabouts. He even tracked down her hot one-armed friend, but she hadn't heard from her, either. It was spooky. It was like she'd never existed at all.

Maybe there *was* a God.

Courtney pushed her secondhand stroller out the door of the photography studio and slapped on her sunglasses. "Bitch," she thought out loud. "It's hotter than a mug."

The southern Indiana heat was cruel and unrelenting. Pulling the sunshade down over the face of her daughter, Twilight Marvinia Daye, Courtney shuffled through the contact sheets, trying to pick her favorite shot. "Three months, Twi," she said to her daughter. "Can you believe it's already been three months?"

It had been a difficult year, to be sure, but Courtney felt like she was finally coming into her own. The cashier's check took a little longer to arrive than Mr. Waxflower said, but it was also slightly larger than expected, so she didn't yell at him too much. Blowing town with close to ninety-five thousand dollars in her pocket, Courtney considered her options and determined that they were infinite. She was free to go anywhere in the world and do anything she wanted.

On her way to Las Vegas, she stopped for gas in Evansville, Indiana, and noticed a For Sale sign in front of a small two-bedroom craftsman a few blocks from an elementary school and a Hardee's, and with a backyard big enough for an above ground pool. Courtney circled the block four times before calling the number on the sign. Something inside her said that maybe she hadn't gone far enough, but then something else reminded her that she wasn't running from anything, so why not just do what made her happy?

She thought about texting Ray, just to let him know she and Twi were okay, but she never did. She was still pissed at him for believing Marvin's letter.

"I mean, toward the end there, Granddaddy saw monsters and shit," she told a new friend in her GED class. "He thought we lived on a boat. He did *not* have his wits about him."

But Twi *was* Ray's daughter. What if he wanted to meet her? Maybe someday she'd show up and surprise him. It was always a possibility.

But a reunion would have to wait, at least until Courtney wasn't so swamped. The Most Beautiful Little Hoosier Pageant (Evansville, Indiana) was less than three weeks away, and Twi hadn't even settled on a gown.

acknowledgments

A big thank-you must go out to the people of Kentucky, my people. I hope you take this book in the spirit in which it was intended. I love you and I miss you. But I'm probably not moving back any time soon.

Even though I dedicated the book to Karen, I feel like I should thank her again here. She is my first reader, and over the years has figured out a way to tell me when something sucks while still being fiercely encouraging. Without her I would probably still be working at Dillards in Louisville.

I have had many teachers over the years who have encouraged my love of reading and writing: Linda Elmore and Pam Bradley; Jeffrey Skinner, who let me take his creative writing workshop, where I met my wife, and who has become a valued friend; Joe Keefe, my Level 3 teacher at Second City, who suggested I write because the acting thing definitely wasn't going to happen. I should also thank Judy Blume, Stephen King, and John Irving for writing the books that defined my childhood and made me love reading.

A big thank-you to Aaron Kaplan and Dan Norton for getting this book sold, Richie Kern for championing it, and my editor, Brendan Deneen, for sticking by it. I do appreciate it.

There are countless friends and family members who have graciously given their time to read different versions of this over the years. I appreciate your contributions and promise to send you a lovely handwritten thank-you note, or at least shoot you a quick text.